I0772429

THE TRIP

LISA LOOP

FALL OF ROME BOOKS

ISBN: 979-8-9909934-7-1

FALL OF ROME BOOKS

Contents

1

Chapter One

October 1982

Callista felt calm again. She remembered her mother screaming, and her father commanding plaintively for her to stop. She wasn't sure which of them he'd been speaking to. Her throat ached, and her ankle bore a thin line of dried blood. Cold light streamed through dust motes below the starshaped skylights. Phillip's Land Rover stood rebukingly in the shadows of the carport, already lightly dusted with pine needles.

The conversation had started out tense, Margaret announcing they were leaving that day, for a weeks-long seminar outside San Francisco.

"Why didn't you give me any warning?" Callista said. "You must have been planning this."

"Mm, not really. Don't overreact, sweetie. It's only for a few weeks." Margaret had had one eye in the mirror, smoothing her blond hair into place. "You have Adam just around the corner to comfort you. If you'd just screw up your courage and ask him to. Boys love being pursued, you know."

"Ah." Phillip appeared, buttoning a shiny new leather blazer. "Hon, it pains me to say this, but we left the keys to my car at the office. She's unlocked, though. If you dropped a lip gloss or anything."

"Can you at least tell me...this trip of yours...?"

"You'll be fine, kiddo." Phillip unbuttoned his top button, studying his reflection. "Mrs. Mack will be coming a couple of days a week to make sure the place doesn't fall to ruin."

Red rage tugged at Callista, a familiar warning signal. The inner voice she called *Vivian* could sometimes be distracted by pain. She pushed a sharp toenail into her calf. "How long will you be away? And why no car?"

Margaret applied tawny cream blush to her cheeks, fingertips stroking in an upward motion. "You have said how much you love Seattle, how superior it is to fusty Fairfield. I don't like the idea of you cruising around there after dark. We all know there's hell to pay if you get the notion that someone has..." She shook her head slightly. "...done something to you you don't like."

"And if there's an emergency?"

Phillip adjusted his lapels. "Impossible, sweetheart. This town hasn't ever had a murder. Why do you think we moved here?"

Callista sighed. "I believe *there's no respect for architecture west of the lake*? If I remember your wording correctly."

"Yes. It's awful here. You've made that clear, many times." Margaret pushed back from the mirror, snapping shut her compact and dropping it into her bag.

"I'm not the one who's off to California. For no discernable reason."

"Sweetheart, you'll be leaving home in a matter of months. Come on, now." Phillip said.

"I agree. You have everything a girl could want." Margaret's eyes drifted to Callista's midsection. "Or you would if you would just put forth a little effort. And stopped trying to make us feel guilty for wanting to live a little. It's time you stopped playing the victim."

Rage erupted. Vivian roared, though in retrospect the details were fuzzy. Callista didn't know how Vivian stored up her abuse, but she was unfailingly cruel. Margaret and Phillip had looked shocked, which gave Callista a hollow kind of satisfaction. Screw them. If they were going to thrust freedom onto her without parameters for success or failure, Callista would decide for herself how to profit from it. She'd find a way.

Water striped the trees outside, under a sky too darkly overcast to suggest how long she had been standing there. She wiped away a tear, banishing the temptation to blame herself for the silence. Fur brushed against her ankle.

"Hey, ugly." She stooped to pick up her brother's leopard cat, Bodhi. But her hands met air. The animal bolted down the stairs in a rush of caramel and brown.

Callista sighed, checked the locks on the front door and the kitchen's glass side door, then went to lie down on her parent's immaculate bed.

When she had finished her Chem homework, Callista picked up the phone in the dark kitchen. The dial tone sounded overloud. She pushed in the number.

"Gamble residence."

"Hey, bitch?"

"Oh, Callista." An older woman said. "I don't think I'm the bitch you're looking for."

"Grace, pardon me." Callista said.

"Heavens, don't be daft." Grace's voice muffled as she called out for Harriet. "You know me too well to think I could be offended by anything you might say."

Callista laughed. The digital clock read 8:30, casting a glow onto the plastic wall organizer. A photo peeked out of one of the pockets, of her and Adam by the lake their first year at Peregrine. She pulled it out and pinned it prominently on the cork square. She had been taller than Adam, then.

"Did you just use foul language on my sweet Maman?" Harriet said. "You vile heifer. I'm the only one allowed to do that."

Grace said, "Hanging up now, monkeys. Callista, whatever you do, try to get this one in some mischief. Her eyes are starting to bug out from hitting the books so hard."

"Will do, Grace."

"Will do, Grace you bitch, I think you mean." She hung up.

Then Callista and Harriet were laughing about plans for the following weekend. Callista could last five days alone. She flipped on the lights, and the kitchen's glass walls slowed their creep toward black, instead reflecting the yellow Formica, and Callista's mane of dark blond hair.

Callista was lying on her parent's bed, textbooks spread around her, the television silently playing a rerun of Sonny and Cher, when the phone rang.

"York Residence."

"I want to get something off my chest." Margaret's voice was off, somehow, slightly wobbly, and higher pitched.

Callista pressed the corner of her Chem book into her outer thigh, hard. Cher swayed in a shimmering lilac skirt and vest combination, her eyelids gleaming purple under black spikes of lash. "Okay."

"We have a right to live."

"Obviously." Callista said.

Margaret paused, maybe taking a sip of something. "I thought giving birth to a daughter would mean having a pal, someone to go shopping with and teach things to. Someone to share my thoughts with. But you. You are just impossible."

"I know, Mother." Callista said, pushing the corner of the book deeper, so it stung. "Sorry I'm such a disappointment. I'm pretty disappointed, too. If you want to know the truth."

Margaret continued talking, but Callista's leg burned. Vivian appeared and hung up the phone. Then she unplugged it. Kneeling next to her parent's toilet, Callista could hear the kitchen and study extensions ringing, but every time she rose to answer, her head was split by pain, and she had to vomit again.

The next Saturday Callista, Harriet, Adam and Brody Knapp drove North to La Conner for a visit to Brody's wild aunt Prudence's house. She spent weeks of each fall out crabbing with her boyfriend and needed her extensive hydroponic garden tended, which Brody was only too willing to do, as he received payment in bags of weed. Callista had heard about these visits to Aunt Prue, but until recently Brody had only invited Bart Frehl, who purchased product to roll and resell at school, or Adam, who always refused to go. For whatever reason, this time Brody had opened up the invitation to Callista, who had insisted Harriet come along. They were too old for Halloween parties. A trip to the farm sounded fun.

By the time they reached Mount Vernon, Brody was already on his third tall tale of witchy Aunt Prue's tinctures and potions.

"Your nonsense is beginning to grate, Brody my dear." Harriet said, changing lanes. A truck horn sounded, but if the rest of them heard, no one flinched. Harriet's tone brooked zero nonsense, and that included semitrucks pushing the silver station wagon into the soggy fields of the Skagit Valley. The windows streamed with rain, the mountains beyond shades of black and green, flames of orange maple licking out.

"To make it up to all of us, I'll treat everyone to the Oyster Bar." Harriet said as they coasted up the off ramp.

"No need for a side trip. I will scurry down to the beach and dig your oysters myself if need be." An unlit joint bobbed between Brody's teeth.

"We want alcohol, stupid." Adam's head leaned against the window. His hand in Callista's felt cold and limp.

Brody met Callista's eyes over his left shoulder. His were light brown, with long white blond lashes and a constant mischievous gleam. Adam's closely cropped hair shaded to honey, but Brody's was like platinum troll doll locks, a kinky crown. "What kind of hooch do you like, York?"

"Something with bubbles, I guess." Callista said. "Just, not beer."

"Hmm. Sparkling wine." He turned back. "Can't promise. My aunt is more of an alchemist than a sommelier."

"About that." Adam wrenched his hand from Callista's and leaned forward. "Is it true she brews actual magic mushroom tea?"

Brody's laugh filled the car. "Of course. According to my cousin, it takes you to another realm entirely. You're never the same."

"Are there dragons?" Harriet downshifted to a stop sign. "Please say it makes you see dragons."

Brody shook his head. "You're such a strange woman child, Gamble."

Harriet turned them back onto I-5 North. "We can't all be as mature as you, Knapp."

"True. So true." He took the joint from his teeth and studied it.

"Put that away, dumbass." Harriet said wearily. She looked left, right, left, her black nape neat beyond the head rest, a pair of silver screw-on earrings shaped like tiny bowls of fruit catching the soft light. Callista always appreciated Harriet's strange touches of glamour, her retrieval of precious things no one else noticed. A day at the Goodwill on Dearborn Avenue was a giddy treasure dive.

"This tea your aunt makes?" Adam's voice sounded clinical, but Callista sensed the desperation in it. "Does it? Change you into someone else?"

Callista studied Adam's face. His skin was pale with an almost constant redness, as if he were perpetually blushing. His blond hair poked stubbornly from his old ski cap, the Alpental insignia vaguely suggestive of trips to old villages where people raised goats. His lips were thin but pretty, pressed into a resigned line that only eased to smiling when he was at school or on the slopes. Callista picked a piece of her own long hair from the back of his sweater. She had given him the sweater the previous Christmas, because it was the same kind of fisherman cable knit their Headmaster wore, from a catalogue in Maine. She opened the window, letting in rain and cold wind, opening her fingers to let her stray hair fly.

She and Adam had fallen into closeness during her first year at Peregrine, and never contradicted peoples' general expectation that since they spent so much time together, they must be dating. As they'd grown older and Adam's affect had become vaguely different than other boys, they had kept on, attending Junior Prom with matching boutonniere and corsage, sitting together at lunch and during events, skiing in winter and boating in summer. Theirs was a comfortable partnership based in layers of inhibition and implicit agreement. They had never kissed, but they held hands often. They had often slow danced, their bodies pressed together in the dark with a kind of halting tension, and she had felt Adam's hardness on her thigh. He was always funny, in those moments, and she knew that while he didn't want her, he also didn't not. He admired her. But...she wasn't his type. She was the girl he would love if he loved girls.

"Frazer. Don't get ideas. There's no need to ruin your liver when escape is only a few months away." Brody pulled the joint down and lit it. He spoke through indrawn smoke. "But to answer your question, I don't know. I've never been crazy enough to drink the stuff."

Harriet laughed. "Goddamn it, Brody. Do I need to stop this car right now and let you walk the rest of the way?"

He handed over the joint, and she took it.

Adam sat back and leaned his head on Callista's shoulder. "I don't know if I handle this world that long."

His hair smelled like baby shampoo. She kissed his head. "Well, you're here now. That's unusual. Did you tell your folks where we were going?"

"Of course not." He whispered. "I snuck out."

She stiffened. "Oh, shit."

"I know. Pain is inevitable. But..." He sighed. "It had better be worth it."

Callista took his hand in hers, opening the palm, exposing its faint lines. "You're going to live a long, wonderful life."

"And what about you, gorgeous?" He said softly, closing his eyes.

Brody sighed. "We stay on this road for about five miles."

"Harriet, go faster!" Callista said. "Every time you crest one of these little ridges, it feels like we're flying."

Harriet obliged, and Brody turned to look at Callista once more. She smiled, her stomach dropping pleasantly with each hill. They gunned it onto a smaller road, flying between fields dotted with hundreds of white shapes that resolved into snow geese, pecking intently at the stubby ground.

Callista always remembered the intensity of Adam's blue eyes as he entered Aunt Prue's cabin, homey with lace curtains and pottery mugs, only a faint thrum beneath the rugs betraying the commercial enterprise below. Prudence had long blond braids and a wide smile. She seemed younger than their parent's generation, somewhere in her thirties, her skin freckled from sun. She'd wore her Levi's cuffed over thick wool socks, moving with brisk energy. "Welcome, rabbits. We have the tide. Make haste, make haste."

"I have to help switch out some bulbs." Brody said, disappearing below stairs and grinning. "Help yourself to some tea. It's only chamomile."

"Hello." Adam took off his hat and extended a hand to Prudence, who shook it, laughing.

"Aren't you adorable?" She took in his handsome face and military-style hair, peering beyond him to Callista and Harriet. "Hi girls. You are all welcome. Any friend of Brody's."

"Yes." Adam "He mentioned...?"

Harriet squinted at Callista. "What's he doing?"

Callista broke in. "I think my boyfriend here would like to inquire about a recipe?"

"Ah." Prue said, crossing her arms. "You come seeking sacred knowledge."

Harriet laughed. Callista touched her arm lightly to silence her. The two girls stood side by side, clasping hands, holding in their laughter as Adam sputtered incomprehensibly.

"Children?" Prudence said. "David is out there putting away some smoked sockeye. How's about you go see if he needs any help, and I'll have a chat with young Adam?"

The door tinkled as they went out the back, where a deck looked through trees onto the channel. Callista happily breathed in the alder smoke, pine, and tidal rot. David was a huge man with hip-length black hair and rubber boots. He was removing rust red fish filets from a rack over a circle of white embers onto a plastic-lined wheelbarrow. His face was handsome, broad, and brown, and he seemed far older than Prudence.

"Anything we can do to be useful?" Harriet called out.

David glanced at them and waved them down a dirt road. "No, no. Go on down to the beach. Yesterday Prudence saw some egrets out on the mud flats. You like birds, yes?"

"Of course."

"There's a rumor of an eagle come back. If you see him...it's good luck." He stopped working and smiled, tipping his head to one side.

"Really?" Callista said. "I thought eagles were extinct."

"You passed the test." David laughed. "Of course there's no eagles left down here. I'm just teasing."

"We're going." Harriet said. "Unless you want to share some of that." She motioned to the fish.

"Go." David said. "This is all spoken for."

Callista's clogs squelched slightly as they approached the brightness of the water. Then they were, three long white stars, egrets stalking through the shallows.

"Don't you love the Sea?" Harriet said.

"I've always thought if I knew I had to die, falling off the San Juan Island Ferry would be the way to go."

Harriet glared. "For the love of god, Cal. We're not even through midterms and you're already turning into Ophelia."

They joined hands again, laughing.

In March, Callista made a circle like David's, on the beach at Point No Point. The wind was high, and her hands shook with cold. The recipe flamed up, as she hoped it would, showing the moon and the sea that she was done with the tea forever. She wanted to make sure her last trip stayed in memory only, not under her skin, like an invisible occlusion. But she would never know for sure. When the paper had disappeared completely, she covered the circle with sand, then rocks, then a handful of dust she had gathered for that purpose, from across the mountains. It was all she came away with, and she would have to content herself with the memory.

Callista had gone looking for a girl. For Leslie McCall, a Freshman she barely knew, who for some reason kept appearing in Callista's trips as if they shared something deep and important. It made no sense. And yet. Leslie had been missing since November. On the early spring beach burning the recipe, Callista had to admit to herself that it might be best, for certain girls in certain situations, to remain lost. That being somewhere else was the only option, whatever means that disappearing required. But she was the lucky one.

"You love to fly." Melusine said on that last visit to her water world. The mermaid's pale skin sparkled, her teal-and-bronze tail caressing the bay's clear waters so the phosphorescence whorled out teasingly. She sat on a weedy rock, like a goddess on an album cover. The sky was apricot and sapphire, with irregular constellations behind thin clouds, and a tea-scented wind carrying Callista's hair behind her, dramatic. Operatic, really.

Melusine had appeared on Callista's very first trip, full blown in her splendor. She was warm, domineering, motherly but in some ways a standard fairy, wanting to barter for every gift bestowed. A bit of a cliché, in retrospect, but compelling all the same.

"Fly?" Callista twirled her hair, which was longer on this dream beach, and gleamed with its own inner light. She made a show of thinking. "I love to ski. And drive fast. That's not the same thing as flight. You know what I want. Where is Leslie?"

"Hers is not your story to write, child." Melusine smiled, her arching, juicy lips almost Gloria Swanson-like. "Your problem is, you always want to fix everyone else's wound, when you have your own. And here I have a fabulous gift for you."

Callista studied her nails. They looked like iridescent rainbow talons. Her torso bulged against her thin cotton gown like a pin up girl's. Very sexy. She hoped the overripe physique wasn't the gift. "What are you offering?"

Melusine rose up like a dolphin on her tail, laughing, her silver hair alive on her naked chest. "To rescue you from evil. To take you with me to where we both belong, so you can be a powerful goddess, as you rightfully deserve."

"Down there?" Callista pointed to the dark waters of the bay. "In your...underwater queendom?"

Meli made an impatient face, her features immediately less regal. "Obviously."

Callista sighed. "You've offered that before. We've gone over this."

"I will show you the freedom, the glory, the magnificence that could be yours...for a price." Melusine reached out her long, sparkling hands but Callista crab walked back up toward the trees.

"Have you and I run out of things to parley with? Aren't you tired of the same old song?" Was *parley* the right word? Somethings kinds did during wartime?

"You think this is an old tune?"

"You offer immortality under the waves every time I see you. No offense." Callista shrugged. Was she going to wake up soon?

"Because that is what you need." Melusine's eyes glittered. "We could make up such wonderful stories. You would be safe."

"Maybe next time." She lied. There would be no next time. "I want Leslie McCall."

"She's made her choice." Melusine loomed toward her. "She wants you to fuck off."

Callista rubbed her eyes. "I know her story isn't mine to fix but...no one else is going to look for her. They've given up and I..."

That was when Melusine started to sing. From the ether a band played, a slow base line and soaring electric guitars. They were great. Callista realized how deeply, irretrievably stoned she was. God she loved Melusine's voice. Like the hoarsest moment of Robert Plant's long, drawn out falsetto, both harsh and seductive, an invitation to new horizons. *Time to ramble. Baby, I'm leaving. Got to roam like I used to*...or whatever that lyric was. Callista could never remember.

And if she listened to Melusine singing, arms outstretched, her face full of welcome, Callista would float right down through the bay and be lost forever. So she stood, unsteady even in her imagination, and did the little jump that sometimes led to a flight. He feet thudded onto the stony sand. She loved flying, in truth. Melusine knew. Callista turned and trudged away, feeling humiliated and queasily sad. She felt like a liar, pretending this wasn't goodbye. Where was Adam?

"Come back!" Mel sang, loud and long and awfully hardcore sounding. "I have not released you, child!"

But Callista didn't turn back. It seemed clear to her that if even her baby toe touched the water, she would never escape. And while the idea of waking up back in the world was humdrum, Callista had decided to do it. The bay looked cold, and wet, and Melusine was so obviously the goddess who mattered there.

Callista was pitched painfully backward onto the rocky beach, elbow hitting something sharp as she crumbled down. Her breath became constricted panting. The water approached inch by inch as Melusine pulled her by the hair. A small girl sat at the water line, hands pushing into the sand, shivering in a wet nightgown. She didn't look up, even as Callista shrieked and poked Melusine's eyes, forcing her to let go.

"That hurts." Melusine, slapped her hands away.

"Oh, my gift. Thank you." Callista said, grabbing the girl's hand. "Come on. You belong with me."

"Oh no, I like that one." Melusine cooed. "She's lost. Like you."

"Fuck off, Meli."

And then Callista was running toward the tree line, the girl keeping pace, the feel of sand and rocks under her feet giving way to smooth dirt path.

"Mine!" Melusine bellowed.

"No! As a matter of fact, mine!" Callista screamed, thrashing from side to side.

"Shush now." Adam said. "Take it easy, babe. It'll pass."

And then she was crying, and sipping mint chip milkshake from a straw, the smell of wheat and distant slaughterhouses in her nose, a familiar rumble under her prone body on the leather bucket seat. Spokane county was passing quickly outside the window, the Palouse like green turtlebacks under piles of milky clouds. She needed to pee.

"That was a crazy powerful dose. You've been tripping for hours. Try to get some sleep, now."

Behind her eyes was violet-burnt orange with a queasy seasick feeling hovering around the edges. But she willed her body to stay where it was, and try to rest, even though rain was falling in and out of view, though it wasn't really rain but tears.

There was no paper left, under the sand and rocks at Point No Point. But all spring Callista dreamed there was, hard as a dinosaur egg, inert but always waiting. And no amount of time would really be enough to bury it.

2

— · —

Chapter Two

November

The mushrooms grew everywhere that fall. Adam and Callista took his GTO for a short ride around Apple Hill on a Monday afternoon, the prefab split-level homes with their green lawns more easily pilfered than in their own neighborhood. The Goat purred, low, its yellow paint gleaming sun-like against the autumn mist. Callista thought of it the way she did the childhood cartoons she still watched occasionally, a candy-coated distraction from the horizontal layers of gloom they navigated from October to June.

"Let's go to Queen Anne." Callista said after their first foray. "Or Magnolia. The lawns are huge, and no one knows us."

"You know I'm not allowed to lurk in the city." He would say, his handsome face betraying no irony. "And I like our local friends and neighbors to see my beautiful girlfriend jumping in and out of my elegant car."

"Thanks, Romeo. Hope it gets back to your folks that our romance continues." Callista pushed the baggie in the glove box but Adam slammed on the brakes and she lunged forward, breaking her fall onto the dashboard with her wrists.

"Are you breaking up with me?" He faced her. "Was that sarcasm?"

She laughed. "Should we? Stage a dramatic breakup for the world?"

He put a hand on her cheek. "Cal. You can't imagine how much worse it would get if he..."

She knew he could go no further. If either of them ever acknowledged that Adam was gay, the fear of being found out and punished would explode. Safety lay in a secrecy so insidious that even they never breached it.

He continued. "Don't worry, stupid. It would be you dumping me, obviously. Not the other way around. Anyway, you're my best friend and I can't imagine not spending this time together."

Her eyes filled with tears. "Sorry."

He brushed them away with his thumb. "I can't believe they left you alone. I mean, I would love it if mine did. But...anyway. I need you to stand by your man a bit longer. Yeah?"

"You bet." Her hands tingled. She hadn't thought about how long their charade would continue. But it wasn't ending now, today. So she was safe.

"Uh," Adam said, reaching out a hand to steady her. "Could you hide those shrooms at your house?"

"Sure." Callista nodded, strapping herself in. "Obviously, no one will find them there."

That week crawled by, each weather report promising higher drifts than the day before. Lesson groups were assigned, rules posted, checks filed in the office. Adam was teaching eight kids, mostly Freshman. By the time students got to be Juniors, they skipped their lessons. If you were a Senior on Ski Bus, people felt a bit sorry for you. The chaperone, Mr. Kling, would force you to sing along with him, and the driver, Miss Lily, would ask about details of your life two years out of date. But it was better than nothing for kids unlucky enough not to have a car.

Tuesday morning, Lake Washington was tossed with whitecaps. The Evergreen Point Bridge swayed, water droplets slapping across the windshield like someone snapping a sweaty towel. Callista, Adam and the twins they carpooled with got to school early, the Goat extravagantly colored as a tropical fish in a row of silver or navy-blue Rabbits and Volvos. The Peregrine School's front hall smelled of rainwater, wet wool, and adrenaline. Kids were sprinting around in a mishmash of backpacks and raincoats. Someone sang the lyrics to Born to Run. *We'll run 'til we drop, and baby we'll never slow down.*

"Here is where I leave you." Adam said quietly, and disappeared into Headmaster Tolland's office.

"Are you in trouble?" She called, her voice disappearing into the morning rush.

"Move." Harriet pulled on Callista's arm and they sailed through the door. "Don't want to be late to Am Stud."

"Hi, Callista. Hi Harriet." Mitch and Will, two seniors, passed.

"Put your pants back on, losers." Harriet said. "You know she's taken."

They howled like sad puppies as the girls pushed their way up the hill to Walker Hall.

She and Adam didn't speak on the ride home. The twins, Thaddeus and Daniel, babbled incessantly about an impending trip to Jackson Hole, where the snow was infinitely superior to the local slop. Once they'd been dropped off, Adam still had nothing to say, and she put her feet up on the dash, watching his hands move over the chrome steering wheel, wondering if they would ever touch another boy the way he'd dried her tears that Monday.

That afternoon Callista reviewed the recipe, scrawled in a refined hand, on a leaf Mobile Gas list paper.

"Be careful," Prudence had said, holding it out with her beringed fingers. "It's magic. Real magic. Not that watery stuff you have on Cap Hill down there."

In the car Brody looked at Adam and said, "Forget that tea. She gave me enough weed to last the rest of the school year. I can share some with you. If you're feeling the strain."

Adam settled back in next to Callista, and said, "Thanks. I appreciate that. But it's...I'm just intrigued by the folkloric aspects of this recipe, that's all."

Harriet whooped. "Oh, Adam. Really now."

Callista kept her eyes on Adam's profile, understanding that he was dead serious.

The recipe had called for ten ingredients, including berries that Brody said he didn't know where to find. But Callista did. She and Adam lived on Mount Zebulon, which was less a development than a wooded mountain slowly given over to small horse ranches and Pacific Northwest designer homes, their horizontal lines in cedar and glass like angular wooden ships gliding between the second-growth trees. Across the road was Carriage Chase Park, a 500-acre forest cut through with wide horse trails and informal deer paths leading to decrepit lumberjack garbage dumps with their old pressed-glass bottles, majestic nurse logs teeming with ferns and saplings, and brush. The recipe called for salal berries, turkey tails, Douglas fir sap, and lichen. Callista didn't have to leave her backyard for those. If you could call the woods outside her windows a yard, which it pointedly was not.

She was glad for a project. Once Adam dropped the twins, and then her, he would return the Goat to his father's garage and disappear until the next morning. He was not allowed out, unless they had a preplanned date, or it was Friday night skiing.

Though they had been pretending to be a couple since tenth grade, Callista had rarely made it past the Frazer's family foyer, with its paving stones shining out like a Medieval fort, simultaneously smooth and hard, vaguely dangerous. The family's German Shepherd Lobo had strained against Mr. Frazer's grip, the man's face almost as forbidding as the dog's. Once he put Lobo away and asked her questions about herself, how school was going, if she had plans for the summer. Something about the glaze in his gray eyes chilled Callista, the way his large hands dangled perfectly still next to the leather belt she knew he used on Adam at least once a week, and more if he found reason to.

"Sir, I am a counselor at Kayak Island French Camp." She said.

"Oh. A good girl, trained in first aid and water rescue." He said. His first name was Aiden she knew. He was from somewhere in Pennsylvania, but Callista was fuzzy about the meanings of different places in the Northeast, the associations, and various forms of status. She only knew that Mr. Frazer had been in the war in Korea, and worked at Boeing. But half the dads in Fairfield worked at Boeing, somewhere in middle management or engineering. It told her nothing.

She didn't want to know. She hated Mr. Frazer for what he did to Adam. It was all she could do to meet his cold, gray eyes.

"Yes, sir. I know mouth to mouth resuscitation." She replied in a good girl voice, soft and compliant. "And I can carve a mean kelp horn."

"Next thing you know you'll start bragging about your prowess at toasting marshmallows, for s'mores." He said. She couldn't tell if he were joking, so she didn't answer. Perhaps he was taking a dig at her weight.

Only Adam's mother Florence, illuminated in the door to kitchen, seemed unthreatening, her hands on a paint-splattered artist's smock, feet in brown pumps. Her lipsticked mouth formed a small, silent oh of surprise when Adam had appeared and took Callista's hand in his. Mrs. Frazer rarely spoke, and when she did her voice had a strangled quality, as if she were forcing herself to break an icy surface. But Callista rarely had to endure such moments of scrutiny. After so long, she was accepted as a fact of Adam's life. A shield against parental disapproval, as he was for her.

Adam and Callista had discovered one another in eighth grade carpool, immediately struck up the friendship they wished they'd had from the moment he moved onto Cedar Street, the year previous. They began letting people believe they were dating in tenth. Not that they ever lied, exactly. It was only that they appeared together at every event, ate lunch side by side, and rode around in the Goat as if one unit. People made assumptions. Which was exactly what they hoped.

Now, getting to the middle of twelfth, Callista rarely thought about the way her relationship with Adam looked to his family. She had let go of whatever code words she and Adam had prepared in case anyone questioned them. Callista sometimes wondered if people had ever fallen for their performance. Adam was far too handsome to be dating her, a rawboned girl who had no lifer friends there, and none left from her previous years of schooling. That wasn't how suburbs like Fairfield worked. In Seattle, kids seem to trade school affiliations and party invitations like they were all one extended family.

Fairfield's public schools were legendary for their champion football teams and raucous garage bands, their hot tub parties attended by kids who spent every spring break on Maui. Anyone depraved enough to decline their chance to take part was incomprehensible. Invisible. Possibly insane.

Callista remembered the deranged football game she'd attended at Fairfield High when she was in sixth grade. A neighborhood girl was cheering on an older crush, and Callista's parents made no objection. Though the Fairfield Fliers were ahead the whole game, everyone in the stands screamed themselves hoarse. It was a kind of delirium out of a historic novel, she thought, the kids around her shivering with intensity, like a tent revival, a religious epiphany. It must have been what the Berserkers were like, drunk on triumph, or the First Crusaders as they unwittingly smashed Christian Villages in old Byzantium, murdering innocents they had convinced themselves were infidels. The hysteria nauseated her, the free license to scream and wail, to let go all decorum for no reason but sport. The Cheerleaders were the most disturbing, shaking their blue spangled pom-poms and high kicking, as sexy as centerfolds. Yet the fans smiled down upon the girls as if they were only teasing generals, commanding everyone to do what they demanded; sing and clap and stomp their feet. As if there were no danger to jumping around seductively and split open-legged on the turf, to showing the world their underpants, as long as they were the same blue as the player's jerseys. *We've got spirit, yes we do.*

Callista felt sick for days afterward. She decided to apply to Peregrine. Margaret approved, and Phillip only made a few noises about how expensive it would be. Spencer already attended, recruited for swim team. The day she committed, Callista felt only happiness. Her brother didn't think to warn her that she would be dropped, overnight, by every kid she knew from the neighborhood.

Luckily, Callista liked solitude. That November was a good time to be alone, in a warm, cedar-paneled house with a built-in stereo system and a standoffish cat. She went to her father's study to put on the first record of the afternoon, Jimi Hendrix' Are You Experienced?, its purple and red velvet tassels caressing down her anxiety. She pulled soy sauce, peanut butter, and spaghetti from the pantry and put them on the yellow Formica counter. Since her parents had been gone, she had become more and more creative about feeding herself. They had left behind plenty of vanilla ice cream, baking supplies, noodles, and Fresca. What she didn't have was anything fresh, salad or fruit or bread. The house was silent, the only sound a steady drip of rain. Callista wished she were back in the city, or looking for mushrooms on lawns, or lounging on one of the squishy couches in Walker Hall while kids practiced speech pieces in the neighboring rooms.

Instead she was looking at Monday night with nothing to do but study. The record ended and she started the next one, the Rolling Stones' Some Girls. It always cheered her, with its lurid tales of life in some imagined city, maybe LA, maybe London, or was it New York? Someplace her parents had visited, back when the world was theirs to explore. She knew they missed their freedom. Living in the woods was part of their rebellion against conformity.

Callista boiled the noodles and mixed together peanut butter, soy sauce, brown sugar and pepper flakes. She missed Spence. He had been the one to introduce her to making up recipes, to ugly soup and cookies invented from whatever they found in the pantry. The gooey disks they baked were lame. But Spence insisted *they're cookies if we say they are. The world is as we say it is.* Their parents worked long hours in their law firm. She and Spencer had experimented a lot. There had always been one housekeeper or another to clean up the mess, but after the third or fourth, a kid stopped getting to know them.

She considered running up some long-distance charges and calling Spence at Stanford, but didn't. There was a purity to refusing to ask for help. When the phone rang, it was as jarring as being shoved. Nope. The only caller Callista was speaking to, other than her brother, would be Adam. And Adam rarely had use of his family's phone. The ringing eventually stopped.

If there had been a grandfather clock in the house, it would have sounded loudly against the emptiness of their pale pine kitchen with its vaulted dining area, its couches and picture windows looking out in three directions. But there was only a digital cube on the wall near the yellow plastic Copco organizer full of message pads for the phone calls her parents expected Callista to note down. It was a childish form of rebellion, she admitted to herself, refusing to accept calls.

Callista poured her sauce concoction over her cooked noodles, and pulled out chopsticks. Her dinner tasted mostly of salt, but the spaghetti was hot, and she was hungry. She let the five-gallon tub of vanilla ice cream melt while she finished the noodles, and then scooped herself out three spoonsful, topping the white domes with apple sauce and brown sugar and a handful of stale walnuts. It was her favorite impromptu dessert. Spence said it was disgusting. She replied that *it was good if she said it was*, and he laughed, his merry blue eyes rolling.

When she had washed and replaced the pots and dishes, Callista pulled out Prudence's mushroom tea formula and put it on the breakfast bar. She donned her parka, and went out into the dusk to collect ingredients.

Later, Callista wondered where Prudence and David had gotten the recipe. David was part Swinomish and had lived on the reservation, but Brody insisted he disapproved of the whole enterprise and had no part in it. The notion of a magic portal had made Brody cranky. "That's all Prudence. She used to be in a cult. I wouldn't believe anything she says. My grandparents have never gotten over her dropping out of Smith. It's nothing to do with David. He thinks all of us are nuts."

By *all of us*, he meant Peregrine students. He meant the weirdo children of local professionals, and old-school preppy families who had been exiled to the land of trees and mountains by the lure of everything fresh it provided, which ended up being money in their accounts, houses on wide tree-lined streets, cabins on islands or slopes, and the club overlooking the lake.

Callista fit in well enough in the exclusive box of misfit toys because her parents were both attorneys and educated back East. And Callista's dour expression, lank blond hair and doughy skin didn't look out of place among the other kids there, the mostly white faces with mostly slender frames with a handful of exceptions that gave the school's public spaces a look of urban complexity. She loved Peregrine, if for no other reason than it let her be invisible. Tall, blond, big, but not enough for the casual observer to recognize her strangeness.

At Peregrine Callista was just another kid worried about getting out of Seattle to college. Unlike at Fairfield Middle School, no one kept track of how popular she was, or commented on how with a chest like hers, she ought to be topless in a hot tub. Maybe it was being with Adam that prevented scrutiny, but she doubted it. Harriet was a Peregrine lifer, and in her twelve years there no one had ever grabbed her breasts, making lewd comments, or pressed her up against her locker.

She brewed the tea and poured it into her dad's green thermos, and then placed it in the nearly empty fridge. By then the trees were near invisible against the gunmetal sky. The house's heat whirred on, and Bodhi appeared at the glass, a miniature leopard seeking shelter from the storm. Callista cracked the door, and he ran straight to his bowl.

"Bodhi." She pleaded, her voice small in the big room. "You could at least say hi."

She found a dish towel and toweled him off while he ate. He looked annoyed, but he had no choice but to let her take off the worst of the wet.

The week continued, each night as quiet as the last, except when Callista went up to the study to blast her and Spencer's records. The phone rang three times per evening, at seven, seven thirty, and eight. She slept in her parent's bed on the upper floor. It had a door that locked. There were no keys to the house itself, or to the cars. They were only lockable on the inside. During the day she had to leave one open, and anyone could walk in. It was the same all over the hill, no one locked their doors. But she felt vulnerable anyway.

All her life, there had been a family sleeping around her. Then that summer, while she was working as a camp counselor on Kayak Island, her parents had gone on a self-actualization seminar in California. They had met some people there from outside San Francisco. The Kirshes. And then, without warning, her folks had announced mid-October that they were going back to the center, and then to the Kirshes' house somewhere near San Francisco. Better weather, they said. Compelling personal growth she wouldn't understand, with freedom they hadn't known since their youth. They had a trial to prepare for and could do that anyplace with a fax machine.

"We need this." Margaret had said, snapping her suitcase closed. It was her biggest case, the one others nested inside. Callista had never seen it used before.

"You need what?" She had asked, but her mother didn't answer.

"Daddy, can you at least give me their phone number?"

Phillip smiled benevolently, his moustache stretching over his teeth. "Ah, sweetie, we don't know exactly how things are going to go. We'll call you."

Then Vivian had taken over, with her sharp wit and mean temper. The first night had been hard. Callista had one of her attacks, when she couldn't breathe or think straight, but she had smoked a couple of tokes off a joint Brody gave her before it progressed to vomiting. She'd been able to fall asleep around midnight in her parent's king size bed, and that had made up her mind not to move back to her single downstairs.

3

CHAPTER THREE

She was used to things the way they were now, a month later. She felt almost safe. The only night sounds were owls, the groaning of tree trunks, or the rare car audible from the street at the end of the gravel drive.

Their house was nearly invisible from the road. Phillip liked it that way, the rebelliousness of refusing to mow a lawn. The unpaved driveway looked abandoned, winding between massive trunks, ferns spilling onto the rutted gravel. Her parents' cars were hidden in a carport behind a woodpile. It wasn't until you came around the circular drive and saw the house itself that you could take in its magnificence, all wood beams, copper lanterns, and walls of glass. The first time Adam saw it, he gasped and took her hand to steady himself.

That Friday morning Callista waited under the branches of a Douglas Fir until Adam arrived. He was never late. She had her skis, poles and pack ready to throw in the trunk. She lay the thermos carefully on its side. They had time to talk on the way to the twins.

Adam picked at sleep in one of his blue eyes, his wavy blond hair freshly buzzed. Callista knew Adam's mother cut his hair, every Sunday after church. Nothing else about him seemed homespun or parochial. If she didn't know him she would think Adam an urban scene maker, someone who bought drugs for Bowie or hung around Frank Zappa's pool. The twins stalked up and dumped a pair of garment bags in the trunk. Their red hair was long and cool, with the careless lack of grooming preppy boys preferred. They went to the club after school on Friday, to learn to dance for the coming social season, so they needed sport coats.

"When's it my turn to drive this beast?" Thaddeus said, thumping the back of Callista's headrest. It was comical, as the twins grew taller and taller, to watch them fold themselves into the back seats.

Adam said. "You won't need a car where you're going."

"Brown?" Daniel said.

"Purgatory." Adam replied, and gunned it.

That afternoon was the first good day of the season. Snow had started in the mountains in October, but it wasn't until the week before Thanksgiving that the powder stood tall enough to make their games fun. Callista took it easy, chasing between moguls and down the black diamond trails until 8:30, when the kids made their way from their lessons back to their buses. By that time she was breathless, her braid a mess under her cap, goggles up over her forehead in spite of the itching.

Adam stood at the mouth of one of the small looping trails on the right side of the run. There was a flat place where the soft mogul field gave way to a rise, and then a small bowl leading down to the lodge and parking lot below. The chair lift poles rose like denuded metal trees into pools of light, scratchy metal roaring out of speakers strung close to serenade riders. Right then the song was *Do You Feel How I Feel*, by Peter Frampton, which had been on heavy rotation for years. A light snow was fuzzing the yellow halos, making Callista feel a combination of nostalgia for when she had been younger and a day on the slopes had been a prelude to a family dinner, and exhilaration, because she was there with her best friend.

The thermos felt heavy in her pack as she vadled over to Adam, who was staring silently down the fall line, though whether at the boys who were passing like soldiers on silent patrol, or the snow gathering down in the parking lot, she didn't know. The ski lessons he gave only lasted two hours, and they he had the chance to take a few runs before they headed home. But not today. This Friday night was special. The slopes were dim gray, light bouncing between the overcast and the snow in an endless loop that would keep the world vaguely daylike for hours.

"You have chains."

He turned. "I do. But I think it's stopped anyway."

He swiveled, and disappeared into the trees, past the snow-laden sign that read, Off Limits. She followed, her skis muffled on the untouched powder between trunks. With the ski day ending, the buses filling, and everyone else loading up their cars to head home, no one would notice where Callista and Adam decided to drink their magic tea. Mr. Frazer might note that they were late getting home, but it was easy enough to claim an accident on the pass. They had two hours, maybe three. She pushed on her feet to keep them moving past the river, frozen into hard gray braids pocked with air bubbles. The pines still smelled sharp over the diesel fumes from buses down the hill in the parking lot. A faint freeway droning was the only other indication they weren't in a primaeval forest. She loved it there, especially because they weren't supposed to ski off trail.

She lost sight of Adam. On every side were wide trunks, each with a dark well of air where the snow hadn't reached, five or more feet deep. One of Callista's earliest memories had been of falling into a similar hole next to the ski patrol hut, and feeling an immediate sense of drowning, of disappearing into something vast and terrifying. Her father had reached in and pulled her out, like taking a dipstick from an oil tank. But they had frightened her since. Adam's tracks led on. She called his name, but the sound didn't travel. She felt alone in a strange, silent world, like an astronaut or a deep-sea diver. It was thrilling.

Adam's goggles sat casually askew atop his forehead, lounging on the side at the base of an enormous redwood. His face was intent but nervous. She, on the other hand, felt elated. It was six days before Thanksgiving, and she planned to spend it alone eating noodles with peanut butter and watching movies. She felt adult, free, fully grown. No one knew where she was. If she got caught here, the only person to help her would be Adam, though he was as likely to light up a joint and settle in, as he was doing, his face dusted with frost from where his gator had failed to protect it. He looked like a baby version of Robert Redford, effortlessly handsome, his blue eyes half lidded with what she knew was excitement.

He had been wanting to drink mushroom tea since the trip to Bow he had been denied by his overbearing father. Callista sometimes wondered if the Frazers had any notion of how enticing teenage misbehavior became to their son, with his life of strict curfews, mysterious groundings and worse things he kept to himself. He'd planned for this foray for weeks.

They made faces as they passed the metal cup back and forth, not stopping until they began to laugh uncontrollably, and then they were far away, in a place of colors and light and giddy glee, like a Peter Max cartoon or Chitty Chitty Bang Bang.

Later, when comparing notes, they called it The Realm. At first, they were simply together laughing, the tree sheltering them above, walled in by snow. Sound carried oddly in the well, intimate, and soft like whispers at a slumber party. Adam talked of going to Stanford, his voice lower than usual because, Callista suspected, he was practicing the speech he would give his father when the acceptance letter arrived. It was around then that she noticed her insides feeling soft and unreal.

She wondered if she and Adam would ever do what they had always promised, and have sex with one another so they could get it over with. It was an old subject, which had grown out of the many times her mother had pressed her on her need for birth control. Callista had demurred, red faced, saying that they were saving that act for a special occasion and not to worry, she wasn't going to saddle her family with the Frazers as in-laws. She had tried to imagine being naked with Adam, but while it was easy to picture his body in swim trunks or cross-country gear, she never saw anything beyond his singular beauty. Her own soft, tall flesh never came into the fantasy. She knew the thought of it embarrassed him, and she empathized.

Callista watched the snow making purplish flames around the edges of the snow well, wondering if any animals lived in the ground below them, and if they found her thoughts ridiculous. She imagined the voice of Lilian Morgan, her

American Studies teacher and Head of Upper School, pointing out the mud-dled quality of Callista's arguments, her lack of logic and crispness. Just what did she mean by *animals under the tree*? Did she mean *living or dead*? *What exactly constituted an animal, in her mind? Did she have a definition? Or was she just hopelessly sentimental, yearning for an underground lair lined with tufted wool, containing prescient rabbits who lived a simple, happy life together with a small fireplace, and tiny books, which they kept on a tiny table like something in the Cotswolds? What a silly notion.*

And then Callista understood, because her hands were not the least bit cold in spite of how long she and Adam had been there, which was either half an hour or half a day, she couldn't tell, that she was high. Really high. So high the world was cotton, and the tiny rabbit fire was crackling below her, and the ski area was exquisitely deserted, and its snow cats soon to head out onto the trails and tamp down the moguls with their dangerously invisible icy flanks.

Callista closed her eyes. She loved the high moguls. She loved the way her knees came up and almost knocked her in the face as she bombed down them, swiveling into the fall line at the precise top, her edges pushing down on the messy chop below until any ice that hid there was not only behind her, but sheared away slightly with the force of her skis. She liked the pick her way across the field the way some people liked to choose what bottle to open or what dress to buy; she wasn't old enough to drink and she didn't have money for dresses, and never had. But she could read snow, and knowing exactly which bumps would allow her to stay in a smooth, steady rhythm, plant, turn, plant, turn, plant, turn, and on and on until the hill just ended at the tree line and she had to whip around, snow flying, and bring her edges behind her into a V and stop for air. That was her moment of power.

And yet. Adam was looking at her and laughing, his eyes smaller than usual, little blue flowers. She unbuckled the tops of her boots, which felt too tight now that she wasn't pressing down on them. Underneath, her feet felt sweaty. They couldn't have been there long, if her socks were still wet with sweat, and probably blood from popped blisters. She never felt them, until she got home.

"I think the tea is delightful." Callista declared.

Adam's laughter rose, childishly, hysterically. She had seen him this high before, though never on mushroom tea. Sometimes he would devolve into crying, heaving and blowing snot, and holding up a hand to silence her if she so much as gave him an inquiring look. So she didn't press.

"It is." He said, wiping his eyes. "Did you bring the crumpets?"

"Naturally." She sighed. "They're in your ass."

His body heaved, silently. Then he whispered. "Of course they are."

Callista closed her eyes. Her body was floating on the snow under her back, her limbs making automatic snow angels. She didn't want to know how he felt about it. No doubt he would find it childish. "I think this is the best party we've ever had."

"Agreed." He said softly. "Do you think that a person could overdose on it?"

"Yuck." She answered. "You'd have to drink so much. Dying wouldn't be worth it."

Adam was laughing so hard she worried he might choke. She reached out and touched his shoulder.

"Don't!" He yelped. "I'm fine."

She removed her hand, torn between concern for her him, and the coaxing of her muscles, which ached to fly, to stretch out and be carried away like a child taken in, sleeping, from the car.

"I can see that you are." She said in a voice like Lilith Vines, their former French teacher. "C'est Claire, mon petit vache."

Adam yelped. "How would you feel about staying here forever?"

Callista flexed her hands in their gloves. The gloves were orange leather with side panels in rainbow elastic that had once belonged to Spence, and she loved them. Were her fingers cold? She couldn't tell. "Are you finally proposing?"

Callista felt the slight hitch of her alter ego's arrival. She watched mildly as another intelligence appeared inside her. It often said better things that she did. It was sharp, and angry, and sometimes mean. She called it Vivian, the person who stayed lucid when Callista was too afraid to take care of herself.

"What's wrong?" He said, leaning toward her in the dark. "Are you okay?"

Callista wondered what Vivian would answer. But she didn't say anything. Callista found that a warmth was spreading across her chest, and Vivian was pushing her toward it. "Do you feel that?"

"Oh yeah." Adam replied. "It's good."

A crack of not-darkness appeared where the snow met the pine needles at the bottom of the well. As they watched, the not-darkness blossomed into light. And then they were digging, laughing, as if the only thing that mattered was getting to wherever the light was coming from. And then they were tumbling, flying, falling. They agreed on that. They had both wanted in, desperately.

4

— · —

CHAPTER FOUR

The Realm was light, color, smells, and sensations. But at first all Callista noticed was music. Her favorite kind of music, the guitar-heavy, harmony-rich rock which had gone out of style just as she was getting old enough to buy records. It made her think of misty mountains and affable boys with long hair and fringed vests, who knew the way somewhere utopian and welcoming, where teenagers were seekers and parents were the guardians of all that was mundane. Boys from camp, or movies.

She and Adam were sitting on soft, grassy turf strewn with flowers, surrounded by trees and gardens, that bore as much resemblance to reality as an animated film cell. There was a sense of adventure permeating everything in the landscape, a presence of sentient animals and mythological beings lurking behind cottages or in shadows, of powerful forces bursting from brooks in the form of pale maidens, or erudite trout. It was like every fantasy book she had ever read, and every cartoon show, combined with all the crazy rock lyrics and psychedelic album covers she had ever studied, swirled together into a universe of loud, technicolor potency, bursting with the promise of quests, of adventures. And each one might lead someplace rewarding, where she might earn something worth having, given by a world that wanted to bestow it. She wanted to cry with relief.

When she turned her head, Adam was sitting in a velvet chair wearing a dandified outfit of breathtaking luxury. Her skin felt warm and smooth, under a white garment that might have been a summer dress or a nightgown. Her feet were bare. She felt the weight of a flower crown on her head, that smelled of lilies. The sky hung with rainbows, which bent into a smooth, clear sea full of islands.

Callista stood, striding around stupidly, looking for landmarks or directions, wondering with a prick of anxiety where they were. Adam was now clad in a pair of swim trunks she had never seen before, his hair under a scuba mask with a snorkel dangling from it, face sober. She blinked, and her body was now clad in a slinky disco dress.

Without speaking, they reached out to hold one another in a way they hadn't since a dance at the start of the preceding year, when a Senior named Jack Shanahan had leaned toward them and said drunkenly, "You win the contest for most annoying fucking couple." It had been a compliment.

Music rose, and they danced. It sounded like Marvin Gaye, though so scratchy she couldn't hear the words. Was he singing into a megaphone? Callista laughed, but Adam, now clad in a sweater and jeans, his hair long and loose, had a maudlin look on his face. He spun her, and she let him, and he dipped her, but his face was grave, as if this performance was for her benefit, and he was doing it only because he had agreed to.

"Hey, you." She said. "Don't you want to explore a little?"

"I do." He said, stopping and letting his hand drop to his side. "But I don't want to go alone. And I don't think you can come with me."

"But. We're together. You're seeing this, aren't you?" She gestured to the sky, which was shading from blue to pink, with cotton candy clouds, traversed by a flock of birds that shimmered like the foil on imported candy.

He gazed into her eyes. "What are you seeing?"

She laughed. "This place, this fantasy world. Come on. Let's go find a quest or complete a mission, or something."

"Would you be willing to kill someone, Cal?" He said, his face somber. "I'm not willing to murder a single monkey. I won't do anything negative to a dragon. No one gets hurt."

The music stopped. The trees looked benign, the nearby hills green and inviting.

"Where are you? What are you seeing?"

But he was gone. She stood alone on a rocky rise above an inlet by the sea, surrounded by Madrona trees and scrubby pines. Below her, waves were lapping on a small beach, and a handful of craggy islands stretched off into the distance. The blues were at their most vivid, and the water sparkled greenish yellow into its depths. Callista could sense whales in the water's depths, and eagles in the trees, otters and kelp below the rippling waves.

A low female voice said, "Every purpose has a price, child. State your deepest desire, and I will tell you the cost."

She looked around but saw no one. Far in the distance, what looked like a version of Kayak Island hovered beneath a canopy of trees, but she wasn't sure if the canvas tent cabins were the same.

"I sense you want freedom, escape, a chance to fly. I can give you those things." The voice ended in a rushing wave sound.

Callista gasped. The sea itself had spoken, maybe the whole idea of the sea, or an unseen creature under the waves maybe. Or had it? She felt fear, and scrabbled inwardly for Vivian to answer, but the sea laughed. It sounded like the roar of surf.

"You sense that?"

"Oh yes. It's obvious. I can see right through you to your heart's deepest, most secret desire."

"That's..." She wanted to say *creepy*. But perhaps she ought to be nicer. "Tempting.

"Come closer." The sea said. "I'm Melusine."

Was that a face? Something silvery, in the water?

"That's okay," She hesitated. "Thank you. Though."

Callista ran up the path toward a campfire circle. Kids were gathering around it, sitting on stumps. The flagpole snapped with colored pennants, and the air felt potent with good times to come. A singalong. Maybe some stories, followed by talk about constellations. For sure there would be s'mores. She saw an empty stump between two kids she almost recognized, but before she could sit down, she was back on the grassy turf again, and Adam was there, wearing a sweatshirt and baggy shorts, his cheeks covered in stubble. He looked like the antihero of a French movie. Was he in black and white?

"Baby. You came." He laughed, a raspy, deep-throated sound so unlike the boy she knew that it gave her a feeling of something like danger. Something playful and dark.

"I was always here."

Now there were other kids in the valley, walking in ones and twos and threes. Callista found it hard to focus on any one in particular. They wouldn't stay sharp. The air smelled like some familiar perfume she couldn't place, and other smells she sort of recognized, a hallway in elementary school outside the music room, that always carried a hint of oil paint, or a scratch of arctic wind that meant winter was coming. The kids slid in and out of clarity, like in a Viewmaster, or a 3-D post card. There was something gold-paper-ticket-y about them. A sense of specialness, or weirdness. For the first time since they'd arrived, she felt truly afraid.

Callista studied her clothing, a pair of piped running shorts and a t-shirt. Was it familiar? A dark-haired younger girl stood near her, dressed in a pair of red corduroys and a white turtleneck. She moved jerkily across some hardpacked dirt in front of a fire pit, like she was in a home movie, flickering and hovering. It was terrifying.

"Go away." Callista said.

The girl smiled, a hopeful look on her long, pale face. It was immediately familiar, though Callista couldn't' place it.

"I'm trying."

"I mean it. Get lost."

"I said I'm trying, Callista. She's coming to get me. We're going to Longbotham and everything is going to be all right. Better than that. Not that someone like you would understand." The girl tipped her head to the side, a curtain of deep chestnut hair falling from behind her ear.

"Going where?" Callista was seized by a physical panic that she was supposed to go there too. She wasn't prepared. She had no passport or travelers' checks.

"Someplace safe." The girl smiled smugly. "They'll never find me."

A cold wind pressed back Callista's eyelashes, and for a moment she was in two places at once, the cartoon nightmare realm, and the tree well. She blinked, and she was on the warm grass again. Adam was walking across the field, his gate relaxed and open. He was wearing old-fashioned Tuff skins, rolled at the ankles like a growing boy, and a pair of conservation boots. His hair was so short she could see his pale skull.

"Where are you going?"

Callista ran after him, her feet touching hard-packed dirt in a comforting way, the trails of summer in the islands, of long sunny days. She felt tears in her chest, her eyes. She ran faster, but realized in that moment that this was a dream, and in dreams there was no running. So she pushed off the ground, and flew to Adam. The voice had been right. Flying was the best thing. She alighted near him.

He ignored her, charging on, his face contorting with tears. Her heart flipped in her chest, realizing that this wasn't her Adam. This boy was five or six. He was smooth skinned and toe headed, and obviously alive with pain.

"What's wrong?" Callista called to him.

But he was beyond words. His arms pumped at his sides, his legs pumping in short, electric strides toward a grove of trees. He didn't seem to notice her. Across a stream, standing on the wooden porch of a tent-cabin, the girl with the red cords stood staring.

"Hey! Where are we now?"

The girl's expression shifted slightly, but she didn't answer. "You know. The place we come. As often as we dare."

"I really don't." The feeling of not being prepared returned in a rush of terror. "Please?"

"Leave me alone." The red-pants girl turned and walked back into the cabin. "You have your own path, or whatever it is Tolland says."

Callista walked slowly back down the path toward the sea, suddenly tired. She found a bench looking over the bay and sat, her feet now clad in beaded moccasins like ones she had worn when she was in fourth grade. The archipelago spread out as far as the eye could see, each island covered in white-barked trees, leaves rustling. There was a strong feeling of magic in the air.

"Could you to come back and explain to me? If you don't mind? Melu...Meli?" Callista called out to the water. "About what I want, my deepest..."

Her eyes drifted closed.

Then her hands were biting with cold, and Adam was cursing, and she could hear the sound of snow cats moving over the trail nearby.

"Fuck." Adam said. "I'm going to lose at least three toes."

Her hands stung, and her legs seem to belong on someone else's body. She heaved herself up from where she had collapsed at the bottom of the tree well, managing to open the back of her neck to a load of snow that snaked painfully down her spine, waking her up with a stream of icy water.

"Idiot." She said to herself. Her mouth was dry, and her nerves were on fire with the assault of circulation as she climbed up the bank back to the trail. The air bit her face.

"Don't look." Adam said, turning to take a leak.

Callista's eyes adjusted to the dimness. The snow cats were thundering on the next run, out of sight. Their headlights looked menacing from below. She guessed the driver could see nothing outside their brightness.

She and Adam carried their skis and poles down the remaining hundred yards to the parking lot. Her feet hurt, both from blisters and the return of feeling. There were ten or twelve cars remaining, service workers or the grooming crew.

They were warm and red faced by the time they reached the Goat, which was painfully frigid inside. They compared notes on what the tea had done to them, as the engine purred and warmed. Adam's experience had been a mashup of his favorite boy's adventure stories, wilderness trips, and memories from when his family lived in Florida. He saw no archipelago, but rather the remote trails his father took him to on the early mornings they went out hunting.

"But I remember dancing with you, Hon." He said, throwing his soaked hat and gloves into the back seat. "In my Realm, you had on hot pants and a pair of go-go boots."

"You're such a liar." She said.

He shook his head. "It's true. You looked like a backup dancer on Flip Wilson."

She shook her head, though she had worn hot pants and go-go boots in fifth grade, as part of a dance costume. "You were a little boy."

He nodded, smile dropping off his face. "Yes. I saw him too. Running away from a whooping, the poor tyke."

"Is that why you were crying?" Callista asked, then laughed. "Oh shit. It was a fucking mushroom dream, and here I am doing investigative journalism."

And then they were laughing so hard they couldn't breathe, and she was afraid she would pee her Levi's, and Adam was thumping her back gently to keep her from hyperventilating. They stayed that way for a long time, tears streaming, stomachs clenched, trying to stop, and then laughing harder.

"Maintain." Adam said the codeword softly and she straightened, the smile dropping off her face. Across the snowy parking lot, two Sheriff vehicles drove off the highway and toward the lodge. One was a Suburban, the other a patrol car, moving diagonally across the rows purposefully.

Callista wiped the last of the tears from her eyes. "We're innocent. Completely."

"That's right. We're just a couple of love birds making out on a Friday night. Is that so wrong?" He said in the fake voice of an upright citizen just trying to keep the country from sliding to ruination. "What is the world coming to when a man can't get to third base with a beautiful girl in the back of a freezing car?"

They laughed companionably, a bit harder, Callista thought, than the joke deserved. But she liked it when Adam called her beautiful. The Goat roared as they bumped and slipped to the highway. Snow stirred in the wind of passing semis. Adam pulled them into traffic, and Callista pushed Jefferson Airplane into the eight track. They tried to figure out if there were rules the to the Realm, as they wound up calling it.

"Yeah." Adam said, "You have to be wasted to get there."

Neither of them had ever taken mushrooms before, or any other psychedelics.

"Maybe all trips are like that." Callista said, leaning her head on the cool window.

"Which explains why there are so many songs about them."

She laughed. "Are you saying the entire rock cannon is about drugs?"

"Not only rock. Books. Adventure stories. This is well known, York. PhDs have been earned. Lectures given."

"So, it's drugs, not magic?"

Rain drummed on the windshield as they plunged down toward Fairfield. Ski bus went all the way to Seattle, so taking the Goat saved them almost an hour.

"Are mushrooms drugs?" Adam said. "Is nature not magic? What is the point of growing up in this fucking wilderness of rain and snow if you don't get hooked on that?"

She smiled, closing her eyes. "Nature is magic. A Pacific Northwest Journey by Adam Frazer."

"And Callista York."

"Illustrations by the cosmic unconscious."

"Gaia to you."

He reached to turn up the volume on Go Ask Alice, and they shrieked along as loudly as they could.

5

— · —

Chapter Five

Callista woke with Bodhi kneading her shoulders like a depressed baker, her parents' bedside phone ringing on and on. She gazed at the ceiling, the fuzzy thirst of a mushroom hangover on her tongue. The cat's fur felt soft as she counted the rings. Ten, twenty...

"Hello." She imagined her mother's face when she heard Callista's voice, ready to plunge into her side of the story.

"Good morning sleepy head. Can you borrow the Goat?" Her brother sounded amused.

"Yes." She sat up. It was 9:46.

"I will be standing in front of the Alaska sign."

"Thirteen Coins?"

"Obviously."

He hung up. She called Adam, and after a few minutes' wrangling, got permission to borrow his car.

They always ordered Denver omelets. Callista noticed that Spencer had started drinking his coffee black, and from how lean his frame had become, she doubted he ate many meals as big as the one they had in front of them in the cushy booth at the Thirteen Coins. His face was similar to hers, a pale round whose softness was mitigated by high cheekbones, a decisive, slim nose, and a large, fleshy mouth. Shadows hovered around his eyes, lack of sleep, worry, or

Callista suspected, obsession. Everyone thought he was easygoing but his sister, who knew well that under his feigned affability lurked a swift, merciless will.

"So, no more swim team?" She poured sugar into her coffee.

"What makes you say that?" He smiled, his face suddenly rueful and cute, a boy.

"I don't know. Your hair's less green."

"Took too long. I'm pre-med now. I know. I hate myself too." Spencer shrugged. "They didn't tell you I was coming home for the weekend?"

She shrugged. "Are they?"

He gazed at her impassively. "What do you think?"

Callista twirled melted cheddar on her fork. "Did they offer you money to come babysit me?"

"I'm financially dependent on them. As I believe you know. But..." He sniffed a pat of butter, then tasted it with his tongue. Callista knew this was to amuse her, and it did. She smiled.

"But...?"

"I had an interest in returning here, for a short time. To check on you, and also..."

"Who is she?"

He sighed deeply.

They took their foil swans of leftovers and she drove back to the house, dimly aware that he was at least as hungover as she was. They didn't discuss their parents, or what was so interesting that it meant skipping the last Thanksgiving dinner before their youngest child left for college.

Callista thought about the Realm, and the snow well, and Adam's face as he had returned to Friday night off the sanctioned trails, and the voice talking about her deepest desires. How would this inner apparition know? Though, Vivian probably did. And Vivian liked to parse out such information when Callista least expected it, when what was called for was action and not reflection. Melusine the Mermaid seemed to imply that Callista wanted something concrete, like a bright jewel or new pet, a definable object. She seemed as hardened as anyone else to Callista's vague yearnings, the ones that came to her in the dark, when the trees were sighing in wind, and a melancholy came over her, so overwhelming it deadened even the relief of tears. It was a yearning to belong somewhere, that much was true. And there was a feeling of reaching out, grabbing for the air, for flight, or speed, or a superpower that would make Callista, not invisible or able to fly, but the opposite. What she wanted was closer to being still, being rooted in a place where she was meant to be, where her being had a purpose, and the drive to hurtle away wasn't always tugging at her like a bodily craving. The thought of her mushroom fantasy being so oblivious made Callista nauseous, even while she understood that an apparition might not be allowed to voice what she herself could not. It might be part of the rules, of her own rules, the inhibition that kept her from knowing herself or remembering things, kept her from being able to speak up in times of threat unless Vivian was there to do the talking for her.

"Are you all right?" Spencer said.

"I am." Callista smiled, though she knew he saw underneath as clearly as she through him.

They went to Fair Square Cinema that afternoon and watched The Stunt Man. They both liked it. At Washington Mutual's pneumatic tubes on the corner of Eighth and Main, he deposited a check in their father's hand and took out a stack of bills. Then they went to QFC and bought hamburger helper, a pound of meat and one of bacon, two loaves of bread, five boxes of Kraft macaroni and cheese, three boxes of cereal, two cartons of milk, two dozen eggs, three each of apples, oranges, and bananas, a head of iceberg lettuce, a cucumber, three beefsteak tomatoes, a jar of peanut butter, a bottle of chocolate syrup, a brick of cheddar, a pound of butter, five jolly rancher sticks in watermelon flavor, five packages of Hershey's chocolate, two jiffy pop pans, a case of Camel filters, and Mad Magazine.

When they had finished unloading and fed Bodhi, Spencer announced that they were going into town.

"Me, too?" Callista's stomach swooped. She rarely crossed back over the lake after dark. He always had, even in high school. Spencer had gone to Peregrine as an athlete, but he had been an excellent student, to everyone's surprise. Callista knew that Spencer was at least part of the reason that she was there at all. The admissions committee had thought she would be something like him. Her grades compared but no one loved her the way they all loved him. She agreed with them.

They obvious shared DNA, but Callista except for her gray eyes and thick dark blond hair that grew straight into her face, her face never looked put together, and he always did. His center part seemed intentional, part of his scruffy look in general, which sat elegantly on his six five frame, shoulders flaring to take up space like an eagle pushing all lesser birds aside. He was a man, skinny and young as he might be. The air belonged to him.

But she was a girl, and her height and broad shoulders were an affront to the room she was supposed to share with everyone else. No one said that out loud, but she saw it in the concerned look on their mother's face whenever they ran into other law partners. Once Margaret had insisted she and Callista wait for the next elevator at the opera house, so the pair of elderly partners and their wives wouldn't have to crane their necks to make eye contact with her.

Margaret was five seven. Phillip, their father, was six three. Callista knew from biology that her five feet eleven inches of solid flesh wasn't her fault but just the combination of genes she had inherited. But only Adam seemed oblivious to it. Everyone else commented, one way or another, either that Callista was lucky, or that she was intimidating. Neither felt complimentary, but Callista thanked whoever had said it, as if she didn't know what she had done to deserve to be so unusual.

They parked the Goat on Broadway near the Harvard Exit, which was playing Heaven's Gate. Callista had already seen it. She was feeling numb with the cold rain of the evening, and the nearness to her brother, which was simultaneously comforting and full of tense silences she knew better than to try and pierce. They ordered drinks at the Deluxe, which was filling with people. Spencer got her a screwdriver, along with a beer for himself. He lit up a cigarette.

"So, what are we up to tonight?" She smiled. "Did mother ask you to get me drunk and admit I need to go on the pill or something? Are they getting a divorce, and don't want to tell me themselves?"

"Can't I buy my sister a drink?" He smiled brightly.

She sipped, the snap of tequila and orange sweetness warming her like electric candy. "So it's a girl."

He sipped his beer, avoiding her gaze. She wondered if he was already high, his eyes half closed, shoulders relaxed in a way he usually wasn't. He was playing some kind of game. She was a prop, and the cocktail a form of payment. Callista took a taste, wondering if she should tell him about the Realm. He might understand. It was the kind of surprise Spencer had always provided, treating her as if her life weren't hers alone. She understood why her parents hated living with her. Without Spencer, all the magic had gone out of their family.

He got another round. They sat watching patrons gather two or three deep at the bar. Men in leathers, older professorial couples, a handful of punks in plaid. Callista wondered idly how much time Spencer needed to waste in order to make it look like they were just running into whoever it was, accidentally. She had seen her brother obsess before.

Callista was thinking about the girl in the red cords when she realized that Spencer's face frozen, lips slightly curled, eyes blinking slowly as if in pain. She turned her head nonchalantly. A girl with long, smooth black hair had walked in, shaking herself off and removing her raincoat. She was slim and graceful, with the face of an actress, bony and still. She handed her coat to a guy with a beard, something soft about him like an older professor. The girl turned toward Spencer, fixing him with a look of such knowing stillness that Callista had to avert her eyes.

Spencer dragged on his cigarette and turned back. The girl continued staring, and she felt some intense energy pass between them. Callista felt her face redden. She should have worn makeup, and brushed her hair for longer, tried to look pretty enough to date Spencer, though the idea of it was repugnant. She knew her brother would do the equivalent to help her get something she wanted. If only there were something, Callista thought, and felt Vivian's cold presence like invisible teeth bared. No self-pity. No whining. The girl and her date moved to a booth of their own, and Spencer finished his beer. They left the bar without a backward glance, and Spencer announced they were going to Belltown.

They settled into a shabby booth at the Two Bells and ate burgers and fries, which Spencer paid for with a new one-hundred-dollar bill. He drank another beer, but she settled for Sprite.

"I wore my dancing shoes." Callista said when the silence between them stopped being companionable, and started feeling more like brooding.

"Mom and Dad are both sleeping with other people." Spencer said matter-of-factly. He fished another smoke out of his breast pocket, but didn't light it.

"I don't care." She said, a feeling of hot tears under her eyes, and beneath that, a yearning to be warm, to be safely out of the rain and in a hot bath, or swimming in a summer lake.

"Mom said we should be glad, because it means they're not divorcing."

Callista stared at him, a cottony numbness spreading through her. "Glad."

He laughed as if she'd made a joke. "That's right. She said it was a perfectly lovely couple they had met at that self-actualization seminar."

"I see." She put her burger back in its basket of fries, wishing the tequila sunrise had been stronger. "Well. That's important."

Then they were both laughing.

"I wanted to ask how they would know." He said sourly.

She raised her eyebrows. "That divorce is worse?"

He moved the cigarette to his ear and ate a fry. "How they would know when they were *actualized*."

"Ah."

"She hung up on me."

"So. They're where?"

He shook his head. "Near San Francisco. The people live there. Ted and Alice, or whomever."

Callista felt Vivian ready to take over.

"So they're having group sex instead of turkey on Thursday? Is that what you're telling me?"

He shuddered. "Dad offered me a lot of money to come tell you. It would have saved him a bundle if you'd answered the phone."

And then she palmed her face. "So the girl at the Deluxe..."

"Oh no. I didn't come here just for the money. She's pretty, no?"

"Gorgeous. Spence. What are you doing for Thanksgiving?"

He shrugged. "Going to Tahoe to ski, obviously. Anyway, Mom and Dad...who knows?"

"Let's not..." She shivered.

"No. Let's never."

They walked down Bell to First avenue. The Vogue was playing Prince and Tugs throbbed with the sound of Joy Division. At Pike street, the wet cobblestones reflected the orange Public Market sign. Beyond the neon glow, two ferries passed in Elliott bay, their windows gleaming like fallen skyscrapers. Callista wished she and Spencer were aboard the outbound boat, heading to Port Townsend, or making the endless rainy drive to Hoh. She wanted to sit in the Water Street Tavern and watch old hippies talking about their glory days on the McGovern campaign, not be contemplating a Sunday with no plans other than to put her brother back on a plane. They stopped under the marquis for the Showbox. The Fastbacks.

"Do you wanna?" He said. "Dad was desperate. I can afford it."

A slow smile spread over her face.

Callista was of the opinion that punk was so successful because the thumping of drums upset circadian rhythms. Music was medicine and punk was the strongest. The louder and more beat-laden the sound, the better it was for your mood. By the second song, *It's Your Birthday*, she and Spencer were in the mosh pit, and by the fourth he had forgotten all about making sure she didn't get elbowed too hard. She got lost in the dancing, her hair hitting guys in the face until they started to laugh, shoving one another around and around, her tallness and advantage, her weight a form of protection. Spence looked like he was meditating, his eyes closed, head bobbing up and down while his hands moved over invisible instruments and his shoulders swayed.

When they got home, sweaty and tired, Callista was ready to fall into her parents' bed and rub the evening's exertions all over it. She wondered if it was worth going downstairs to get her own toothbrush, deciding to forget any form of cleanliness that night. Her ears were ringing, and her hair was soaked. The note taped to the front door almost went unnoticed, as she and Spencer entered via the kitchen door like always. But she had to pass it on her way to bed, and the envelope made a darker rectangle against the glass.

It was written in memo form, on Fairfield Police Department stationary.

To: York

From: Officer R. Franklin

Re: Missing Peregrine Student/Leslie McCall

6

CHAPTER SIX

"**I** got a thing from the cops!" She laughed, though it wasn't funny.

"About what? Did they get news of your burgeoning tequila habit?"

She grabbed the paper back from Spencer's hands. "Do you have a number for them?" She meant their parents. "This seems like the kind of thing you need a lawyer for."

He shook his head. "Nope. I asked and they…"

"Never mind."

She read aloud, "*Dear Yorks, please call me at your earliest convenience.*"

He grimaced. "That sounds…very murky. I wouldn't call."

Callista found a paper towel and wiped off some of her sweat, turning on lights, putting water on the stove to boil. She tried to remember Leslie McCall's face, then moved to the wall organizer by the phone. In the hand-stapled school directory, Leslie was listed as a Freshman.

When the phone rang, Spencer answered it immediately. Callista didn't have time to explain why she couldn't risk speaking to their mother. He didn't know about her attacks, or at least, he thought they were something she had grown out of.

"It's for you." He held out the receiver. He mouthed the word "Adam".

"Hey." Callista tried to keep the surprise out of her voice. It was eleven forty-three. Adam never called her that late.

"Did the police come to your house?"

His voice was shot full of anxiety and performative energy. His father was obviously listening from another extension. She realized with creeping guilt that Adam must have been calling her for hours, and Mr. Frazer had no doubt been asking where the car was.

"Spencer came into town and we went out for dinner and to a movie. I think there was a note on the door from a detective asking about Leslie McCall? I don't know her. Obviously, I will tell them anything they want to know. But, I guess I figured Dad would want to read it before I did."

Spencer watched her, his face a combination of admiring and puzzled. She shrugged. She had never tried to explain the complexity of her situation with Adam. And Spencer had always insinuated that he knew, anyway. Such arrangements were not unknown at Peregrine.

"Leslie is one of the kids from my ski class Friday night. She didn't make it onto the bus, apparently."

"Oh no." She said with a bit more concern than she felt. Her ears were ringing pleasantly, and her shirt had dried stiff with sweat. "Any idea what she did instead? Are they sure she didn't just grab a ride with a friend?"

Callista imagined the mountain, the darkness, the wind blowing snow onto oncoming semi-trucks. It was not a place for fifteen-year-old girls, even if she and Adam had fallen asleep there.

"No idea. Class was normal. We worked on staying in the fall line. She showed improvement." Adam said, all business. "I don't take the kids to the bus. They leave straight from our final run. So wherever she went, I wouldn't have that information. Unfortunately, since I'm sure her family must be frantic."

"Of course." Callista said woodenly. "They're sure she wasn't on the bus?"

"Miss Lily didn't remember seeing her, and neither did Mr. Kling. Her stepdad was waiting at school I guess, but she never got off."

Callista wanted to say that Miss Lily was far too occupied with the misery of driving through the frozen dark to be paying attention to roll call. And Mr. Kling was a bit of a joker, a sing-along-leading weirdo, not someone you'd depend on. But she decided to wait until she and Adam were together in person.

"What do the police think happened?"

Callista heard a sound on the line, a faint clicking. Someone listening in, or hanging up after listening in.

"They didn't say. But naturally they were wondering if I had seen anything."

He didn't say, *if I had anything to do with her disappearance.* Callista waited for him to mention that they had met after his shift ended. Obviously, he wouldn't volunteer that they had been high, or flying through a colorful fantasy realm or anything else compromising. Admitting they had driven home together after hours, after some rare alone time was an alibi, wasn't it? Should she admit to that? Give the listeners the idea that she and Adam had been up to something romantic in the back seat of his car, something less damning than drinking mushroom tea? She never knew exactly what his father saw as an infraction. She decided to play it straight.

"Do they have any theories as to who she might have gotten a ride from? There were lots of skiers. Maybe she ran into a friend."

The silence stretched out, full of tension she wasn't clear on. Her head was beginning to throb. Spencer motioned to boxes of tea, and she indicated the market spice flavor. He took down the old tea pot their mother had bought at the Fairfield Art Fair when they were in elementary school, covered in the impressions of fern leaves in thick clay.

"Her skis and bag were aboard the bus."

The line clicked emphatically.

Then Adam whispered, "I told them you and I were late because we were breaking up. I don't know why." And hung up.

"Well for fuck's sake." Callista said, replacing the receiver. "After your romantic proposal of marriage."

"Trouble in paradise?" Spencer said, reaching into his backpack for a small tin, from which he produced a joint.

Callista pulled down two cups. "He just is so afraid to be caught doing anything. His father has this insane need for control of every detail of Adam's life. It makes him crazy. Like, he wants me to be his girlfriend but then he wants to make it seem like our relationship is on the rocks. Our imaginary relationship."

Spencer studied her, rummaging in the drawer for a match.

She was too tired to blush. "You knew."

He lit up. After holding in the smoke for a minute, he said, "He doesn't honestly think anyone believes the two of you."

She poured the orangey scented tea. Something akin to relief washed over her, with the steam. "It's not that simple."

"It never is." Spencer studied her.

Vivian spoke before Callista had any awareness that she had appeared. "So. I call the cops tomorrow and out my boyfriend? Or I lie and say we weren't tripping off trail? Because let me tell you the psilocybin this season is...whoa."

He passed her the joint, his blue eyes swimming with amusement. "Little sister. It's all so complicated with you."

Vivian sucked in the burning leaf smoke and laughed, letting the hoarse feeling in her throat merge with the shredded feeling in her head. "It's very simple. Never tell the truth and nothing bad can happen."

The kitchen filled with an unfamiliar haze.

Callista ignored the note. She told people at school that her father was taking care of it. "Being an attorney and all that."

No one seemed overly worried about Leslie McCall. As scuttlebutt trickled around school, she learned that everyone who had been skiing on Friday night had been questioned. When the detective finally caught up with her on Wednesday morning during her free period, Callista felt confident her participation was perfunctory.

Officer Franklin appeared by Mr. Kling's side after French. "Callista, you're a hard girl to catch up to." Mr. Kling said, grabbing her sleeve. She wrenched it back. Kenneth Kling was the school's Lacrosse coach and ski school chaperone and an object of scorn. He smiled sheepishly as she wrenched her arm back.

A man stood next to him, in a crisp uniform, hat under one arm.

She stopped in her tracks. He was the kind of guy she avoided talking to, cute, mid-twenties, blond hair shorn around the neck in the way soldiers continued to do after they left the military. They were the ones who started nice, then began pressing for advantage, then began with insults if she didn't respond. Still, that wasn't quite fair. She didn't know him. He certainly looked worth a few moments time.

"You were with Adam Frazer after his ski class last Friday?" Franklin said.

She wondered what her father would tell her to do. "Yes, sir."

"I've been speaking to witnesses in the art room."

She suppressed a smile, imagining their assistant head of school, Valerie Mayer, relegating Franklin and his uniform to the art building, which was used only for elective classes in afternoon blocks. Ms. Mayer would want to hide him. And the gold embroidered Fairfield Police patch ablaze on his chest.

He moved slowly, seemingly self-conscious.

They mounted the stairs past batik flags made by the elementary schoolers and entered the room where Corning Aster taught drawing and painting. Charcoals of a semi-nude model hung from clips, breasts at various angles, crudely rendered by lower classmen. Franklin sat at one of the long tables. Callista's intuition told her to wait, and she felt vindicated when he picked up a clipboard, gathered a pen, and cleared his throat before motioning gravely for her to sit.

For some reason, she didn't want to make things easy for him. But at that moment, she couldn't have said why. "Any news on Leslie?"

Franklin looked at her with large hazel eyes of surprising intensity. Callista was aware that he hadn't expected her to speak first, or to ask questions.

"I know everyone is very worried." She said.

"Are you worried, Miss York?" He said softly.

Callista thought of drama class, of exercises Beatrice Hollymore had taught them, to modulate their voices in resonance with the text. She decided to learn what she could from him, if for no other reason than the school seemed to breathe as easily after Leslie's disappearance as it had before, and that bothered her. Obviously, she knew nothing. But this young man might.

"Of course I am." She matched his tone. "I was there on Friday night. It was cold."

He looked hard at her. She met his gaze. In her head was a faint echo of her father's voice demanding to know why the police weren't out solving the crime instead of harassing his daughter. Her parents were real estate attorneys, not criminal ones. But still.

"Friday night at the pass. What time did you connect with Adam Frazer?" He looked at his clip board. "He said he gave you a ride home, but I am confused about how precisely you met up."

Callista had been thinking about this question all weekend, and had settled on a lie that was almost true. Something simple. "May I depend on your discretion, Detective?"

He blinked. Then he blinked again as if she were completely out of line. *Dammit,* Vivian said in a sarcastic tone. *He's one of those kind. Smarter than everyone, especially girls.*

He spoke loftily. "Of course, Miss York. What can you tell me?"

She sighed, looking around at the naked torsos around the room. "Adam and I have been seeing each other."

Franklin smiled, his eyes wrinkling just slightly. He might be 24 or 25. Not much older than she was, but out in the world, seeing whatever dark underbelly Fairfield let slip. "So I've been told."

"Well. I am convinced that Mr. Frazer has the wrong idea about us."

"The wrong idea?" Franklin shifted in his plastic chair.

"Yes. He has intimated..." She pushed a strand of hair from her face. "Mr. Frazer has implied that he thinks Adam and I are..." She allowed her face to finish the thought. Embarrassment and mortification rose, feelings she was sure applied to both the truth and the half-truth of her words.

"Having sexual intercourse?" Franklin said softly.

She covered her face in her hands. "Yes."

Vivian laughed inwardly. A long, tense moment passed. Then she removed her hands.

"The thing is, Officer Franklin. No one would believe us if we said that we weren't."

He gazed at her, then said in a voice that betrayed perhaps a tiny measure of admiration, "I'm sure some people would believe you."

Was he impressed that they weren't having sex? She suppressed a laugh. Then let go another sigh. "Mr. Frazer is...suspicious. He seems to think Adam is doing something he shouldn't."

"And meeting you to ski off trail is something he shouldn't be doing, is that it?"

She shrugged, and tried to change the subject. "Do you know what it means to have your father's disapproval, to a kid like Adam?"

Franklin looked up suddenly. "What?"

Callista wondered how much to say. Something about the fact that Franklin was police, not only police but the authority from where she and Adam lived, made her want to tell him everything. The mornings of Adam being blue around the face, the endless rules of when he could and couldn't leave the house, Lobo growling, Adam muttering about getting the belt, calling it a whuppin. The shining floor reflecting his mother's ridiculously formal shoes. How would you get a man busted for exerting exacting, brutal discipline in his own home? Still. She wished someone in authority knew.

"It means that his father can refuse to pay for college next year. And Adam is one of the brightest kids here. So...if his dad thinks we've done something he disapproves of, or risked something terrible..."

"Going to the U is that bad?" He tipped his head to one side.

Maybe she had gone too far. Did police go to college? "Of course not. But this is Peregrine...it's not why our parents paid so much tuition. You know?"

"Why did your parents pay for you to go here?" He said, his head moving slightly toward her, eyes dropping to her chest.

"I guess they have high hopes for my future, sir."

"And Adam's dad doesn't want his future decided by a baby."

Callista was surprised by the heat that rose in her body. She cleared her throat, and Franklin looked away. "Adam's dad doesn't want anything to distract from Senior year. Which is fine. But the truth is, Detective, the bigger distraction would be a big breakup. You know? It would disrupt everything."

He clipped his pen to the clipboard. "So you and Adam, are you going to stay together, then? Or, should I say, was that your plan, Callista?"

She burst out laughing, realizing how nervous it sounded. *Where was Vivian?* But Callista was still the one talking. "My plan is to get through the year, just like Adam. That's it."

He gazed at her. He was handsome, she decided, everything about him muscular and intent, reflexes coiled to spring. "Did you know Leslie McCall?"

Callista explained that she knew Leslie as well as she did any Sophomore, someone she might say hello to at the movies or on the street, but never at school. She had met Leslie's step-brother Joseph, who was her age, when he had gone to Peregrine, but he had transferred to boarding school bast East. Their huge Tudor house was close to school and they belonged to the Club, which was typical but not what Callista's family did. Her parents thought the Club was stuffy and silly, a place for people who cared about bloodlines, which was ridiculous. And that was all Callista knew of Leslie.

"Was she pretty?"

Callista laughed again. "Leslie?"

She tried to remember what Leslie looked like. Dark hair, a pale square face, and a weird way of hunching her shoulders so her stomach stretched in and her back grew broader, like she was always cold. Had Callista ever even spoken to the girl?

"I don't know." Callista said.

"Not as pretty as you?" He smiled. "Not as...attractive to a kid like Adam?"

The heat drained from her neck. "What?"

He sat back, putting the clipboard between them. "Okay, Miss York. Would you be so kind as to give me your home phone number? It's unlisted."

Vivian smiled. Had the school actually declined to give this police officer the directory? Vivian finally spoke, softly, with deliberation. "Oh, shoot. My folks would kill me. They're very protective of their privacy, you know. Being attorneys."

His eyes flashed. "Oh."

"Sorry." She stood to leave. "I sure hope you find Leslie."

"Do you?" He rose. "Thanks. I sure hope your boyfriend isn't leading you down a path you don't want to go."

She smiled. "Oh. Don't give it thought. Our paths are straight to college. That's what I've been trying to say." "Thank you." He said, rising from the desk to usher her out.

7

— · —

CHAPTER SEVEN

Outside, rain had begun to slant across the bricks, blackening the branches. Callista felt a cloak of something dark and angry slide over her, a feeling of rage so overwhelming she wanted to break the trees in pieces and throw them through the cafeteria's picture windows. Instead, she hurried to French.

That afternoon after they had dropped off the twins, who knew Leslie McCall and doubted she had a boyfriend to go home with, Adam and Callista pulled over onto Bridle Vale road and smoked a joint. They hadn't smoked much that year, which was ironic since the Goat provided such a perfect spot to light up. Who knew when Mr. Frazer would decide to sniff around and come up with a reason to punish Adam?

Once, when Callista and Spencer had been younger, their mother had come into the kitchen while they were cooking tacos with Spice Island flavoring and ground beef, and flown into a rage that they were obviously covering up the smell of their drug habit. They had watched with round eyes as she paced, enraged, telling tales of kids who were sent to juvie and worse for such behavior. It was a gateway. It was illegal. It was the sign of unmotivated, spoiled children who would wind up freaking out on acid one day.

When she had clomped into their parents' wing, Callista and her brother hadn't even laughed at first. They simply watched, intrigued by their mother's assumptions.

After a long time, Callista asked in a whisper, "Does she really think this is what pot smells like?"

And then they had been laughing, so long and so hard that when their dad came in from whatever he'd been doing outside, Callista was sure it looked like they were every bit as stoned as their mother thought.

On Bridle Vail Road it was raining in earnest. Adam passed her the joint, which she knew he had bought from Bart Frehl because the rolling paper contained a tiny metal thread that bent into a roach clip as the smoked, though she hoped not today. Sharing a whole joint with Adam would get her higher than she wanted to be. She didn't even like pot. Neither did he, really.

"Feeling the strain of suspicion, are we?" She inhaled.

His eyes narrowed. "Depends on who you mean by *we*."

"Who do I mean by we?"

He puffed sourly. "They're sniffing around Bolt."

Callista felt the shock from the cottony distance of her high. Bolton Tolland was their white-haired, erudite, benevolent head of school, and Adam's mentor. The idea of Bolt doing anything hostile to anyone was ludicrous. She couldn't even imagine him raising his voice, except in excitement about the teachings of Epictetus. "Are you kidding?"

She thought of the small blond hairs on Franklin's neck, like the head of a child. The rage came again, but muffled, by the smoke, just as Adam had planned.

"That annoying cop has been to see him three times. Others have come. They all wear their uniforms, of course. They leave their squad cars right out front. It's like they don't stop to think how it looks. To have so many authorities wandering in and out."

Callista gazed at Adam. He had stopped passing her the joint, and it had gone out. He rolled down the window and tossed it into the rain.

"Hey." She put a hand on his shoulder.

He dipped his head. "You're going to say it looks like he's taking Leslie's disappearance seriously. Which is good."

She removed her hand. Adam was always prescient like that. "I was going to say that I can see you're worried about Bolt, but he is brilliant and well connected, and he is going to be fine."

"I'll get you home." He said in a small, overly calm voice, as if she were being hysterical.

"I mean, a girl disappears. It's good that they notice. Right? Good that they care?"

He pulled her close, kissing the top of her head. "Don't think about it. It's not going to happen to you."

Callista gagged. She was having an attack. How had he known? He always saw it before she did. He started the engine, but didn't pull forward.

"It's okay. I'm not sick." She said. He nodded without looking at her.

Then she opened the door and vomited onto the muddy gravel below. The vomit tasted sour, hot, and familiar.

Adam waited until she had sat back upright and clicked on her seatbelt before pulling away. She felt bad leaving trash behind them, though the rain beat down hard enough she was sure by morning nothing would be left but the shining line of the joint's internal thread.

The headache, which was sometimes the first sign she was going down into herself for the duration of the attack, flared like a dawn. She felt that stupid way she always did when sickness suddenly sprung out of her gut, as if she should have seen the sun that now came to shine onto her with its merciless glare, the ache that pressed down with a concussive threat. Tears began to fall down her cheeks as they turned onto Mount Zebulon Road, passing three girls on horses by the side, plastic ponchos over their helmets.

"Feel better." Adam muttered miserably as she let herself out of the car, bending to retrieve her book bag.

"I always do." She waited until he was out the drive and back past the trees before hauling the bag over her shoulder. Shoots of pain trailed down her shoulder.

Mrs. Mackie had been there. The house smelled like Lysol and cigarette smoke. There was a new carton of milk in the refrigerator, along with a bowl of macaroni and cheese. Corn bread sat under foil. No note. Mrs. Mackie had precise handwriting that looked similar to what Callista had been tasked with doing in first grade, Gs with tiny loops at the top, even end strokes. But she didn't like Callista, even when she was thirteen and Mrs. Mackie had come to replace the Taiwanese girl that had lived with them. Ginger beef and rice was replaced by hamburger helper and shake and bake. Callista didn't really mind. But she had made the mistake of forgetting to greet the old woman when she came home from school the first day, instead running to grab a cookie off the place on the counter, and Mrs. Mackie had been livid. She had struggled to explain that nice girls said *thank you*, and were grateful, for all the wealth and abundance that surrounded her. Callista had stared. No one had enforced any such ruled on her before, but Mrs. Mackie had been outraged. She said the word *spoiled* under her breath, and Callista had escaped with another cookie, waiting to come back to the house until she had gone.

When Spencer was home, Mrs. Mack, as he called her, would coax out of her stories of riding the rails during the Depression, the friends who had been killed in terrible accidents while they all traveled the railroad looking for work or food. She would smile, the tip of her cigarette growing longer and whiter, until it threatened to fall onto the counter she had just wiped down. But it never did. She would rescue it just in time, ashing into the garbage disposal, then rinsing it down.

Callista knew Mrs. Mackie didn't like her, but she still appreciated that someone had been in the house. The sheets on her parent's bed had been changed. The dryer was spinning pleasantly in the background. It was something, that tumbling noise. Evidence that a family still lived there.

She went to her mother's drug supply, in a shoe box under one of the master bathroom sinks containing over the counter medication, and whatever prescription drugs had accumulated over time. Callista didn't know what any of them were for but the Percocet. She sat with the bottle in her hand, hoping Mrs. Mackie was really gone for the day and didn't walk in, as she once had, and assume that Callista was stealing drugs. Her headache had begun its inevitable descent into her spine. It wouldn't stop there. She knew.

The phone rang. This time there was no question of answering it. Callista wouldn't be able to say more than a word or two before she threw up. She slumped to her side, holding the bottle. It was too much effort to open it, then.

The ringing phone had been the deciding factor. She replaced the unopened drugs under her mother's sink, and went to the toilet, where she spent the next few hours patiently allowing her body to purge her of anything that it held, until she sat in the shower crying, her head exploding with pain, letting the now-cold water run over her until she could no longer stand it. Then she wrapped herself in a towel, and fell asleep in her parent's big bed, soaking the pillowcase.

Callista felt emptied in the morning. She hung up her towel and opened her mother's closet. She might be reprimanded for borrowing clothing, but it seemed so hard to go all the way to the other side of the house, down the stairs, to her own room. It would be cold down there, dark and silent.

She picked out a blouse to wear over her Levi's, and a pair of clean socks. She opened a drawer and sprayed on some Chanel Five, which she loved enough to tolerate the overwhelming nostalgia it raised.

Adam leaned over to unlock the door. "You look like shit."

She pulled her cap over her hair, which she realized she had forgotten to brush. She hadn't eaten, either, but the emptiness inside felt floaty, almost pleasant. Who knew if she could eat yet, or if the sickness would return, as it sometimes did? Luckily, the rain had given way to weak sunshine, which streamed cheerfully through the evergreens.

She rarely saw his teeth in the Goat. They wordlessly descended into a color-less, windy day. The trees whipped. From the twin's driveway, the lake looked like a rushing river, white with foam.

"Are you okay?" She said, with terrible timing.

He turned to her, his face a mask of bland duty. "All I think about is getting to Stanford. Literally all. If I can make it through this.."

He motioned toward the lake, with Peregrine waiting just across the bridge. His wrist snapped. He hugged it to his chest self-consciously and sounded the horn. But the twins were already mounting the driveway, their red and white athletic bags over their shoulders, laughing at their private jokes.

School was festooned with mimeographed sheets advertising Leslie's disap-pearance, pleading for clues. In homeroom, Ms. Meyer announced an all-school assembly to be held after lunch. Callista sensed motion in the kids around her, something foreign disturbing the normal flow of their days. Eyes turned toward her. She realized her face looked grim already, no need to try and convince observers of her worry about Leslie. Though, when she tried to conjure Leslie's face, all she came up with was a white beret she had once seen on a dark-haired girl. Callista wasn't even sure the girl had been Leslie.

She began the climb to Walker Hall, wondering if she ought to put her own hat on against the mist, deciding against it. She still felt the sting of her sleepless night, the floating of her empty body. The sky was a tepid pearl, admitting only a few yellowish rays, like the moment of feeling well again after a long sickness before you realize you just want to go back to sleep.

"Hey, fat ass!" A falsetto sounded behind her, and she felt a sharp pinch on her left butt cheek. Harriet's smiling face appeared next to hers. "Wake the fuck up."

Clarissa made an effort not to smile. "You can kiss my fat ass."

"You wish." Harriet said affably, matching her pace to Callista's. Her unathletic, slender body was surprisingly agile. She was wearing a trench coat and silk scarf that Callista assumed must belong to her mother, or grandmother. It suited her. Harriet was unapologetically eccentric, like every other Peregrine lifer. She often wore red lipstick or a neckerchief, which made her look like a children's book illustration. "What happened to Les? Any theories?"

Callista shrugged. "I don't know. Why does anyone disappear?"

The tears she had shed the night before sprung up again out of nothing. Harriet had been her first friend at Peregrine, and could be trusted not to judge if Callista showed her real feelings. That fact alone was a balm on her jagged heart.

"Do you think this means Morgan will relax the grading curve? I heard they talked about it in the faculty meeting."

"You're going to get an A anyway, you feckless whore. What do you care?"

"I'm thinking of you, dumbass."

Callista laughed. And then she was unable to stop, tears rolling down her face, snot threatening to erupt from her nose. Callista was an even better American Studies student than Harriet, a source of unending irritation to her friend.

"Thanks for the charity." She said, her voice rising. "You're a goddamn font of generosity."

"Well." Harriet said, wiping her own eyes. "Someone has to look out for you. God knows your boyfriend is busy enough trying to keep from getting caught with his hands down Tolland's pants."

"Oh God." Callista said, imaging Adam and the Headmaster together.

Harriet was stating a fact that most everyone suspected that there was a romance between the Adam and Dr. Tolland. But Callista usually avoided the actual mechanics of it. In truth, Adam had implied that the feelings between him and their headmaster were unrequited, and even if they had been returned, Tolland would not allow any physical contact between them. But the notion of a romance between them was more salacious and exciting, and Callista guessed people simply preferred a sexier version.

"Did I offend you?" Harriet said, her voice incredulous.

"A dirty cow like you?" Callista rolled her eyes. "Say what you like about my boyfriend. We know what we feel for one another."

They laughed, entering the huge, peaked door of Walker Hall, all carved oak and iron knockers, preeningly gothic. Callista loved the place, every threadbare oriental carpet and nonsensical stained-glass window with scenes of St. George.

"Is Adam okay, though? He looks more than ever like he's about to throw himself dramatically into the sea." Harriet said in a low voice as they settled into seats before the grand fireplace.

"I guess. I don't know. Listen though, for what it's worth…" she wanted to say that Adam's problem wasn't at school but at home, but they were almost at their classroom. She trusted Harriet, but Adam didn't. Callista could say nothing.

Only she was aware of the tight control over Adam's time. He would have no opportunity for romance with their headmaster, even if his love were returned, which she suspected it wasn't. If there had been something physical between the two, they would have had to get together during school hours, in the office or some other such corner of school. It was impossible. Other teachers had engaged in sex with students at Peregrine over the years, though they had been required to get married after graduation. At their rival school, Cedar Point, there were such couplings at least once a decade. But they were always between a male teacher and a female student. Anything else would have been deemed unseemly. Adam couldn't marry Tolleson, though in an odd way Callista liked the idea of them together, the white-haired, gentle scholar and the ruddy cheeked, fierce misfit in his yellow muscle car.

But more than love, Adam wanted escape. She envied him the clarity of his yearning. She wanted him to have his freedom above all, if for no other reason than it gave her hope. No mere college could release her from her own cage. What ailed Callista was nameless and invisible, clear only when she was having an attack, and then disguised as her own mild insanity. If there was an institution that would unlock that, and free her, she had yet to find it on a list. At least Adam sympathized. The whole point of their friendship was to confuse matters for the outside observer, to strew crumbs down a false path. Callista wouldn't give away any details of Adam's life. Just as she knew he would never admit to people that she would be spending Thanksgiving alone, but for the cat her brother had left behind.

In the end, Harriet must have either spoken to Adam or questioned Callista's easy tears, because that afternoon her mother Grace marched over, pearls clacking, and insisted Callista come over on Thursday.

"You know what, my darling?" She called out, her gray page boy falling smoothly across her cheeks, lips shining glassy pink. "Just inform Phil and Maggie that you're having two meals. You need it. Look at you, you're fading away."

Grace was being sarcastic, Callista knew. Her parents never went by Phil and Maggie. And Callista's body was ripe and womanly under her Levi's and vest.

"You're right. I am feeling a bit under nourished." Callista said, smiling.

Grace blinked a blue eye. "Bring wine. Whatever you do, don't cook anything."

Callista was relieved to have her school day end on such a good note. They had suffered through an excruciating assembly, all five hundred students crammed into the gym on folding chairs within the ancient, creaking bleachers. Tolland had stood like a tweet-jacketed Gandalf, pleading in his quiet way.

"My friends, imagine if your family was wondering about your well-being. Think if the missing person were your sister, or your brother. The hole such uncertainty leaves in all our hearts. The sense of incompleteness we feel at any tarnish to our health and safety as individuals, and as a community. I implore each and every one of you to search your memories. Especially anyone who was skiing last Friday night, but all of us. Ask yourself anew, if Leslie mentioned anyone she had met, a friend at a different school perhaps, or someone she knew from camp in the islands, or in the equestrian sphere. The authorities are doing a most thorough job of querying her friends, teachers, and so forth. And yet, Leslie is still not back with us, her smiling face shining out, as it should be. You are the key, now. It is imperative that you redouble your efforts to summon any half-forgotten thread of a clue, any idea that may have been dismissed as being foolish. I assure you, you might have a shred of information that helps bring Leslie safely home. Please."

Then he held up the photograph that had been copied in black and white and stapled up on all the bulletin boards. This one, the original, was in color. Leslie stood staring into the camera in a white fisherman's sweater and red corduroys.

She was back in the Realm. The girl was standing on the wooden porch of the canvas cabin, staring at her. In her red pants. Leslie's face, her long cheeks and prominent nose freckled from sun, matching her golden-brown eyes.

Callista shook her head to clear it. Franklin was standing to Tolland's side, watching the students' reactions to Tolland's plea. His wide stance and dark uniform looked otherworldly. Callista pictured herself telling him that she actually had seen Leslie the previous Friday, but it had been in a dream. Or to be accurate, that she had been tripping on mushroom tea.

She felt fingers on the back of her elbow. Adam was sitting behind her, sensing her tension. But she didn't turn. They would talk about it on the car ride that afternoon. But that afternoon, her locker bore a stickie note in Miss Webber's hand. *Adam was called away. He sends his apologies for not being able to drive you home today.*

Callista almost enjoyed the Metro bus ride down Madison street past the small central district shops and hair salons, the radio towers, then Seattle University with its trophy-like buildings. It gave her time to brood. First and Pike felt muffled and quiet compared to its usual dangerous energy. Callista had once been mugged there by a hoard of other kids who insisted she hand over her money, then they took her book bag and kicked it into the street to be run over by a passing car. Some of the parents had come together afterward to make sure Peregrine kids had a network of carpools and ride shares. So in a way, it was Callista's fault Adam had to drive the Goat.

The market sign shone orange in the watery air. On another day she and Harriet would meet at Frederick's for Frango milkshakes in the basement diner. They might paw through the discount makeup section, where Callista had bought her mother birthday perfume before she understood how second rate the products were. Today, she felt satisfied to mount the rubberized accordion bus taking her over the I-90 bridge, to Old Fairfield, past Jafco which made her think of all divorced dads buying new stereo equipment for their new waterbed apartments, Bang and Olufsen or RCA. It was closed now, with none of the low-slung German sports cars that usually dotted the parking lot. She got off the bus at Hunter's Glen, with its seedy 1950's ranch houses.

A boy she had once ached for, Chris Lansky, lived in that subdivision. They'd taken the same bus to Cascade Junior High, his winged, glossy brown hair riding his high cheek bones in waves. Once at a school dance, he had asked her to partner with him for one song after another, until she was breathless, and Rail and Company had taken a break from their covers of Chuck Berry and Aerosmith tunes. Chris had simply walked away, leaving her standing alone on the now-silent gym floor. She had looked to see if anyone was laughing, if his friends were putting him up to it. But she saw nothing in the darkness but couples and stoners, people who had come to see the band, like she had. She loved Rail and Company. But she couldn't decide how to feel about what Chris Lansky had done.

Days later, someone had written *Chris L plus Brenda C* on the bathroom stall, and Callista had felt a combination of dread and relief. Brenda was the prettiest girl in their class, a cheerleader, larger than life. Callista assumed, knowing it was taking herself a bit too seriously, that Brenda had written it there just so she would see it, so she would know that Chris was taken. But it had never occurred to Callista to try to be with him. It had been terrifying enough just to dance together.

She had never spoken to him before, and afterward, he continued to saunter onto the school bus and ignore her completely. She trudged on, wondering if he had changed now in high school, and if Brenda was still or ever really had been his girlfriend. Callista had always wondered what would have happened if either one of them understood that Callista was no competition, never had been, could no sooner poach another girls' man as fly to the moon. She never spoke of the interaction with Chris Lansky to anyone, not that she had many friends in junior high, beyond the librarians. Callista had found that not speaking was the key to survival in the brutal and bewildering place. Especially after the thing had happened. After the thing, for a long time, only Vivian was able to speak at all. And no one liked being around Vivian. Not even Callista.

She pulled her cap on. She was wearing a wool sweater and down vest over her jeans, and a pair of nylon Nikes. They weren't ideal for walking in wet conditions. She wished for a pair of gloves. She only owned the orange ones. Maybe she would go to college someplace where a person wore thin, dark wool gloves or even red leather. But when she thought of college, darkness loomed. It seemed like something for other people. Something she would have to force herself into like the terrifying halls of Cascade Junior High. The thought made her feel like an unexploded ball of tears. The urge to hide was so strong that she had to force herself to keep breathing and move one foot past the other.

A name for the feeling appeared in her mind. *Self-pity.* But at least she wasn't sick. She was hungry, and chilly, and full of childish woe, which wasn't acceptable. Callista sighed at how quickly she had come to her action of last resort, the only surefire way to come back to sober reality. Resigned, she reached up and slapped herself across the face, three times, as hard as she could, so hard her cheek snapped to one side, and then the other. Cars passed with their lights on. Families going home for dinner. She wanted dinner. She wanted light and cooking smells, and homework time with the news on in the background. No doubt Bodhi was hungry, too.

The lighted sign for Mount Zebulon shone out from the brick platform where its oversized, carved placard rested, as if their sprawling suburban development were a national monument rather than a collection of comfortable homes and hobby ranches of a few acres each. She had to choose between walking up the forested path, or traversing the few inches of wet undergrowth between the main road and the rainwater ditch. The forest was rumored to be dangerous, with a bogey man who would chase girls and rape them. But if a car sideswiped her in the shadows between streetlights, Callista would be up to her knees in cold, muddy ditchwater. She was very familiar with the trail. And if she took the road, a well-meaning neighbor might stop to offer her a ride. She was tired and hungry, but the humiliation of their questions would be unbearable. Out of the corner of her eye, she saw a police cruiser begin the first hairpin turn down from the top of the hill. Her decision was made.

The woods were black velvet, the only sound dripping branches and the sucking of her feet on the muddy trail. She followed a thin line of moonlight trailing between branches above. Her feet felt cold and wet, but the fresh smell of wet needles and horse manure was comforting. She thought about the feel of a horse under her, that terrifying weight and girth, the way she never liked bossing the giant beast. When she was little, she'd had birthday parties and play times and sleepovers with kids all around. When other girls talked of their horses as if they were almost people, friends with personalities and preferences and a right to attention, Callista found herself yawning.

Callista no longer had friends on the other ends of all the trails that ran through her neighborhoods like miniature dirt roads. Those kids now would only greet her stiffly, or not acknowledge her at all, not ask her how school was, or offer any information about theirs. In eighth grade, when word had gotten out that she was switching to Peregrine, everyone lost interest overnight. People who had known her name suddenly forgot it, looking through her, as if the invisibility she already felt suddenly became real. Now, four years later, only the adults seemed to recall that once, Callista had been a girl like the others, who rode horses and did levitation at sleepovers and laughed at The Return of the Pink Panther. The trees shifted, dripping water like rhinestones in the moonlight.

Callista accepted being forgotten. She liked being alone, in the woods, with no friends and no family. Like a dyad, or a sylph, someone whose body could be removed, slipped off, like an ill-fitting skin, and left behind on a broken branch for birds to eat. Vivian whispered that she was thinking all wrong. She slapped herself again, three times, as hard as she could stand it, so hard that her nails caught at the edge of her eyes, and tears came. She pushed them back in with her will, angry and hard. Her feet were cold and wet on the muddy ground. She forced them on.

The woods clicked with animal sounds, with the creatures who lived there, racoons maybe, opossums and wood rats, the occasional feral cat. There were too many birds to count, owls and hawks and wrens, the robins she detested, the scrub jays she should hate but didn't. Their screeching reminded her of her father's father Grandpa Eugene, who lived in Ohio and played golf. He had loved it when she went to Peregrine. He was proud of her, had asked why she wasn't preparing to be a debutante. Callista had been embarrassed when her parents told her, offhanded, her mother snickering about buying a gown at the awning store. Callista hadn't understood until later that it was a joke about her size, and not something else wrong about her.

Callista's hand poised in the air, ready to strike again. She breathed in and out. No. She was okay. She thought about what album she would listen to when she got home. She had been wearing out Songs in the Key of Life. But she was in the mood for The Ramones, she thought. She would make herself dinner, and put on her headphones, and go to sleep with the sound turned up.

"Miss York." A voice called out from fifty feet behind.

8

——·——

CHAPTER EIGHT

S pooked, Callista ran. She had only one idea. Escape. The whole world became that one thought. She had no keys to make into a punching fist, no hard shoe soles to kick with. And she knew what happened to girls who didn't fight. She knew. She knew. She knew.

Her breath came in loud bursts, a song of trail runs and mogul fields. She knew an almost invisible path that led off to the right in a hundred feet or so. It went to the Cahill's barn, which was only a short distance from their house. Their living room walls were mostly glass. Their lights would be on. They would be eating dinner. They had been her friends once, she had ridden with them, back before the thing happened. They might recognize her face, even now. She would go there.

"Callista!" The voice said behind her.

He was trying to convince her he wasn't following her. But she knew better. No one who called her *Miss York* would be in that forest, two nights before Thanksgiving.

And then she stopped running.

It was Detective Franklin. It had to be Franklin. And her cold fear was replaced by a combination of anger and curiosity. And Vivian came out, like a dragon from the pages of a book in a cartoon, breathing animated fire.

"Are you kidding me?" Callista said, though it was Vivian's voice, because Callista was still panting and trying to get her limbs to stop trembling.

"I'm sorry." He said. "May I approach?"

"What am I, a judge?"

She regretted saying it. But it was his fault, for arousing her wrath. For scaring her.

"I'm going to walk closer." He said.

"That much is obvious." She said. "What other plans do you have, Officer Franklin? What else do you have in mind?"

She backed toward the Cahill's trail, knowing it was both futile and unnecessary. Franklin was not there to hurt her, she knew. She knew. And yet.

He was walking toward her, his pale face incongruously young in the moonlight, dressed in the kind of street clothes she pictured sailors on leave wore, cheap dark jeans and a chambray shirt, under a rain slicker so out of fashion it made him look almost preppy. She couldn't help laughing, and letting him see her laugh.

"Is this a humorous situation?" He said, his voice strained.

Then she was angry again. "You tell me, Officer. You tell me."

She crossed her arms over her chest and glared.

"I was patrolling, and I saw you disappear into this dark trail, alone. As I said, the department is on high alert right now." He sounded irate. "Are you in the habit of walking alone in the woods at night?"

"I see your point, sir." She said, knowing how arch she sounded and liking it. She sounded like her mother, practicing a speech. "But I think since you are the one who snuck up on me, it behooves you to explain yourself, and not the other way around."

And then he was laughing, nervously, though she couldn't see his eyes in the semi dark.

"Oh boy." He said. "I can see you're not used to having to justify yourself to your elders."

"You sound like a two-bit preacher. And you're what, twenty-five? Not really that much my elder." Vivian said in Callista's voice. She must have heard that on television. Callista didn't know what two-bit was. Money, maybe? Someone cheap and worthless? In truth, she had no feeling about him at all, other than that he was cute, and she was glad he seemed to be concerned about where Leslie had gone. He had insinuated something weird at school that day, something about Callista being jealous of Leslie. Now, he just seemed out of place, a guy in a world of horse girls, someone who used the word *elder* to describe himself toward a girl in the dark, as if she owed him respect. What else did he think she owed him? She turned to walk away, her back prickling with fear. She just wanted to get away, get to the pantry, to the headphones.

"I apologize if I scared you." He called out, again not moving closer. "As I said, I was keeping an eye on things around here."

She whirled, several ideas occurring to her at once. "Why? Why here?"

She saw him deciding how much to tell her.

"I…" He sighed.

"You're watching Adam. But he could hurt me any day of the week if he wanted to." She turned away, letting her voice rise over the space between them. "Or maybe you think I know something about where Leslie is? Which is great. I applaud you for exploring leads."

He trailed after her, like a man breaking a colt.

"That is correct, Miss York. I…the truth is that I haven't been able to stop thinking of our conversation."

She interrupted. "Right. And you're in this dark park, following me, because of your investigation? Is that right?"

It dawned on her that his sole reason might be her. Vivian breathed slowly, a hunted animal weighing her options. Her mind scrambled for some threat to make, some action she could assure him she would take. But her parents, the lawyers, weren't there to back her up. She could not have her father call, or her mother petition for a restraining order, or whatever lawyers would do in this situation. They had never been helpful in times like these. They didn't see that Callista had ever needed help, or ever could. She was invisible. To them. But not to men like Franklin. Her thoughts flitted to Margaret's father, her grandfather who lived only fifteen miles away, who was a Federal Judge, a man of importance who could pull strings and make heads roll, she had heard it said. Vivian would have none of it, and forced Callista's attention back on the man before her.

"Why are you following me?"

"You're not afraid of being out here, alone?"

"For fuck's sake, officer." Vivian snapped, "I'm hardly alone. You're here."

He flinched, visibly even in the dim light, holding up his hands in a show of gentleness. "Okay, you're right. I see that I scared you. Glad you've at least got enough good sense to be nervous. Not everyone is trustworthy, you're right. It's just, I have been thinking about what you said. Something in your statement felt like a cry for help, to me." He sounded annoyed. "Plus. This is a public place. No jury in the world would find fault with me for being here."

"Okay! Have it your way." She said, finally reaching the Cahill's fence. She stepped onto their narrow path, which she felt with her cold feet, a kind of dip in the moss, made by their ten-hand quarter horse, Moses. In fifteen feet, an open gate indicated their property line. She stepped through it. "Now I'm on private property."

"Miss York. Callista. If Adam Frazer isn't responsible for what happened to Leslie McCall, that means there may be a kidnapper or killer on the loose. But you don't seem at all worried about that."

She backed away one more step. "You can't know that. You have no idea how I feel or what I worry about."

"Come on. What would possess a pretty girl like you to take the risk of walking here alone, at night? Are you putting yourself in danger intentionally, for some reason?"

"Is that what happened to Leslie?" Vivian was overheating with outrage. "She chose to put herself in danger, intentionally? And now she's simply vanished off the earth and other girls are expected to go the same way? Because we choose to? Is that what you're saying?"

"Why are you so mad? Did someone do something to you?"

She gently closed the gate, breath jagged in her throat. What was he seeing? The gate squeaked quietly and then latched.

Vivian's voice was scornful. "I am walking home from school, sir. I am returning to my home after a day at my place of learning. Which is, I believe, a perfectly ordinary and legitimate thing for me to do. And if you suspect that

I am up to some kind of bad behavior, which clearly you are, I suggest you take it up with my lawyers."

He pushed the hood off his head and scratched his scalp. "You know, I would. But I can't seem to get them to return my calls. Their assistant claims they are out of town."

Her body flushed. "Well, if that is the case, then I suggest you leave them a message. I will be. I will be letting them know exactly what happened tonight. And it wouldn't surprise me one bit if they took it up with your superiors."

He gasped, and even in the dark she could see him flinch. "Geeze. What is your...? Don't you want Leslie to be found? Don't you want to be safe yourself?"

"Are you kidding me." She said with cold fury. "Are you making some kind of connection between me walking to my own home in my own neighborhood to the disappearance of Leslie McCall? Please explain."

His hands moved as he struggled to find his words. "The connection is, you're taking an awful risk. That's all I meant. It's dark here. It's lonely."

She gazed into the middle distance as he trailed off. Through the trees, light filtered from the barn onto the Cahill's riding ring. Someone was working there, brushing Moses' coat, or cleaning tack. Maybe they were smoking a cigarette and looking at a magazine, enjoying the smell of hay and horses.

"I'm sure it appears that way to you. But this is my neighborhood. I grew up here."

"Not on this trail. At night."

Callista turned her head to stare at the cavity in his hood where his pale face shone out, his features blurry. "Detective Franklin. Surely there is someone you should be talking to besides me, who had no classes with Leslie and barely knew her?"

"I understand that you didn't know her well, Callista."

"So I'm not Miss York, now?"

"I know you didn't know her well. It seems to me the only connection you had to Leslie McCall was via Adam Frazer."

Vivian started to laugh before Callista could stop her, a deep laugh of such derision that it couldn't fail to insult Franklin.

"Okay, take it easy."

"No, no. I'm sorry." Callista gripped her fists until the pain of her nails in her palms calmed her. "It's just...if your theory is that I harmed Leslie, because I thought she had something going on with Adam...it's both funny and infuriating."

He stepped back from her, his head sinking from his shoulders. "Has anyone ever told you you're awfully...articulate?"

"I'm a high school Senior in my last trimester before I apply to college. I memorized a ton of words for my SAT. Next week is finals. That may not mean anything to you. But Peregrine students are working our tails off. Our entire futures depend on what we do in the next handful of weeks. So if you think that I am sitting around plotting against a Freshman girl because my boyfriend teaches her skiing for a few hours a week, you are fucking out of your mind."

The trees dripped water onto his hood. She crept backward slowly.

"Jesus you people are awful."

"We're just articulate, Officer."

"Will you be alright getting home from here?"

Callista laughed. "If you're so concerned about safety, maybe you ought to learn the trails system. I am almost to my front door."

She turned and walked down the path, away from the forest, between the Cahills's barn and their house. Her fear sloughed off her with the heat of the encounter, and by the time she was inside, her whole body was shaking.

She ate microwaved SpaghettiOs for dinner and poured her mother's bath salts in the hottest water she could stand. The steam helped take the smell of adrenaline away, replacing it with lilac. She wrapped herself in her father's thick robe. By the time she had done her homework there had been no time to listen to music. Sleep came easily.

The phone rang. It was 6:30 a.m. The detestable robins were chirping their stupid song. Light streamed through the trees, which were soft green and lacey. No rain.

She picked up the receiver. "What?"

The click of someone hanging up sounded too loud, like they were in the next room. She replaced the receiver and stared at it, thinking about all the prank calls she and her friends had placed in their younger days, how annoying it was to be hung up on.

Bodhi chose that moment to jump up on the bed, purring affably, as if he hadn't been in hiding for three days. Callista rose, pulling on her dad's robe, and went to feed him. He purred like a demented fur engine. She made herself instant coffee with cream and sugar, then found herself cooking an actual nutritious breakfast of scrambled eggs, orange slices, and cheese toast. She felt almost cheerful. Had the robins gotten to her?

She washed her hair and raided her own closet for clothing, tossing the things she had been re-wearing into the wash for Mrs. Mackie. Then she studied Chemistry until the Goat honked in the drive.

"Oops. Peptide chains were so fascinating I got lost."

"Just remember to talk about amino acids defending against predators and you'll get enough extra credit for two final exams." Adam kept his face turned away. "Sorry about yesterday."

"My darling, I know you had a good reason. But."

"But what? Did something happen?" He turned around in the drive.

9

CHAPTER NINE

"That maniac of a cop followed me from the bottom of the hill. On the dark trail, like someone out of a true crime novel."

"Are you joking?" He said flatly.

"I wish I were. He snuck up on me behind the Cahill's. Scared the bejeezus out of me. He implied I might have done something to Leslie because of a love triangle. With you."

Adam pulled down a side street that led to some newer houses, out of sight of the main road. When he turned to face her, she saw blue and black on the left side of his face. His cap was pulled down over a cheekbone covered in makeup, by concealer and powder. It would fool no one. Her chest made a swoop, then fell to burning rage.

He raised one hand in a beatific gesture, like an early Renaissance saint. "It's not important."

"What? Franklin's suspicions, or your broken face?"

He closed his eyes and sighed, and she realized he hadn't slept. "My...situation. It doesn't factor into the subject you just raised."

"Debate skills aren't going to help us, A." She slumped, pushing her knees onto the dash and blinking back tears. "We can't intellectualize ourselves out of this."

Two cars passed, fathers on their way to the city. A black Volvo, and an orange Audi. She couldn't see the drivers in the reflected sun on their windshields. Adam smelled like his mother's Youth Dew.

"Out of what? We haven't done anything. I know we are both the type that takes on the guilt of the world, thinking it will somehow prompt people to be better. But trying to change others never works." His voice dropped to a whisper. "We have to just let this go and worry about our own happiness."

She straightened up. "So your solution is, ace finals, get those essays in, forget about Leslie?"

"Yes, if you insist on making me sound heartless. What is wrong with that?"

"Nothing. It's just that..." The girl in her trip dream flashed through her mind, the dead look in her eyes.

"It would help you to commit yourself mentally, you know. Just imagine yourself on a campus somewhere. Try it. It might give you some focus."

She nodded. "I know."

"But...?"

"Adam. Your face is covered in bruises. You've obviously not slept. The police think we're criminals. And you're concerned about where I'm sending my SAT scores?"

"Stay focused, Cal. Don't let them confuse you, bully you, or otherwise deprive you of self-determination." The slightest rueful smile hovered on his tight lips. "Do I make myself clear?"

She slumped further into the bucket seat, straightening her knee sock under her jeans where it was slightly off center. "What would help you right now?"

"Me?" He started the engine. "I've made a decision. I am going to take a radically different approach from here on in."

She sat up. "Really?"

"Yes. Saturday you and I are going to go out."

"Where?"

"You'll see." He pulled onto the road. "We need to make some more of that tea."

School was only half populated that day, and let out at noon. The twins had already left for Jackson Hole, so Adam and Callista had time to drive around Magnolia looking for mushrooms. It was a gloomy day, with few people out, and they filled a baggie in half an hour. The bridge blew about in high winds, spray whipping the windshield, but their moods were buoyant.

"Do you have any lipstick, Cal?" Adam asked slyly. "Or...whatever. Gloss."

"Yes." She laughed. She had rarely worn makeup since Junior High, when all the girls layered on mascara and shiny roll-on lip gloss. "Why? Do you want me to doll myself up on Saturday or something?"

Callista thought he must sense it, the blank space where her desire ought to be. She thought Adam was the most beautiful person she had ever seen. But his beauty was like her house, or the brooch her grandmother had given her for her sixteenth birthday; meant for someone she wasn't, but was merely pretending to be, because to drop the chore of being that imaginary Callista would leave her empty, bereft, and above all, disappointing. If the people who loved her understood the monstrous dark chasm that was her real self, they would all cease to love her. All but Adam. And that was only because his predicament was also one of pretense, of leveraging peoples' expectations to avoid being known. A form of peace, in exchange for the sleight of hand of showing up, in the right clothes, with the right girl, and doing the dance, as expected.

"It's going to be a special night." He smiled. It looked painful.

That afternoon, Callista was surprised to find herself waiting for Adam in Peregrine's light-filled foyer while the last few students filed out, and the office rang with faculty laughter. She sighed and waited, rereading the Missing poster, Leslie's face fading from the mushroom trip, copied over by the pale girl in the photograph. She heard Adam's voice mingle with that of Headmaster and Mrs. Webber. She loved the sound. It was like Adam, to make these adults laugh, to make them delight in him. How could his parents not see that to change him was to ruin something rare and amazing? When he appeared, red-faced and breathless, she thought she had never loved anyone as much as she loved him, at least in that moment. It would pass. Strong emotions always did. His blue eyes widened.

"You okay, Cal?"

She nodded. "Just listening to you suck up, you hopeless brown noser. Good god, I want some lessons."

He smiled. Harriet sauntered by, pulling off her Walkman. "What are you two sweaty teens slobbering about? No one wants to witness your foreplay."

"Harriet, the spy." Adam replied affably.

"The bruises don't become you, love." Harriet said, tucking a lock of her black pageboy behind one ear. "Senioritis is déclassé so early in the school year. After March 25, obviously we will expect you to look a bit rough."

"Fuck yourself senseless, Harry." Adam replied, grinning. "Because god knows no one else will."

The office window shut with a small snap of displeasure.

Harriet beamed and turned toward Callista. "Do not be late tomorrow, bitch. And pack a little suitcase if you have those things in Fairfield. Or, what is it you suburbanites use? A gym bag?"

Harriet only carried canvas totes with her monogram.

"You want me to bring something exotic from the country? What, a sapling or two? Did your grandparents forget to leave you any when they logged the peninsula?"

"Oh, they left me some all right." Harriet sighed. "I meant pack some decent pajamas. We're doing scrabble with the 'rents. And I expect you to know some words, you little grind."

Adam looked quizzical.

"I'm sharing the holiday meal with the Gambles. I've told my folks, and they are delighted I'll be fattened up even further."

Adam said. "Just don't evangelize too much about Penn, please?"

Harriet snorted. "I can't afford to encourage multiple applications from this place. Brown may love us, and Cornell may consider us a wee, provincial feeder. But Penn has no notion of Peregrine, and I can only imagine how badly they'd want the beautiful Miss York if they could get their hands on her."

Callista blushed.

"Look at her." Adam said. "Is it your beauty or your attractiveness as a potential undergrad that makes you squirm?"

"Shh." Harriet said. "She's very shy. You know that."

Callista was stalking out the door to the Goat.

"Cal. Have you given any thought to my suggestion? Where are you applying?" Adam caught up with her.

Vivian smiled. "Oxford or Harvard. Which do you think has better food?"

And Adam let the subject drop.

10

CHAPTER TEN

That evening, after listening to Avalon three times and The Sky's Gone Out four, Callista noticed the distant, tinny vibrato that was the telephone. She listened to records in her father's study, on his hard, scratchy Danish modern couch, looking at his overburdened bookshelves the way she might a painting she had been looking at all her life, long past noticing detail but loving the unchanging nature of the tableau.

"York residence." She said.

"Callista?" Her mother Margaret's voice was mellifluous under normal circumstances. Now, it had a husky undertone that made Callista wonder if her mother had been smoking something.

"Hi Ma." She said.

"Is it really you?"

"Yes...?"

"Callista?"

There was a pause while Callista tried to intuit her mother's mood. Then she felt irritated. "Were you not expecting to get me? I can hang up and we can pretend you weren't able to get through and have the rest of your evening in peace."

"Oh stop it." Margaret said. "We've tried to reach you at least a hundred times. This receiver is practically a new limb for me at this point."

Callista laughed. She was angry. But the image of her mother with a telephone glued to her ear was both funny and somehow perfect. Margaret's natural habitat was the phone.

"Well, you got me."

"Phillip. She's there!"

She heard her father say something in the background.

"He sends all his love."

"Ah." Callista said. "Where are you?"

"Oh that. Well. There's so much to tell." Margaret trailed off.

Callista could hear muffled voices in the background. "It's not a complicated question, Mother."

"Of course it isn't. We are in Sausalito."

"With those people."

"Excuse me?"

"Spencer mentioned new friends."

"Oh. Yes. Spence has met them. He may come by tomorrow, though I got the impression he had a better offer. You know your brother. Very independent."

"Right."

The line buzzed softly, white noise, all the wires between them carrying nothing.

"Darling, I gather from Spence that you aren't planning to join us, either?" Her mother said, making no effort to disguise her discomfort.

"Join you?" Callista said, fingering her father's jar of paperclips, a large crystal bowl engraved with something in Latin. "Not to be peevish, but was I invited?"

"Yes, that is a bit peevish." Her mother continued quickly. "As we haven't been able to reach you, dear."

"Ah." Callista said.

"We even sent you a post card. Did you not get that?"

Callista felt hot tears on her cheek. She was too tired to slap herself, too weak to fight. "You know Mrs. Mack brings in the mail. I haven't looked."

"Well, look. For heaven's sake, Callista. It's only a day."

She let snot run down her lips rather than risk letting her mother hear her sniffle.

"Of course. Only a day." She was about to explain that she had an invitation, that she was going to Harriet's, but her mother said, "All right, then, Sweetheart. We love you. See you later."

And the line went dead. Callista mouthed the word, "When?" but no one was there.

Pinch was closing the door on Grace's Mercedes station wagon when Callista arrived, red-faced and chilly from the walk from the bus stop. Foil catering containers peeked from under a plaid blanket. Their Rat Terrier, Maude, was scampering merrily atop their luggage.

"Maude, you mangey mongrel!" Grace called out mildly. "Get off the turkey!"

Pinch smiled down at Callista, his eyes kind behind round wire rimmed spectacles, his bow tie straight under a button down, topped by a Cowegian sweater stitched with black bears. "My dear, we should have come to fetch you."

Callista smiled. "It's okay. I had time to catch up on some reading."

"Oh. What do the Socialist degenerates at that school have you learning, child?" He tucked his tall frame into the passenger seat.

Grace drove to the ferry, while Callista found herself in a dense discussion of the Russian writers with Pinch. She liked Tolstoy, but he urged her to read Chekov's short stories. "It's such a shame what happened there. And now all they do is get drunk and play chess."

She didn't know what to say.

Callista had been to house parties at Loon Landing, as the Gambles referred to their second home, but never an intimate gathering. It was an enormous, slightly rundown 1903 hunting lodge, dark brown gingerbread detailing and an old grove of Douglas firs crawling with moss and turkey tails. The porch was wide, its wood ceiling varnished as smoothly as a racing shell. Inside, enormous taxidermized elk, moose and stag heads looked down with glassy eyes, shot by the original owner, Bainbridge Gamble, who had come from New York for the Alaskan Gold Rush and stayed to strip the surrounding hills of their trees.

Callista's room was large and frigid, wallpapered in cheerful yellow rosebuds, a corner of the room devoted to a massive armoire with a tarnished mirror that reflected the waving forest outside in chaotic green waves. She and Adam had spent at least two nights staring into the mirror's otherworldly rendition of summer twilight, like a never-ending Vera scarf forming and reforming, while their highs wore off. The bathroom bore a sink from the 1920s with a neoclassical pedestal that somehow elevated the rustic vibe to one of lofty pleasure, so that her morning hangovers seemed groovier for being at the end of the earth with a gorgeous boy she had slept next to but not with. That had been in the summer before Junior year, when his father forbid him from staying overnight anywhere but tournaments.

She deposited her small suitcase on the folding rack, and left her toiletries case on the marble-topped dresser in the bathroom. The radiator clicked, its ancient mechanisms beginning their work of heating the large house. It wouldn't be enough, she knew from past experience. The stairs were soft with old carpet, and the massive chandelier black with tarnish. Every exterior door was open, and Maude was scampering around barking randomly, in case any predators were about to appear from around the large doors off the entry hall.

"Come on, fat ass!" Grace called. "Mommy needs oysters!"

They drove fast to the Port Denham Grocery, through canyons of tall trees and long, neglected driveways. "Oysters, salmon and crab."

Callista smiled. "The basic food groups."

The Grocery was crowded with other shoppers finalizing their holiday meals. Harriet, who had chosen a camel-and-red plaid swing coat and a silk scarf she wore tied under her chin, like the queen, picked up the order from the fish counter, then threw in a box of Cap'n Crunch, whole milk, triple cream brie, licorice whips, pringles, and two packs of Benson and Hedges Golds. When the bags were in the car, Grace suggested grabbing a cup of coffee at the Rhododendron Bakery.

"I think I'll pick up a pie, as well. Mommy always gets a cranberry cheesecake from the Surrogate Hostess, which is wonderful. But really. Oughtn't we have one pumpkin-y dessert?"

"Let me get it, please." Callista said. "I brought Chardonnay but it's from California. I'd love to at least offer something good."

Grace laughed. "Have you ever had a drop of Chardonnay? In your life?"

Callista shook her head. "My mother thinks California wines are the only kind that exist, you know."

"So naturally you won't try them." Grace said, moving to place their order. "I understand they're delicious. Honestly. Of all the hills to die on, honey."

Callista paid for the pie and they ordered Earl Grey tea, sitting under spider plants next to the fog-framed window facing Front street. People stood talking in small groups, families, couples, older folks in nice outfits. The sight of it felt like someone tossing pennies at Callista's chest, with an annoying, painful plink.

"Did you bring any..." Grace studied her tea leaves. "Refreshments for us?"

"Depends."

She had packed a couple of joints Adam gave her expressly for the holiday, in the lining of her suitcase. *Ammunition*, he'd called it. She could see he felt left out. Callista wondered how he would fare, with his parents and much older sister Rebecca, who belonged to a religious community, and ate only carob, tofu and sprouts. Or so Adam said.

"He told me about your new concoction, by the way. It sounds...delicious?" Her dark eyebrows rose to meet each other.

"An acquired taste." Callista grinned. "It takes a while to properly digest."

"I know. And I am too much of a coward to take that particular journey. But...weed?"

"Of course, your needs are provided for. Is it okay if I stick with champagne? And sugary cereal, of course."

Grace laughed. "Always."

The Sutherlands, friends of the Gambles, appeared at 3:30 bearing heaping platters. Grace smiled affably over the one dish she had managed on the old-fashioned stove, mashed potatoes, and they all went to the parlor to drink and eat seafood by the fire. At some point a local woman and her teen daughter had appeared to staff the kitchen. Callista and Grace were left to fill glasses and answer the usual polite questions about the college application process. Whenever Callista was asked where she was applying, she smiled at Harriet and said, pointedly, "Penn."

The Sutherlands had known Harriet all her life, and Callista was relieved to be mostly left out of the conversation. She worked a puzzle on the oak game table, while the family's elementary school age sons Buzz and Hud took turns floating a Frisbee across the darkening lawn. The puzzle bore a sketch of the City of London, and must have been at least fifty years old, made of wood and hard to solve. Callista had just put the gilded urn atop the Monument when the dinner bell rang.

Grace had excused herself to go smoke one of the joints, but her reddened eyes were the only indication that she was less than completely present. The dining table, set with white linen, crystal and silver, bore small cut-glass ashtrays alongside the wine coasters. Laughter rang down the long table, and she joined in, not because she understood what was funny, but because she was part of the group. It was enough, to be with people who knew how to feel happiness, or at least felt the necessity to feign it. She tried not to think of her parents and what they were doing in California, in some hot tub with middle aged strangers, or at some pseudo Italian vineyard that catered to the childless elite. No doubt, they were happy not to have to keep trying to get her to answer the phone.

Vivian appeared, inquiring in her smallest internal voice whether Callista needed to take herself upstairs and slap herself back to composure? Callista smiled and banished all thoughts of her parents. When her pie came out with the rest of the desserts, looking plain but perfectly appropriate, Callista found herself near tears. Grace looked at her with a somber expression Callista couldn't read, but she knew was kindly meant. Then the older woman looked away, making a joke with the others, and Callista felt an unfamiliar combination of humiliation and gratitude. She was a charity case, and glad to be one.

Then the other mother, Jane, sent the boys to watch television. "Okay now. Time for theories. What happened to Leslie?"

11

CHAPTER 11

By the time the plates had been cleared, she felt drunk and overexposed, as if she'd been examined thoroughly and found rather less interesting than expected. But at least she had been telling more or less the truth. Whatever buzz was traveling around town about Leslie, it wouldn't be made any worse from anything Callista had said. One theory had it that she had gone to Alaska to work on a boat. Another held that Leslie and Mr. Kling were secretly having an affair, which made Callista and Harriet lock eyes. They finally rose to walk around the porch in the cold, while inside voices grew more animated and laughter shook the old leaded windows.

The next morning was dark, gray, and miserable. Harriet dropped her at the ferry, leaning over to peck her on the cheek, and said, "I apologize. They're a bunch of fucking vultures."

"It's fine. I mean..." She shrugged, shouldering her bag and hefting her case. "At least people are passionately concerned. Let's face it. If I disappeared, you'd be the one person to notice. One of two, anyway."

Harriet's face shifted in a way Callista had never seen. She looked as if she were about to cry. "Don't get me started."

"Hey. Tell Grace and Pinch that they're the absolute bees' knees, and I adore you all."

"More than reciprocated, stupid."

The Mercedes flashed silver as Harriet drove off.

Callista sat on the thundering ferry deck drinking coffee as the Seattle skyline approached with almost ludicrous cheerfulness. There were few passengers on the day after Thanksgiving, which she appreciated. She tried to force herself to read, but in the end she just sat watching the port's angular cranes. The walk to the bus stop was cold and miserable.

A taxi slowed on Post Alley and rolled down his window. "Where you going, Miss? Can I get you there faster?"

She had only taken taxis in other cities, and then with her parents or Spencer. "How much to go to Fairfield?"

"Fairfield?" The driver said, as if he had never heard of it. "How far is that?"

"It's six miles. Maybe seven from here."

He told her the price.

In the warm black vinyl interior, the driver was listening to Marvin Gaye's *What's Going On*.

"I love this song." Callista said brightly, then wondered at herself. Had she said that, and not Vivian?

The driver smiled, teeth vividly white against his dark skin, and turned up his radio. His face was thin, covered in acne scars, and handsome in a weathered way. They spent the drive singing along, first to Marvin Gaye, then to Stevie Wonder, and then to the Brothers Johnson, harmonizing with the high notes. It sounded good. She noticed the driver's growing anxiety as they climbed Mount Zebulon past its small ranches with acres of white fencing, then into tall trees, ending at her gravel road. It must have been hard to figure out where she was going next, so far from where they'd started. Callista gave him all the money she had.

"You have a wonderful day, Miss." He said. "And try not to walk around by yourself. The world is not a safe place. You know that, right?"

She smiled. "Thank you."

The yellow cab disappeared, a setting sun on the drab street. Bodhi was standing inside, with his face pressed to the glass door as if he'd been trapped for days. Another note had been taped there.

"Please call me." It gave his number.

She pinned it onto the organizer by the wall phone, as the cat attacked her legs with purring, his body weight pressing hard on her in a way she had only seen him do to Spencer. She checked his food and water, but they were the kind that automatically refilled, tended by Mrs. Mackie. He was just lonely. She scratched his head for a few minutes, and he flopped down on the counter to watch her.

The mushrooms were in their baggy behind the gallon size tin of soy sauce in the pantry. Callista turned on an old Cream in the study and let the sounds float down as she brewed. Cream always felt mildly psychedelic, reminding her of when she had been little and all the references had seemed mysterious and wonderful, instead of what they were, reminiscences of acid trips and trysts with groupies. It didn't matter. The music made her feel good, and it drowned out the robin's cheerful chirping.

The afternoon was perfect for cooking. While her recipe steeped on the stove, Callista brought up the new food processor that her father had given her mother the previous Christmas. It was still in its box. She made herself carrot salad with raisins, and then toll house cookies. While they were baking, the phone rang.

She regarded it coolly. Vivian seemed to be floating right under her skin, vigilant, ready to step in. Was she desperate? No. Callista risked answering.

"Hello." She said with force. "The offices are closed. May I take a message."

"Callista?" An old man said. Her mother's father, Wesley Pierce Couley, no doubt alone in his waterfront house in Fauntleroy. Callista's skin crawled. "Is that you, Callista? What do you mean, *the offices are closed*?"

She thought about the house, his easy chair, the ferries that went to Vashon Island, only a short way from the one she had just been on. You could almost see his house from the boat, a few miles to the south of downtown. Maybe he had spent his holiday there, alone, wondering where his daughter was and why she no longer hosted Thanksgiving dinner. Or had Margaret explained? Blaming Callista, as she always did? Vivian was there a lion, ready to roar, to take a person's face off with the pasta server, push them bodily through the windows to the ground.

When Callista returned, it was to the smell of cookies cooling. The phone was back on its cradle. The kitchen was spotless, but for the enamel pot of tea on the stove, dark brown and smelling like a haunted basement. Vivian had made chamomile in Margaret's clay pot. She had placed the cookies in precise rows on a rack, and apparently washed, dried and replaced the baking sheet. Callista checked her body, but aside from the fact that she had changed from socks to slippers, everything was the same. It took her a second to register that no record was playing. The light was waning, and the birds had settled.

The old green thermos was ready. Callista poured the tea into it, looking at the phone on the wall, wondering if she could figure out how to cut the wires, like a bandit in a movie.

She went to her parent's liquor cabinet in the dining room. It was dusty with disuse, the cooking wines and unopened duty-free scotch bottles giving off a faintly desperate feeling. There were three kinds of whiskey, she knew because the bottles said the word. Scotch, that her grandfather liked. The worst smell in the world. Sherry, vermouth, gin, vodka, and crème de menthe.

She took the crème de menthe into the kitchen and poured it onto vanilla ice cream. Then she went to watch reruns of the Carole Burnett show until it was time for Mary Hartman, Mary Hartman, and then a nature documentary about the African Savannah. She knew the baby elephant would eventually unkink his little lame foot in time to evade the big cats. But she enjoyed seeing the older dames fretting, their trunks soothing the baby like gray hands. She checked her body, again and again, for sickness. But Vivian had shut that feeling down, and the threat had passed.

When she woke, her head ached faintly, and the sun was almost as high as it got in late November. But something was different. As she sat up in her parent's bed, Callista realized with a surge of joy that it was snowing. Flakes gathered on the higher elevations of tree branch, making weird white tendrils on the deck, which to her amazement didn't melt.

It was going to be a snow day. She picked up the phone.

"Hello?" Mrs. Frazer said in her quavering voice.

"Hi Mrs. F." Callista said with a familiarity she didn't really feel. "Any chance Adam is available?"

"Oh dear. I'm so sorry. He and his father are out hunting. I don't expect them back until midafternoon."

The notion of Adam hunting was both comical and deeply sad. Callista left a message. She already knew Adam would want to go out that night as planned, no matter the weather. His excitement over snow had always been transparent, even as his demeanor had grown more opaquely cynical. Add to it the ordeal of having to take instruction on how to be a proper man all day, and he would be frantic with need to escape.

12

— · —

CHAPTER 12

T he snow kept falling all morning.

At 11:30, Callista called Franklin's number. After five rings, an exchange operator picked up. "Fairfield Police department. Officer Franklin's line. Name and number of caller, please."

"Officer Franklin? Is he not Detective Franklin?" Callista was sure he had said he was a Detective.

"It depends on the case. Are you calling to report a robbery, or a missing person?"

"Will he be in on Monday?"

The woman sounded a hundred years old. "I believe so, Miss. But he checks messages."

"It's not necessary. I'll try again."

"Thank you for calling. Good day."

The line went dead.

Adam appeared at 7:30 that evening, the Goat a rumbling yellow monstrosity in the pale world of her forest driveway. Callista picked her way to him. She had worn a pair of her mother's waterproof dress boots, reasoning that wherever they were going, she would have to walk in snow. She had also spent an hour and a half curling her hair and putting on her mother's makeup. Margaret had used to love it when Callista did that, complimenting her on how pretty the cosmetics made her look.

"You should wear makeup every day, darling. It draws the eye to your face."

Meaning, away from your body.

Adam stared. "Holy smokes, Cal. You look like the whore of Babylon."

"And you look like Handy fucking Andy."

In truth, he looked insanely handsome in dark slacks, a turtleneck, and what had to be a leather blazer of his father's.

"Aren't we going to boogie down at the discotheque?"

"I meant that in the best possible way. You look luscious. And we are in fact going to boogie down at the discotheque, and then fucking some."

The Goat slipped all the way down the hill, but somehow Adam kept them from winding up in the ditch. The main road was clear. From the bridge, Laurelhurst gleamed in the last of the cloud's reflected daylight.

She didn't ask where they were going. Capitol Hill was clogged with pedestrians just like every Saturday night. Broadway was a parade of punks, cross dressers, students, and people she didn't know enough to identify, but who walked stiffly, clearly just beginning their highs. They passed the Deluxe. No one was waiting to see King of Hearts at the Harvard Exit.

They parked in a covered lot by the community college, which to her amazement Adam paid for.

"Okay, now I am stumped."

He laughed. "You brought it, obviously."

She pulled the Thermos from her backpack.

When they had drunk the stuff, he spritzed her mouth and then his with Binaca, and locked their things in the trunk. He threw his wallet in on top.

"Do I need money?" She asked. But he was already walking away, laughing, making a dismissive motion with his hands.

"Hon. We are on a date."

"Oh. So boy pays?" It wasn't their usual arrangement.

"Boy pays. Man pays." He reached for her as she neared. His voice was mocking. "Come on. Stick by your man, and I'll take care of you."

But he didn't. Of course he didn't.

Later, when she tried to remember how they got separated in the huge, loud, light-stippled night club, the only images that came were of going to the bathroom and finding half-naked men with caps on their heads and straps on their torsos, snorting coke and laughing as she pushed by to pee.

"Honey that is not what we do here." The taller one said. He was both smirking and sympathetic.

"Only Ragers welcome." Said the other, his blond hair falling into his face in spite of the thick layer of jell he'd clearly used to try and give himself a fashionably tall crown.

"Please?" Callista smiled. "Just for a sec?"

The blond man groaned, and Callista saw that his jeans were unzipped. She pushed past, hurried to finish, flushing just as the lights went off, and the men laughed with devilish basso profundo voices. How many were there? She felt their hands grabbing at her as she found the door, but they were only pawing at her with no real intent. Just to scare her, like at a haunted house.

She found Adam talking to a pale man in plaid with a Greek fisherman's cap and a brushy moustache that looked pasted on. He was leaning down to talk, one arm against the wall, and was clearly drunk. Adam smiled when he saw her and ducked away, grabbing her hand and dragging her onto the dance floor, which was remarkably disco-like with jelled lights and sparkling mirror balls.

She and Adam danced as a silver-spangled drag queen called Lady Midnight performed I Feel Love, starting with somber intensity and ending with tight gyrations and grand arms gestures, which filled Callista with so many emotions she had to turn away. The air smelled like copper and sweat. She wasn't the only girl there, but the others were dressed in sequins and feathers. It made her feel perfect, invisible, unremarked upon, like a statue in a garden. Nothing could touch her, on the dance floor, under the swirling lights.

The Greek fisherman tapped her shoulder, speaking loudly into her year. "You're a lesbian, right?"

She looked into his brown, dilated eyes. He was doing what the men in the bathroom had tried to do. Scare her.

"I might be. Who wants to know?" She said, swaying to Pull Up to the Bumper.

He staggered slightly and made a face she couldn't read. "You're not welcome in here. This place is for us."

Before she registered what was happening or had a chance to find Vivian's steely calm, Callista had burst into tears.

Had Adam been there, by the standing area with round tables near the exit then? Or had he already disappeared?

She remembered him speaking into her ear at one point, some explanation about another room, someone special who was going to turn up there. She was fine at that point. More than fine. Her body felt like woolen mittens, soft and warm and finely made. She danced alone, and with other drunk strangers, whooping and clapping and laughing while some people blew their whistles. And then the men caught up with her, and told her she wasn't supposed to be there. Another place she didn't belong. Another person saying Callista's presence was ruining their fun.

And then somehow she was standing in the alley, watching fabulous people stagger away on their platform shoes or in work boots, their smiles and comments over-bright due to drugs and drink, her buoyancy fizzing like fireworks under the streetlamps. The snow had all melted, replaced by slush. She was still stoned enough not to feel cold. Callista felt like a ball of salty, unshed tears, nothing more. And even a drunk leather queen could see it.

Adam wasn't there.

She felt the tingling in her hands as they readied to strike the self-pity right off her face.

"Hi there. Do you need a taxi?"

When she turned, a boy was sitting on a tall stool. The doorman. He was too young to have so much authority, Callista thought. He might have been a year older than her brother, twenty-one, maybe? He was narrow and graceful, with coiling hair that shone dark copper in places. He wore a black motorcycle jacket, jeans, and boots. His smile was both kind and knowing. Like Adam's. He was very like Adam, in fact, his blue eyes amused, his skin not yet hardened from shaving.

"I'm Kevin." He held out his hand. She shook it. And it felt like her own hand.

13

— ◆ —

CHAPTER 13

Later, in his apartment on Grant Street, his kiss felt that way, too. Like what she would kiss like if she were kissing herself. His hands were on her, but she found nothing wrong with that. He put on the Tom Tom Club but they didn't dance. They kissed, and he fumbled for her buttons, and she threw her mother's boots across the room so they skidded underneath a chair. Kevin laughed. His mouth tasted sweet, like caramel candies and cigarettes. He watched her, and seemed to find her excitement unsurprising, and he pushed her further, as if testing to see how far she would go. She felt the increasing levels of daring, and took them, one by one, unhurried, amused, watching herself as she shed her clothing and helping him shed his own. She was surprised by his naked body, slender, hairy, perfectly proportioned though smaller than her own. His skin seemed to contain her hot tears, her tea-soaked explosive feelings. She saw that nothing could or would shock him, and while he was young, he was not the least bit innocent.

How long did the first kisses last? They exploded, one into the next, time standing still, the Realm a window she didn't walk into. He moved his hands over her, and for the first time in her life, Callista was free to so where a pair of hands led. She pushed Vivian, and memories of other moments at other times. Kevin's confidence teased an eruption of desire out of her, giddy and gleeful.

She couldn't be naked enough. All the sensations of the apartment should have been unpleasant, the cold air, the faintly fetid smell of moldering bud, and under that a watery tinge, of pipes and rust, and abandonment. But instead, she felt alert with need. Her skin was white under the ceiling's bare bulb, which he declined to turn off. He just stood, cigarette in one corner of his lips, slowly peeling back his jeans to reveal hairy skin, and no underwear.

When he touched her between her thighs, with sure and practiced hands, she felt she was on the top of a high slope, but instead of the drop feeling cold and swooping, it was a sudden murmuration of swallows, gathering and unspooling into an iron gray sky. He moved her to his bed, fingers inside her. His breath drew in.

"Wait. Sweetheart." Kevin said as he readied himself for what came next. She was trying hard not to come back down, not to let Vivian arrive on the scene and ruin everything. Her breath was ragged. The apartment was dusty and shabby, the bed no more than a mattress on the floor. She wanted what was next, though she didn't want to imagine it, or admit it, or name it. She wanted him to take her where he so clearly knew how to go.

"What?" She whispered.

He licked his lips, hesitant. Callista realized he didn't remember her name. He spoke with deep, amused awkwardness. "Honey. I'm...no offense, but are you a virgin?"

Vivian smiled wickedly. "Aw. Here and you seemed like the lad for the job."

Kevin startled, eyes widening. "Well. I would. I guess..."

But Callista, burning, hating the smell of ashes in her nose, was already stooping to pull on her panties.

And then she was on the street, stopping in a doorway to tie her shoes, walking and walking until she found the parking garage. Adam wasn't there, but the Goat was unlocked. She climbed inside, reclining the seat, and let the rest of the mushroom tea wash through her like a dark tide. Her mouth was full of caramel and salt. She remembered then touching Kevin, the weird soft and hard feeling of him, the lack of fear or shame. Vivian had not been there, had she? It was all Callista.

And then Adam was shaking her. But she was still asleep, and instead of opening her eyes to the car, she was in the Realm from the last trip, the place where she had seen Leslie. This time it was just like the inside of the night club, only they were in a glade, and Leslie was dancing, and laughing, and she turned her pale face toward Callista and said, very clearly, "I want to stay here. It's better. Joe can't find me here."

And then she was shivering, and Adam was driving. It was early morning, and the trees in front of Dick's Hamburgers sparkled with water. Callista tried to see Adam's face, but he hid it from her. Later, what she recalled most clearly was the sound she had never heard before, and didn't want to hear then, of Adam sobbing, hoarsely, flatly, as if whatever hope he had started the night with was not only unrealized, but worse. Far worse.

"I can't go home. It's...it's too hard, Cal. I can't take it. And when I try to make it better, I'm no good at that, either. I just, I don't know what I want. To have sex, to just do it, get it over with? Do I want to...make this real?"

They drove around for a while, past the line of people buying burgers after being kicked out of the bars, past the Egyptian Theater and the Paramount, which was still lit up, its marquis reading Paco de Lucia and Al DiMiola. Roadies were loading amps onto a truck.

"Real? We hate real. Don't we? Isn't that the point of the tea?" She was trying to get the feeling to return to her glacial hands and feet. "We have to stop doing this outdoors, Adam. I'm going to wind up with hypothermia."

Her voice came out so flat and whiny that they both started to laugh.

"I didn't get very high at all." He spoke with unusual intensity. "Did you?"

She studied him. Obviously, he was high at that very moment. They were inching toward the wasteland of warehouses and old brick apartment houses between the freeway and Lake Union. Above them, the old mansions of Capital Hill shone out like exotic lanterns. The Space Needle pointed to the future, or what the future had looked like when they were babies. They passed the Monastery, runaway kids standing beneath its gingerbread eaves in the cold smoking cigarettes and looking for their next offer. A police car was stopped, and someone within was speaking to a handful of girls wearing fishnet tights and thrift shop overcoats like heroines of pulp fiction. One of them had on wraparound sunglasses and smoked from a long cigarette holder. The Goat coasted past, as conspicuous as a parade float.

Callista closed her eyes. "I was as high as I've ever been. I had a grand adventure. So fun. This has been such a long night. Have you ever had such a long night?"

He slumped, his face growing pinched. "My adventure may go on for quite some time, if the rumors are true."

She sensed it had something to do with the shifting torsos in the club, the copper sex smell, the lights, the movements happening in shadowy corners. "What rumors?"

"Have you heard? A sickness that only attacks the gays."

She had never heard of anything like that. But where would she? He was almost the only person she talked to. "They're just trying to scare people. What sickness?"

"It has no name." He sounded shaken. "But I have it on good authority that now is not the time for me to...become an adult. In the carnal sense."

"Adam, where were you?"

He laughed. "Someplace good, my love. So good. Paradise, really."

She closed her eyes again. The world floated by, invisible.

"Did you bring any money, in the end?" He said. "I lost my wallet."

"Your wallet is in the trunk, stupid." The hot air pumping from the dash felt almost tropical against her hands and knees now.

14

— • —

CHAPTER 14

They parked on a gravel parking lot on Fourth and entered the Doghouse. It was quiet, the lounge closed with a narrow plastic chain in front of the cardboard placard for Dick Dickerson. Callista and Adam had sat in front of Dickerson's organ last April, drinking rum and cokes and waiting for someone to ask them for ID. But no one did. Tonight the booths were crowded with kids and old men. One table held a group of women with big hair and eyeliner, listening to someone tell a sad story.

Their waitress dumped the menus and stomped off, which made Adam smile. They didn't need to open the menu, covered in fifties-era cartoon illustrations of reasons a fellow would be sent to the Doghouse: *blondes, bowling* and *lodges.*

They ordered fried egg sandwiches with a side of sliced tomatoes, French fries, and coffee. Across the room, Callista saw a boy she had known in elementary school. He peered over at her as if he might recognize her, but they both quickly looked away. Someone laughed loudly in the next room. Adam's color had returned, but he seemed bewildered, breathing through his mouth, and blinking slowly.

"How long have you been awake?" Callista pulled napkins from the chrome holder.

"I don't know. We got up at four to head over the pass."

"Let's call it twenty-three hours. Did you kill anything?"

His eyes met hers and looked as if he might cry, again. "I don't know."

"Who were you looking for tonight?" Her fingers traced gold flecks in the linoleum.

"It's embarrassing to say. I'm sorry I abandoned you. You must have been waiting in the car for a very long time. Why didn't you...I don't know. Leave?"

He squinted at her pityingly.

"Are you feeling sorry for me?"

"Guilty." He said. "You're such a devoted friend. You have been..."

"Stop." A calm, weary knowing flowed through her. "I did leave, Adam. I was gone for hours."

"Into that trippy place, you mean? Are we still calling it the Realm?"

"There, too. But no." She tried for a smile, though it probably looked half-hearted. She felt the exhaustion tugging at her, inviting her to lie down. "You know...there are other men in Seattle."

He looked at her with an expression she had never seen, a kind of snarling annoyance. "What are you insinuating?"

Did he really think that he would take her to a place of such heat and motion, and expect her to remain inert? Clearly, he did. She wanted to stab him in the hand with her fork, get his attention.

"I also experienced Paradise, you egotistical nepse. I went home with Kevin, the doorman."

Adam's gawping stare was both insulting, and gratifying. "You what?"

"I think it was his leather jacket that got me. In any case, I had a pretty memorable night while you were off wherever you were. Thanks for asking."

"Oh, honey." He said quickly. "Please god tell me you didn't fuck Kevin. He's a skank. He'll sleep with absolutely anyone."

She laughed. "Oh, and whoever you were with. Is...a sterling character, I assume? Someone with standards."

Adam's face flushed, and he leaned across the table. "Don't be hurt. He's cute. I can see why you'd kiss him, but these days you have to be careful." He sighed.

The waitress placed their food in front of them.

"I thought you said the rumored thingy only affects gays?"

He held up his sandwich, letting the yoke drip before he bit. "Let's just say, don't fuck any boys you don't know."

"Oh. And you?"

He leveled a gaze of such sadness she felt her own eyes tingle. "Not even me."

"Obviously, that's not what I meant." She sat up, realization dawning. "You...did you risk your life tonight?"

He shrugged, "We are constantly risking our lives, both of us. We don't seem to be able to live any other way. But no. Not tonight."

"This is what those boys in the bathroom were talking about. Oh my god.."

"Choices in life are hard, sometimes." He spoke softly. "When we leave for college, I think it's going to be best if you forget you knew me."

She sipped her coffee, numbness descending. "Oh, I don't think it's going to take me that long."

"Are you mad?"

Callista opened and closed her eyes. He should be able to almost read her mind. He always knew what she was feeling. She told herself he was just really, really stoned. That was why he acted like her fear of losing him was anger. "How could you ask me something like that? Because you might get sick, you might die?"

He hung his head. "Because if I do, it's a kind of my choice..."

She took his hand in hers. "You didn't choose this. I chose you, and you chose me, and it's too late to worry about forgetting one another now. I don't care who you fuck, and I am choosing to believe you're being a snob about Kevin because you thought I was always going to be your imaginary girlfriend. But if you think I wouldn't notice you disappearing, you clearly don't even begin to understand what a fucking insult that is."

He dried his eyes with a napkin. "You're right. I'm sorry. I don't deserve your feigned love."

And then they laughed, bitterly.

"I guess you don't." She said.

"Why do you, though?" He whispered. "Love me?"

She rolled her eyes. Something delicate was being broken. Her egg yolk looked sick under the restaurant's fluorescent lighting, and her coffee was cold. "Who else have I got, Adam? Really? Who in this world would drive by my house and notice, if for some reason I wasn't there?"

The ride home was fast. Something had broken loose inside her, a delicate mechanism she hadn't known was there. She felt like a rocket engine jettisoned, falling free through space. The Goat flew across the empty bridge, through the endless green light of the exit, and up the hill toward the forest.

When they reached the bottom of Mount Zeb, Adam said, "I almost forgot to tell you. Leslie came to me tonight. I must have been high after all."

Callista didn't answer. She wondered how she had spent so many hours in the passenger seat, feeling safe, when the safety was only temporary, and how long he had been thinking about that fact, while she just played along.

15

— • —

Chapter 15

Callista slept most of the day, a dreamless, restful floating in blackness. She woke, feeling unexpectedly guilty, wishing the phone would ring. She felt Kevin' hands on her, inside her, and was torn between wanting to recreate the feeling, and shame at him asking about her virginity. She called Spencer's fraternity, but the kid who answered only said that he wasn't around, and no he couldn't take a message because he was too busy right then, and could she please say something dirty?

She said, "Mud oozing from your every orifice." And hung up.

She looked for something to clean, but the house was already spotless. She searched every drawer in her mother's study, but it was as always full of meaningless legal documents, reference books, and half-used yellow pads. She went into her own room and stretched out on her bed, thinking about Kevin, half glad she had already forgotten his last name, and had never given him her own.

If he wanted to find her, he would. Seattle was like that. People would know who she came with, and where they went to school, and someone would give him her information. But she doubted he would ask. In the light of day, trying to get some of the floaty flying feeling back by touching herself, Callista remembered his crooked teeth, the way he had stumbled going up the wide stairs to his building. She recalled the buzzing of someone trying to get into the apartment while they were wrapped around one another, his hands under her clothes and then on her naked skin, how he had shown no curiosity about who was outside in the cold. Another lover, or someone else who expected to be let in, at 2:30 in the morning? She could imagine his excuses. His explanations.

No. Callista wouldn't see Kevin again. His words as she left, returned like a misbuttoned seam, reminding her of embarrassment. *Sweetheart, are you a virgin?* Almost approving, excited by the thought. And the answer, which she had not formed into words before bolting back to the deserted street.

Am I?

She lay back on her bedspread and reached out her mind to Vivian. Callista was still high, even so many hours later, because the defensive side of her was asleep, biding her time. A spider had installed itself in the windowsill above her bed, and she was mildly surprised to notice herself not feeling frightened by it. It was almost a friend. At that moment Vivian crept in, softer than usual, almost unfelt but for a stronger sense of breath in her chest.

Am I a Virgin? Callista asked.

And then her breathing changed, and her darkness began to rumble softly, like a snowbank collapsing from warm rain. Her chest tightened, and she remembered the sound of her grandfather's voice on the phone. *Callista is that you?*

And she went to the shower, stripped and stepped into the hot water, and vomited until long after the spray ran cold onto her naked back, and even then she couldn't bring herself to stand and hobble over to a dry towel.

The snow returned that afternoon and lasted until morning. Callista dressed and packed her school bag, but when she had picked her way to the street, the trees and pavement were unbroken white, and kids from the top of the hill were already sledding down the cul-de-sac to the gulley.

She turned on the radio in the study, and heard the announcements of snow closures all across King County. They wouldn't mention Peregrine, but their schedule was pegged to the Seattle district. No school that day. More precipitation, most likely continued snowfall, expected for the foreseeable future.

She studied for a while, drinking tea and eating toast with peanut butter while the cat strafed her feet. She washed her parent's sheets and her own laundry. She caught up on her reading, outlined a paper for Am Stud, and looked at her study guides for Chem and French. All afternoon, the snow coursed down, until the trees were so thickly blanketed their shadows were steel blue, and etched with cartoonish fuzziness.

After lunch, Callista put on a pair of old ski coveralls and her hiking boots and went for a walk in the undeveloped land behind the house. There were trails snaking all through the gully, unbroken by tracks. Callista wore a soft cap over a braid. Between her cold, red cheeks and her getup, she imagined herself looking like a forest sprite. When she had been small, she had dressed this way for skiing. They all had. Then styles had changed, and she switched to a scratchier hat, jeans, a bandana, and a pair of plastic aviator frames with rainbow sides, and yellow-lensed goggles. The coverall was warm, and she understood why younger kids wore them. As she walked deeper into the gully toward Adam's house, she imagined Leslie in a pair of coveralls, and wondered if she were remembering a real time when she'd seen the girl. The coveralls in her imagination were blue with orange piping, and a ribbon emerging from the bib to hang tickets on so the wearer could discard their parka on warm afternoons.

Why was she remembering that? Was it a pair she herself had once worn?

Then she heard a sound and was snapped out of her reverie. A stippled brown owl looked down on her with majestic indifference. It was so big that even from the ground Callista could see the beautiful orange amber of its eyes, feel the breeze from its wings as it wheeled from its perch and flapped away. She felt like an invader. And yet, like Leslie in the realm, Callista wanted to stay there forever. The owl disappeared into a grove of Alders. Far off, there was a sound of someone starting up a chain saw. A tree had fallen, and one of the dads was turning it into firewood.

As the trail emerged by the T, Callista saw the curl of smoke coming from Adam's chimney. Here, a car or two had emerged earlier in the day and left tracks now half-filled with snow. But the sky was clearing, and off to the West the sun was beginning to shine on the points, and the lake beyond.

Callista walked to Adam's street, a dead end with three brick houses with white gables. His driveway had been cleared and swept. A neat pile of fresh wood had been stacked on the side of the building. The drapes were open, and the smell of woodsmoke made the scene look so sweet as to make her grimace. Mrs. Frazer's blue VW Rabbit sat off to one side, heavily laden with snow. The Goat was obviously in the garage. A gang of younger kids walked by, their faces bright red.

"Lobo is a crazy dog." A boy of eleven or so said helpfully. "I wouldn't go onto their property if I were you."

And they ambled on, someone beginning a story about that one Halloween when Lobo had bitten a kid trying to go to the door for candy. Callista wasn't afraid of Lobo. She had walked by Adam's house for years before they'd met in ninth grade, when the Frazers were new to the area, and the German Shepherd had run at her growling. But Vivian had kicked it in the mouth, and told it to get the hell home. And Lobo had obeyed. Grandpa had taught her that trick.

How old had she been, then? Ten, eleven maybe. Before. Before the thing had happened.

She stood in front of Adam's house for twenty or thirty minutes, then walked home by the road. The sky was darkening, and the air was cold. She walked in the center of the road, waving hello to the handful of neighbors who were sweeping or building snow men. One called out. An old lady named Mrs. Ware she had once sold girl scout cookies to. "Callista, dear, aren't you cold? Would you like a cup of cocoa before you catch a chill?"

Callista smiled stiffly and blew a kiss, as if she couldn't quite hear Mrs. Ware but was sending love. Vivian snorted derisively, but Callista ignored her. Later, she changed into warm clothes and her father's robe, then dialed Franklin's number.

16

CHAPTER 16

"**T**hank you for calling." He said. "Unexpected."

"You did leave me a message."

"Oh." He sounded puzzled. "I meant that for your parents."

She looked at the paper. It said *The Yorks*. She sighed. "So you don't want to talk to me. Okay."

"No, Callista. Don't hang up."

She laughed. He sounded so much like a boy, like a regular boy, not a man, a cop, someone trying to and capable of ruining Adam's chances for Stanford. Her own chances, of whatever it was she wanted.

"Listen. Franklin,"

"It's Randy."

Randy?

"Randy. Listen. I've been thinking about Leslie. I assume you're still looking for her? I mean, I haven't been to school since Wednesday morning, so for all I know you've found her...?"

"No. Unfortunately."

Something about his tone confused her. He had been so adamant when he'd stalked her in the forest. Was he so focused on Adam now that he didn't care about her input anymore?

"What's the latest?"

"About Leslie?"

"Yes, about Leslie, Randy."

"Sorry. It's just. I didn't put it together. Who you are, Miss York. Callista. I...I feel like an idiot."

"Okay." She didn't ask why, if it was because he was embarrassed about his zealous actions or her threats. Something was up, but she persevered. "Listen. I have been thinking about Leslie."

"Oh sure, right."

"And it seems to me...have you spoken to Kenneth Kling? The man who chaperones the ski bus?"

"Kling? Oh. The lacrosse coach?"

"Yeah."

"Of course. We've spoken to anyone who could have come into contact with her. But Mr. Kling was on the bus last Friday. So he is not a suspect. Are you implicating him in some way?"

"Implicating?" She felt a sneeze rising. "No. I just know that he's a person who was there. Who was present, you know?"

"You're still worried about Adam being a suspect?"

"Not really." She lied, a numbness ringing through her. A suspect? "We talked about Leslie, though. Adam said he suggested she race. As a way to improve her form, you know?"

"Her form?"

She touched her cheek. It felt like someone else's hand on her skin. Was she getting sick, again, so soon?

"Her ski technique. Adam told me she was keeping her feet too far apart, which is a typical intermediate stance, you know. But not, an advanced skill. So he suggested she race. So she'd stop being afraid of the fall line. And, as I'm sure you know, Mr. Kling is in charge of the racing. And Leslie refused to even consider it. So I thought...I should let you know."

"Any idea why Adam himself isn't telling me this?"

"I guess because it hasn't occurred to him that such a minor piece of information would be useful to you. And because he is afraid of you."

His laughter was surprisingly deep. A man's laughter.

He laughed again. "I will think about Kling, for you Callista. I just found out who your grandfather is. Such a powerful man. I will of course obey your slightest command."

"I haven't spoken to him in years."

"Why not?" He said. "This is his jurisdiction. Don't tell me he's too busy for his family."

"I'm not threatening you." Unaccountable tears hovered in her eyes. "I just worry. That no one is trying to find her. Really trying. Not just gossiping and being catty."

"Are you okay?"

She hesitated. "You asked if I'm worried about Adam being blamed for Leslie's disappearance, but I happen to know for a fact that Adam had no motive to do anything to her, or any..."

She didn't finish the thought.

"You think Kling might know more than he's telling. And you're asking me, nicely, if I will look into it. Is that right?"

"Don't tell him, though." She whispered. "If he finds out that it's me who put you onto him...it doesn't matter who my grandfather is, or my parents..." She didn't want to say the truth, that she was alone in her house every night.

"As you wish, Miss York. Because you asked nicely."

He hung up. When the phone rang again, Callista felt underwater.

"Hello."

"Callista, is that you?" The woman's voice trembled.

"Mrs. Frazer?"

"So it is." She said in a sing song voice, as if she were talking to a kindergartener. "Dear. I saw you, standing in front of the house, today?"

"Oh, yes." Callista tried to sound normal. "I didn't want to disturb anyone..."

She closed her eyes, feeling the pull of the dark.

"Oh, no. It's right for you not to knock on our door."

"Oh."

"We feel that it is inappropriate for you and Adam to spend so much time together." Mrs. Frazer went on, woodenly. "And his driving privileges have been revoked until March 25, and then shall not be reinstated unless…"

March 25 was Ivy League college letter day. "I understand."

"Good."

"So, how will Adam be getting to school, if I may ask?"

"No. I don't think you may. The twins have already agreed to carpool with Marcus Van Zee. You will have to find your own way, from here on in. Good-bye." Her voice rose to a squeak, and then the line went dead.

The dread that had been hammering at Callista ebbed. She was surprised. Something about not being so responsible for Adam's daily life felt like a relief. And yet, it was only because he'd been so hot and cold to her on Friday night. She still loved him. She yearned to reach out and stroke her finger along his ruddy, smooth jaw.

But she was glad not to be between him and his parents anymore. The moment he'd looked at her pityingly for kissing Kevin, she'd stopped wanting to pretend. The something that had flown out of her that night under the doorman's hands wasn't coming back. She wasn't the same person. And her desire to be an accessory to whatever Adam was doing behind closed doors was gone. Still, she worried. In a way, he was more alone than she was.

She called school, and amazingly, Mrs. Webber was in the office. After some explanation, Callista was offered a place on the school bus that picked up at the bottom of the hill. A twenty-minute walk under the best of circumstances, through muddy trails. It would have to do.

"And ski bus, dear?" the older woman said.

"Pardon?"

"Shall I put you down for ski bus Friday? The weather report says rain. But the snow, you know. Lovely fresh pow, as the kids say."

"Yes. Thanks, Mrs. Webber. I'd love to do ski bus."

She called Harriet to ask if she could sleep there on Friday. Harriet said she couldn't understand why anyone would subject themselves to December night skiing when they could be home reading a book. But obviously Callista was welcome.

The next day, she found a pair of old boots and her good shell, and arrived at the bus stop ten minutes early. There were only two other kids aboard at that hour, and they were cramming. There was an accident on the bridge, so they crawled along, buffeted slightly in the wind. She sat and looked listlessly at her French vocab list as the lake passed below. The reeds in the Arboretum were the color of dried blood, trees like black baby's breath in the mist.

They were so late getting to school that she had to run to homeroom. The buildings of upper campus were as bright and lively as a small city, kids full of energy for the exams to come. Adam was already in his place by the fireplace, but he didn't look at her. They had no classes together, and he ate lunch in Headmaster's history classroom with some of the other kids in AP Western Civ. They didn't speak for the rest of the week.

17

⁓ • ⁓

CHAPTER 17

She watched him walk down the hill at the end of the day on Friday, deep in conversation with Brody, while the skis were loaded onto the yellow bus for the trip to the pass. Not teaching ski lessons today. Of course he wasn't. She felt stupid not to have thought of this, and how it might land with his parents that he'd lost his part time job right when he needed it for college applications.

"Hi there, Cali!" A man's voice said.

She didn't respond immediately. No one called her Cali, or hadn't since she left public school.

She turned to find herself face to face with Kenneth Kling. He was a tall man with a reddish winged haircut and flared brown sideburns. His smile was square, like Theodore Roosevelt, which contrasted oddly to his modish hairstyle. His face struck Callista as slightly vampiric, his hair hanging in waves from a deep widow's peak to his collar. He had an air of pugnacious swagger, like the bookish fellow at camp who challenges all comers to arm wrestling, then gets angry when someone turns out to be stronger. Callista remembered Mr. Kling refusing to hand her skis over until she smiled, back before Adam received the Goat. She gave him the same gritted-teeth expression now.

"Hi there, Mr. Kling. How are you holding up?"

"Holding up?" He said breathlessly, voice rising and falling. "Fine, I guess. How are you holding up? Haven't seen you on the bus for a while. What happened?"

"I got a better offer." She matched his sing song intonation.

He laughed. "A better offer. That's a good one. Well, take a seat. I have to help the littlies. Good to see ya, Cali."

She sat in the back with the two other Seniors she knew well, Ben and Mitch, affable nerds who spoke only in horny double entendres, and rarely moved their eyes from her body to her face.

"How's it hanging, losers?" She called out, settling in for the ride.

They both blushed. The bus moved. Someone played old rock songs on a boom box, and people sang along. They made good time across Mercer Island into the Cascade foothills, the Snoqualmie River a ribbon of rocky, cold white. Beyond black lace branches, the mountains' fat white fangs bit into a pale gray sky.

Without thinking about what she was doing, Callista leaned her head against Mitch's shoulder. He recoiled. She laughed. "Oh, sorry."

"Callista!" He said, his glasses catching on his voluminous black curls. "Good heavens."

Ben laughed, his small hazel eyes furrowing with embarrassment. "Be careful. A girl like you is likely to make him go off unexpectedly."

Mitch laughed along.

"Oh?" She smiled.

The joke continued for a while, Callista pretending to put her hand on Ben's knee and him pretending to be driven wild by it. He was only half pretending, and Ben was watching with an intensity she knew wasn't feigned.

"Not much has happened for you two since tenth grade," She said. "Has it?"

"Not enough!" Ben said.

Mitch agreed, leering. "Not nearly enough."

They went on talking, but Callista's eye was drawn to Mr. Kling's shaggy head as he wandered the aisle, speaking to kids, sitting down on random empty seats. As they began to climb toward North Bend, the music stopped and Mr. Kling appeared, standing with his guitar over his shoulder, and began strumming.

"Uh oh." Mitch said.

"Mr. Kling, really, you're far too good for the likes of us!" Ben called out, but Mr. Kling didn't react.

He began to play. Callista's lips moved silently to Wooden Ships and Teach Your Children Well, but all she could think about were the previous times Mr. Kling had done this. She had thought nothing of it at the time. Now it struck her as pathetic, forcing a captive audience of high schoolers to sing along with your C-D-F-G chord progressions. They were going skiing. It wasn't like their morale needed lifting.

As they passed through the tunnel that marked the beginning of the ski areas, quiet descended again, and then zippers closed and rucksacks rustled.

Callista turned to Mitch and Ben. "Be straight with me, boys."

They met her eyes with an eagerness to please and an undisguised lust.

"Did Mr. Kling have some kind of fascination with Leslie?"

And to her surprise, they nodded and made small noises of agreement.

"You ride to the top with me?"

Mitch leveled his brown eyes at her, waggling his unruly brows. "Could you please repeat the question?"

And Ben dissolved into giggles.

The sun hovered like a Mento candy above the summit as they rode three abreast. The slopes looked tantalizingly lush with soft, deep-shadowed runs strewn with light powder. Callista felt the familiar pang of yearning for those runs. But she had to make use of this time.

"What was going on between Leslie and Kling?"

Mitch tapped his ski with his pole. "He just had a special interest in her. You know, the usual kind. But it was obvious she wasn't interested."

Snow fell from Ben's ski onto some kids below. One of them flipped Ben off. Ben smiled with delight and waved.

Mitch said, "But he didn't kill her. No way. We rode home with him two Fridays ago when Leslie disappeared. He was normal. Just, he asked if she had gotten there yet."

"Gotten where?"

"To the bus."

"Wait. You're saying Kling asked if Leslie had arrived, yet?"

"Right. Like he wasn't sure if she was already there, which makes no sense." Ben shrugged.

"He said," Mitch quoted, "Anyone seen Leslie? Has she gotten here yet? I don't think we should leave without her."

"But you did leave without her."

"Yeah when Miss Lily got there we just went. We got back to school at the normal time. Which is good because my mom would've been pissed if we kept her waiting again."

"Again?"

They air grew colder as they glided up. The sound of turning wheels grew closer, then they surmounted a pair of metal poles, and the churning grew faint again. Ahead, a wall of fog stood cottoning the mountainside.

"There were other weeks when the bus was late. I think it was because Leslie was late. Klingon would always blame her. You know, she's on her period, or she had to call her mom, or something. He always made it seem like he was doing Leslie a big favor by not leaving without her."

"Do you guys...know Leslie?"

They shook their heads, which were whitening as they entered the fog. And then they were in it, completely engulfed in opaque air, inches apart but invisible to one another.

"So every week this winter so far, Leslie has been late getting back to the bus, and Mr. Kling has made excuses as to why?"

"Just about."

The chair stopped, abruptly. They slid back imperceptibly, then sat rocking back and forth until their chair came to rest. The cold bit into Callista's gloved hands. She pulled her bandana over her mouth and lowered her goggles, so only a narrow strip of her forehead was exposed. The boys did the same, pulling up gators and zipping up their parkas.

"Where do you think she is?" Callista's voice was muffled under the blue bandana.

"I hope someplace with better weather." Mitch laughed.

"Yeah, Klingon said he thinks she ran away."

"Why would he say that?"

"If I tell you, can I touch your boob some time?"

Callista took her pole and pretended to push open his binding with it. "Never in your wildest dreams."

"Oh my dreams can be pretty wild."

"Why did Kling say that?"

Ben sighed, signaling defeat. "Because he thinks she was planning to leave. He said so that night. When she disappeared. He said she was a really unhappy person with a lot of problems, and no one would miss her."

Callista's body turned cold fire.

"And I assume he told the police all that. As well. So they wouldn't think that anything bad happened to her."

Mitch scratched his nose, which was poking over his black gator comically. "Did something? You kind of sound like you know something."

The chair started up again, lurching them forward. Someone behind them cheered.

"No. I guess, I am just worried about her. Kling might be holding back information that could help."

"She'll come back." Mitch said cheerfully. "How could anyone walk away from all this? He motioned with his pole, to the invisible slopes, including Callista in his gesture with a lascivious flourish.

She laughed. "Right."

18

— · —

Chapter 18

The skiing that night was so sweet Callista found herself wishing Adam were there to share the delight. She took run after breathless run, lights yellow circles in the gray fog, the snow uniform light powder that flew from her edges with no quiver from hidden ice below. The mountain was almost empty. Her outer thighs burned with the rare thrill of turning in and out of gravity without regard for anyone else's safety. Her breath was an even, greedy rhythm. Her goggles fogged. She left them on, feeling her way down. The music that night was annoying, Rod Stewart and Steve Miller, but it didn't diminish her enjoyment. By the end of the night, the sky and snow were one.

She slid to a stop on the side of the trail where she and Adam had snuck off to get high, pushing a wide arc of snow to the side out of sheer obnoxiousness. She hated to leave, wished he were there to drive home with in the warm Goat, listening to an eight track of Chaka Khan and bragging about the night. She looked sadly at the passageway they'd taken that night. It looked completely transformed by snowfall, the trees poking right up out of deep drifts, their branches invisible below thick layers of iron gray under the evening sky.

Was Leslie out there? Callista imagined her inert in a tree well, covered and recovered by snowfall, her red pants disappearing into white. She thought of the Realm she had first dreamed of that night, or whatever she had done, hallucinated, fabricated. She didn't know.

Though the Realm had felt as real as this mountain, this trail, this snowy forest. The speakers began blasting Tequila, which was a signal for everyone to come in for the night. Callista sighed. The longer she stood there, the colder her feet grew, and her fingers were fully numb. But she wasn't ready to go yet. This was the only thing in her life that felt real. The only time she felt alive, truly alive, not like someone acting out the role she had been given.

She pictured Leslie's white, pinched face, gazing out with an inscrutable expression that must have been hiding her true self. Callista felt sad. And then her icy bandana was wet with heat from her tears. And she felt angry with herself, that it was time to go, and she had to move her feet and slide the short way to the parking lot and the bus, but her body refused to do it.

Is that how Leslie had felt? Like there was nothing worth going back for? Like she wanted to dissolve into the mountains and the forest, ooze into them, like snowmelt in the spring, disappear into the clean ground and never come back out again?

She bent forward and shook her banana, and ice fell onto her ski boots. The fabric was too cold and wet to replace on her face. She had to go. It was time to get back on the bus. But something held her. Was it Leslie? If the girl had been following her and Adam, wouldn't they have noticed her? But Callista didn't remember how she woke, or how long she and Adam had been in the tree well. If Leslie had been there, wouldn't they have noticed her?

Callista's stomach sank. The mountain stood blank and white as a movie screen.

Callista thought about the Sherpas on Mount Everest and the bodies they left, unable to bring them safely down. No way a teenaged girl would be uncovered by Spring thaw, a hundred yards from where the drivers sat smoking and reading magazines. She wasn't here. Callista felt nothing like what she had sensed in the Realm, the calm presence of Leslie's will, stating that she would not be moved.

She shifted her feet, flattening her soles to the angle of the snow, and began to glide. When she got to the slight rise before the bottom, she pushed with her feet to smoothly shoot over the top and slide to the dirty slush in front of the lodge. A handful of other people were swarming to the parking lot. Callista was the last aboard.

The bus smelled like sweat and wet wool and cocoa. She sat in the front, next to the driver, Miss Lily, a middle-aged lady with a thin, brown ponytail that reached to her hips, a Sonics sweatshirt stretched over her bulky torso. She had a sweet face and a kind disposition and liked to tell kids that they had a "particularly golden aura." She said it to everyone. As far as Callista knew, Miss Lily never left the bus except to smoke Virginia Slims menthols by the blue-veined snowplow cliffs around the perimeter of the parking lot.

"Callista!" She called out, "You look half drowned. Sit down and warm yourself. My goodness."

There had been no time to ask what Miss Lily knew about Leslie before they started out of the lot, the bus lurching violently from slushy parking lot to wet pavement. The wipers swiped frantically at snow, and as they descended, fine rain. Kenneth Kling stayed in the back, his head pressed against a window, eyes closed.

"How is your friend, Adam, dear Callista?" Miss Lily called out, half smiling as they rolled past Denny Creek, and the road flattened out.

"He's fine." Callista said. "I can't wait to tell him what a great ski day he missed. How are you?"

"Fine now, thank you." Miss Lily winked in the large rearview mirror. "I don't love when it's freezing rain at night. But at least the kids are tired."

She was right. The bus was almost silent, most people either dozing or talking quietly in the dark.

"Thank you for being such a safe driver, Miss L."

She beamed. "What happened to Adam's pretty yellow car?"

Callista sighed. "I don't know."

"Oh, I hope the two of you didn't break up. So sorry if I'm bringing up a bad topic."

"No, no." Callista smiled. "Everything is the same as usual. But it's kind of a busy time for us, you know."

"Oh, yes. Same every year. Finals and then college applications. And the SATS, did you already take those?"

Callista nodded. "Yes."

"So you and Adam are going to be separated anyway, isn't that sad? Next year."

"It looks that way." Callista said. "Can I ask you something?"

"Oh, anything. The drive is pretty easy, now."

Outside, the lights around Lake Sammamish shone, illuminating the suburban homes flanking the park where Ted Bundy had poached one of his victims, a dark patch in the stretch of sparkle.

"What kind of search did they do when Leslie went missing? Do you know?"

"Oh, poor Leslie. I'm glad you brought that up. I didn't want to. But, here you are skiing alone, without Adam. And we don't know what happened." Miss Lily waved a station wagon on as it passed, a good twenty miles per hour faster than the bus, sending out sprays of water from its wheels. "Go on, enjoy yourself, you numb skull. Anyway. I think the search was very thorough. They combed the trails, and the surrounding woods all night and all day the next day. The found nothing but a couple of old, rusty bindings and about fifteen pole baskets. It's a big forest, but apparently the trails all lead to the same valley and it didn't snow that night at all, so if she had left tracks they would have found them. Poor thing. She was seen in the lodge, just before we left. Mr. Kling said she told him she had a ride home. And not to wait for her. And I..."

Miss Lily's face fell into a grim expression, and she suddenly looked much older.

"Really? She told him to leave without her, and he did?" Leslie said. "That's..."

"Nothing to do with you kids." Miss Lily's face looked long and sad in the mirror. "Have they been bothering you and Adam, Callista? I'm sorry. They came after me three times, asking and asking if I knew anything about Adam's whereabouts. But of course, you both drove in his yellow car. It was sitting there, when we left. Where were you?"

"We were in the trails, just skiing. You know. It was a clear day, and we stayed behind for a while. But we didn't see her. I just...feel awful."

"Oh, I know. Honey we all do." Miss Lily pulled the huge wheel with her small, fat hands, turning north. They turned off the freeway onto Lake Washington Boulevard, passing Leschi Marina on the right. Lights shone on the lake's still waters, gilt glass ellipses that stretched into infinity. "None of us will be able to sleep until we find out...well. Where she is. Now...and, that she is safely home with us."

"You're the best, Miss Lily." Callista patted her shoulder. "I'm glad no one is giving up hope."

"We surely are not. Bless you for asking, Callista. You are grown up enough to consider how hard this is for all of us. A real lady. You're going to do wonderful in college."

Callista sat back down, a tiny tendril of shame burning through her. She hadn't thought much at all about how hard Leslie's disappearance was for the staff, or her family, or anyone else. All she had thought of was Adam.

The image of his bruised face and pulled-down hat flashed into her mind. There was plenty to think about, there. Or there had been. Now, with no car rides and no pretend dates to share, maybe it was all over between them. His college applications were due January 1. That meant he'd spend break in his room writing essays. After that, they had one half of Winter Tri left, and then Spring Tri, which he was planning to spend biking in Italy with the rest of the Latin nerds. They didn't have prom to look forward to.

It hit her with a hollow thud. Her relationship with Adam had been winding down, all year. She had been too wrapped up in their charade to notice. But Adam was smart, in just the ways she wasn't. He had known. He had always known. He wasn't waiting until Stanford to escape. All the more reason she was no longer needed. No longer useful. She sighed. It didn't mean she loved him less. It only meant she needed to adjust her expectations. To nothing.

Callista felt a prickle, and knew that Kenneth was looking at her. She turned, and he smiled his troll's smile. She showed her own teeth, then turned back. Miss Lily's eyes met hers in the mirror, her expression blank, her eyes wary.

When they disembarked at school, warm, miserable rain drifted down. Kenneth smiled as he handed kids their skis, bidding them each a special good night. No one answered, just took their things in silence and shuffled away, half asleep already.

"Mr. Kling, when does Lacrosse season start up again?" She had practiced the question, deemed it a logical one.

"January, though most of the Seniors have projects Spring Tri, no one goes out for Lacrosse." He handed over her skis. "These yours?"

"Yup."

His eyes traveled over her, and then the length of the skis. "You don't want the new shorter ones?"

Callista grimaced. "No."

Kenneth laughed, his mouth grotesquely wide between his sideburns. "A purist. I get it. The boys like to ski with you. Because you're an old-fashioned ski queen."

"What?"

"I've seen you. Vadleing like an alpine maiden. Like the girl on the cheese label. The braid is the perfect finishing touch." He growled like Tony the Tiger. "I like it."

Callista almost stumbled. "Thanks."

"Will we have the pleasure of your company next week, Callista?"

She shivered. "You bet."

She waited until he had turned his attention elsewhere, then shouldered her skis for the walk up to Harriet's.

19

CHAPTER 19

She showered in Harriet's bathroom, a brightly tiled expanse that brought to mind black and white movies with girls preparing for their wedding, or their formal introduction to society. Harriet was asleep.

Callista had left her wet things on the porch, using the spare key to enter, greeting Maude, who licked her with sleepy dutifulness. The television was on in the den, and Callista poked her head around. Grace was on the couch, wrapped in a caftan, an ashtray and empty martini glass by her side, a half-finished game of solitaire on the table. Johnny Carson's voice droned. Callista considered turning it off, but she was afraid Grace would wake up and be disturbed by the sight of a drenched, sweaty girl in ski clothes. She settled Maude on her little bed and crept up the stairs, past the line drawings of Paris.

After a shower, warm and clean in the trundle bed beside Harriet's four-poster, Callista couldn't sleep. She felt weird touching herself with Harriet in the next bed, so that route to relaxation was out. She tossed. The bed was comfortable, the sheets old and smooth, and though she couldn't see them she knew them to be printed with quaint read and white toile scenes of ancient China. She had slept on them many times. But Kenneth's grotesque smiles kept appearing in her mind, his confession that he had watched her ski, the names he had called her, the simple knowledge that he was classifying her for his own pleasure. She sniffed the sheets, comforted by their powdery fabric softener scent. She was safe in this bed, where she had once gotten her period, and Grace had showed her how to get the stains out using cold water, without shame or getting annoyed, and Callista had watched the little red pagoda emerge from her menstrual blood, as clean and perfect as ever.

The bare trees on 36th dripped like hands outstretched to the rain. Her body was tired, and she was hungry. The two PBJ sandwiches she'd packed had come nowhere near satisfying her hunger. She wondered if there were any old candy bars or a forgotten box of raisins in her pack. The thermos with its half-consumed tea was still there. Callista didn't remember why she'd thought it a good idea to bring it, except for a vague hope that Adam would appear after all. The pack was damp, and smelled lightly of wet nylon. The thermos clunked as she pulled it toward her and eased open the stopper. It smelled foul. And also, weirdly familiar, a combination of mildew and yeast. It already felt habitual, like a favorite food that had once been an acquired taste. She stoppered it and felt around in the bag, but there was nothing to eat, only the empty wrapper from a long-ago stick of juicy fruit.

Harriet shifted in bed. "Go to sleep, York. You'll catch your fucking death. And I have too much Chem to study to be bothered with your funeral."

Callista laughed. She closed her eyes, trying to remember the good parts of the previous Friday with Kevin. Adam's face crept in once or twice, but she banished it, thinking of him in the snow, laughing, while Leslie was lost somewhere. How little either she or Adam had cared, when they'd heard. It was like hearing about the troubles of a stranger, when they had so many of their own to worry about. Kids got lost all the time, disappeared into the white like letters into an envelope. Just never anyone they knew.

The next morning she slept late. But Harriet was the most marathon sleeper Callista had ever known. She peed and snuggled down to doze some more. But by 11:30, her head ached from caffeine withdrawal, and her stomach was contorting with emptiness. She crept downstairs.

Grace was in the kitchen watching The Galloping Gourmet and smoking, stirring something in a copper pan on the stove. The room was huge and old-fashioned, cluttered with mysterious pressed glass or French wire implements, the ceiling hung with baskets. A frontispiece displayed novelty tea pots with colorful finishes, copper molds, and serving pieces Callista didn't know the use for.

"My darling, you scared me half to death. I had to go and make sure you got in all right. Why didn't you wake me?" Grace's deep voice carried its usual tone of detached amusement.

Callista took the cup of coffee she offered and sat in the breakfast nook. "You looked so peaceful. I was afraid you'd wake up and think you were in a horror movie and stab me with your..." She took a guess at the thing in Grace's hand, "Whisk."

Grace laughed. "Cheeky. Girls disappearing. Coming in late at night. Did you carry your skis all the way up the hill? At midnight? In the rain?"

Callista smiled. "We all miss Adam's car. Me most of all."

Grace fed her a cheese omelet, dripping with sharp cheddar, and a piece of toast with currant jelly. Afterward, Callista was still so hungry she had mandarin orange slices from a can, and part of a hunk of smoked sockeye Grace had been saving for Sunday dinner. She turned off the stove and came to sit at the table, picking up a newspaper.

"Thank you. I must have skied fifty runs last night."

Grace looked at her inscrutably over her glasses, half studying a crossword puzzle in the folded-over newspaper. "You say that as if I have the foggiest notion. You could say a hundred and fifty, and I'd believe you."

"The weather was cold and foggy, so no one showed up. The snow was perfect." She smiled. "I had it all to myself. Heaven, Grace."

Grace snorted, filling in some squares with a small gold pen. "Please God let Heaven not be anything like that."

They talked for a while, around the subject of Harriet, school, and their college search. Grace clearly knew everything Callista had ever told Harriet, which was strange to Callista. She hadn't confided in her mother in years.

"Wouldn't you like to stay here for a while, Callista?" Grace said after Pinch had come in wearing his tennis whites, said hello, then roared away in his old green MG.

"Oh, I'm fine. Thank you." Callista smiled.

"Are you, though? Fine?" Grace peered at her, smiling. Callista loved her square, strong-boned face, the way she didn't cover her gray streaks where they sprouted near her temples. She looked like the kind of lady who ought to be writing on a typewriter in a flat in New York City, or Chicago, not stirring a pot in a backwater like Seattle. "I hear you and Adam…?"

Callista's face burned. She found herself inexplicably speechless.

"You needn't tell me, don't worry. And if I don't watch myself Harry will get miffed with me and my big mouth."

"But she's told you…" Harriet trailed off.

"I know you're a capable young woman, Callista. And I know Harry thinks the absolute world of you. But."

Callista held her hand to the corner of her right eye, to stop it from leaking.

"…No one knows what happened to Leslie. Not that anyone suspects Adam of anything." She placed a special emphasis on Adam's name, to heighten the absurdity of his threat. "But of course everyone is feeling the strain."

"Do you really think that something…sinister?"

Grace shrugged and looked at her puzzle, delicately ashing her cigarette into a cloisonné dish. "I know Leslie's family. Everyone around here does."

She waved her hand, indicating the neighborhood. Callista caught the implication, that she and Adam didn't live around there, so they wouldn't be privy to relevant gossip.

"And, what does that mean?" Callista asked in a small voice, feeling meek. Feeling like she was floating.

"Nothing, just, they're not the kind to run away. Do you know what I mean? I think you do. You're not the type that disappears when the going gets tough. Right?"

Callista felt a bolt of humiliation go through her, though it had to be an accident. Grace was writing again, very normal and relaxed. She was talking about Callista's parents. Nothing else. She couldn't possibly be talking about anything else.

Harriet appeared in the doorway, her black hair humorously askew, looking like a girl from a 'thirties advertisement for soap. "Mother. It's too early to discuss the murder."

Callista felt her face grow wooden. "Murder?"

Grace laughed. "You're frightening the horses. We don't mean murder. We're just suspicious of the theory that Leslie ran off to San Francisco or New York City or someplace."

"Is that what people are saying now?"

"They're saying everything you can imagine. But the most prevalent theory is that she thumbed a ride to distant horizons. Or ran off with some local yob no one knows."

"But people who know her don't think she ran off?"

Both Grace and Harriet shook their heads. For the first time, Callista saw the resemblance between them, their heavy brows, their pale green eyes.

"She's not the type." Grace said. "Not a risk taker. Not the girl to slide off the track with a boy."

Callista's face burned. "So at least you know Adam is innocent."

Harriet laughed. "Innocent of doing anything to do with Leslie."

They went on that way for another half an hour, Callista watching herself numbly fumble for a way to present herself. She was comfortable, happy and warm there. But the sense of impending gossip suicide wore away at her, the feeling that if she slipped up, she'd supply their whole locality with rumors and innuendo that might run out of control. It was a game they played much better than she did. She was tired when Harriet drove her home, the Mercedes roaring over the thick coating of slush that appeared as soon as they turned onto Mount Zebulon.

Adam's house looked cheerful. A string of early Christmas lights shone out in a multi-colored row on the gutters. His mother's car had been replaced by a mummy-wrapped Goat-sized object, which still bore a light dusting of snow.

"Where did you wind up deciding to apply, doll?"

"Me?" Callista smiled. "I'm going to leave that a mystery. But not Penn."

"Of course not Penn, you daft cow. I am asking about you. I thought we were friends." Harriet said, sounding genuinely annoyed.

"The truth is, Harry, and don't spread this around...is that without my parents to pay for application fees, I can't apply. And my parents are in California. They..." It felt strangely good to admit the truth, to herself as well as Harriet. "They seem to have forgotten that this is my Senior year. Or, any year, really. They seem to have forgotten that I exist...more or less."

The car felt still even as it mounted Cedar street and pulled into the circular drive. There, as if to rebuke Callista for her words, sat her father's Land Rover, doors open, filled with grocery bags, and her father in a woolen cap and a plaid shirt, cheerfully unloading them.

Harriet stopped the car. "I see someone decided to show up after a long vacation. Cal, I am not an idiot. So listen. Promise me you'll get Phillip to sign some checks, while you have him here. I see you worrying about Leslie and Adam and all that you see before you, when what you need to be worrying about is your own future. Promise me."

Callista turned her face to her friend. "Please tell Grace thank you. I promise."

Harriet started speaking again, but Callista was already closing the hatch back, and carrying her skis to the house.

20

CHAPTER 20

"Darling, I want to hear about everything." Her mother said from the kitchen counter. She was replacing the tea pot in its place in a high cabinet. Callista felt a pang, as if it were her tea pot, and she should decide whether or not to put it away.

"Hello, Mother."

Mrs. Mackie moved behind her mother, continuing a conversation as if Callista weren't there. Margaret, who looked tan and relaxed in a white outfit that contrasted starkly with the dark weather outside, laughed. "Maureen, hold that thought. I want to have a quick word with my daughter."

Mrs. Mackie looked over as if she couldn't fathom why. She was a pudgy, red-haired woman of indeterminate age, who wore orthopedic shoes and royal blue polyester scrubs, as if she worked in a hospital. She nodded her permission.

Callista sighed and stepped over the threshold.

"You're not bringing those in here?" Margaret said. Callista saw she was wearing eyeliner, and her gray eyes burned with an intensity Callista found enraging. They were focused on Callista's hand, which still held her skis and poles.

Callista sighed and went back into the yard, descending the outdoor steps to the lower level. Her level. She let herself into the utility room and hung her equipment from the proper hooks on an interior closet. She changed into clean clothes and brushed her hair, which was oddly buoyant from Harriet's unfamiliar shampoo.

From the kitchen above, she heard Mrs. Mackie saying something about Callista not caring for the cat. Bodhi herself was watching Callista from the door, her tortoise shell face impassive, tail flicking as she entered her room and rubbed up against her leg.

"It's okay, baby. You're still alive in spite of me. Aren't you?"

The cat purred. Callista flopped back onto her bed and stroked her belly, the two creatures hiding from so much sudden activity. Bodhi kneaded Callista's belly, affectionately, reminding her that it was there, that her too abundant flesh was always going to be there, canceling out whatever other qualities people saw in her. She started to cry, softly, and Bodhi began to purr.

Fifteen minutes later, Callista mounted the stairs to find her parents drinking coffee and eating cookies before a roaring fire. The sunken living room was like the gondola of a low flying zeppelin crashing slowly into evergreen trees. Margaret and Phillip looked as if they had always been there, two people perusing legal briefs, glasses perched on both their noses. Callista struggled to see any part of herself or Spencer that seemed to have come from the matched set of self-satisfied beings before her. She and Spencer both had their mother's dark blond hair, but while her brother had the prominent chin and long hands from Margaret's side of the family, Callista's face was rounder, with high cheekbones and thick brows. Something burnished and electric emanated from Phillip and Margaret's seated forms, that Callista found wholly unfamiliar. She wondered why they had ever decided to have children. They seemed complete just the two of them.

"Mother. You wanted to speak to me?"

Her parents put down their files and turned their attention to her. Callista felt naked. Phillip smiled.

"You're looking awfully well, Callista." He said in his mellifluous voice. "Fresh snow in the pass, according to my information. Was it a delight? Or somewhat overrated?"

"Fabulous, Daddy." Callista sat on the Moroccan pouffe. "I skied my head off."

"In spite of the news, you're still doing the Friday thing?" Margaret appraised her. "Girls going missing, I understand? How are you still around?"

"Meg." Phillip said.

Callista felt dragged down by her mother's glare, though Margaret's face remained mild, the only sign of her real feelings a slow, deliberate blink that had always stuck Callista as the purest form of contempt. She noticed with a chaotic feeling in her gut that not only was Margaret wearing eyeliner, her eyes were lined on the insides of the lids, smudged black, like a groupie at a rock show.

"So sorry not to have been kidnapped or murdered." Callista said tartly. "I could try to lead a riskier life, though that will be harder now that you're home."

"Don't be sensitive." Margaret laughed. "I'm only joking."

"Of course. And you have such a distinct sense of humor. I guess I forgot, you've been away so long." Callista said.

"Stop it you two. It's too soon to pick that back up again." Phillip smiled. "You managed all right without us, pet? You seem to have. Mrs. Mackie says you carried on as always."

"Oh, did she?" Callista looked around to see if the housekeeper was lurking. "She's like a ghost. But apparently she was keeping tabs on me. Good for her."

"Are you angry that someone was looking after you?" Margaret said incredulously.

Callista studied her mother. She let a long moment pass. "I had no idea that Mrs. Mackie considered herself my caretaker. Silly me. I do appreciate you sending Spencer and his stack of money, though. Next time, if there is a next time, I need the keys to one of the cars. Because what with girls being nabbed and all that, I really shouldn't be out wandering."

Phillip said. "I apologize. We had no idea things would get so hazardous around here."

"Okay, Daddy." She said. She knew that her mother didn't want her driving. Margaret said if Callista or Spencer wanted access to a car, they could find a job and buy one. What would she say if she knew where Callista and Adam had been? Where had Margaret been, herself? Callista didn't really want to know. She had missed the idea of a mother, someone like Grace, who saw into her and cared, or Adam, who automatically sympathized with her problems. But Margaret had never been like that. She almost seemed to avoid looking at Callista, even now. What did she see, when she looked? A daughter who wasn't what she had hoped for, a girl too large and too troubled, whose moment of growing breasts and getting her period had come along with the thing that happened, and the day Callista had tried to tell her, and Margaret had said, "Hush now, baby elephant. That's my father you're speaking of." And Callista had run outside, into the rain, and been unable to speak again for weeks, months, until finally Phillip brought her to a speech pathologist, who said there was nothing wrong with her.

Even now, Callista found it hard to speak to Margaret. Bodhi came and sat on her lap, like a comforting little fur blanket. It soothed her. She could let the hope go, that Margaret would ever be the mother she hoped for. Margaret had probably known she would, eventually, surrender. Her mother was a famously canny negotiator.

"What about Adam's car?" Her mother asked, opening a file on her lap. "I thought your paramour drove you wherever you wanted to go."

"Adam is not, and never was, my paramour. In any case, he is no longer available for my use as transport."

Margaret made her mouth an oh, her chin disappearing into layers of skin. "Handsome Adam? Never your paramour? What a shame."

Callista turned to her father. "Listen. If you're tired of parental responsibilities, I understand. But I think I should know. Do you intend to pay for my college?"

Her parents both sat forward, as if watching a horse race that had just gotten exciting.

"Of course, darling." Phillip said. "Obviously."

Margaret's face reddened.

"Mother." She spoke softly. "I am not interested in talking to you about my relationships. And I really, really don't want to know what you've been up to with your friends in Sausalito."

Margaret began to object but Phillip held up a hand to stop her.

"You obviously have your own lives, irrespective of mine."

"Darling, don't be such a drag." Margaret said.

Callista smiled. "Statement of fact. Based on evidence."

"Stop that." Margaret said, eyeing Callista up and down. "You're such a big, strong girl. You obviously handled yourself, and whoever is looking for victims has decided you're too much woman to be worth it."

Phillips sighed audibly.

"Thanks for that evaluation." Callista smiled. "While we're critiquing, let me say that that kohl looks very silly on you. We're not in a production of Godspell. You ought to try a lighter color, perhaps silvery gray to match your roots. Might come across as a bit less desperate."

"Callista." Phillip said. "Both of you stop it."

She turned to him, serene in her rage. "Her father called, by the way."

Margaret made a sound in her throat. "Your grandfather, you mean. Did you finally relent, and speak to him? Have the two of you made up?"

Callista coughed. "I hung up on him. Though, just a guess? He won't appreciate your slutty makeup either. He likes natural girls."

Margaret's eyes widened. Her voice came out a scream. "How dare you? This nonsense has to stop."

Callista stood and watched as her mother's face went from white to red, and then she was crying into her hands, dramatically. Phillip looked imploringly at Callista.

"What? She just needs to be less sensitive."

And Callista ran, stopping only to grab her parka and boots, out into the rain, down into the trails, to the gulley.

21

CHAPTER 21

The sky was already darkening. Callista walked to the road, then past the entry to Adam's cul-de-sac, though she didn't turn to look at his house, past the T, toward the long hill down.

Around the place where the power lines crossed the street, she realized with growing clarity where she was headed. She turned toward the power line, following its alder-lined passage to the elementary school. The low, modern building lay like a dark brick in the dusk. Only its flagpole and name plate were illuminated. She went to the play structures where she and Adam once played the suffocation game, which they called Hyperventilation when they were thirteen. She had hyperventilated so many times since, she no longer thought of it that way. It was a stupid pastime that kids played before they discovered drugs.

The little wooden house kids used to climb onto the slide was dark and empty, and smelled like cedar. Callista sat in its comparative dryness and pulled her feet up off the wood chips. The trees on the other side of the mud play field looked almost comically dark and dangerous. The play courts looked like triangular monster heads, perpetually open to swallow.

She pulled on her ski hat and dragged the thermos out of the bag. It smelled nasty, but also weirdly enticing. She poured herself a quarter cup, reasoning that it had only been accumulating magic and power over the preceding week.

She drank it down. It burned unpleasantly, causing an instant sense of regret and sadness. She dragged her hand along the bottom of the pack, finding the soft rectangle of ancient unchewed gum, long separated from its foil case. She put it into her mouth, lint an all, chewing desperately, until the juicy fruit flavor mingled with the dank mushroom tea. She replaced the cap, pulled her legs up under her so she was truly invisible to anyone who might pass the lonely playground while walking nearby trails. Then she suppressed a cough of nausea. No one would be out so late, on a cool, wet night, in early December. She was alone. And even Adam wasn't going to come join her.

"Get rid of the bossy lady." Meli's voice whispered. "Kill her, and you can come to me whenever you want."

The realm was different. Darker, in colors from a kaleidoscope rather than a cartoon show. Stained glass refracting over the islands, meadows and valleys. Callista felt Leslie's presence, like a bird flying in front of the sun, unseen and unsettling.

"What lady?"

"You know the one..." Still unseen, Meli drew out the words like a singer. More Patti Smith now, low, and hoarse and poetic. Callista hated the sound.

"What is this fucking music?" She said.

Meli laughed. "Come closer."

"Oh, I would be happy to." Callista moved toward the shore, her feel gliding, a choppy dream like state, as if in the real world her body was shivering with cold.

The face under the water rose, and it was terrifying. But Callista had asked for it, and when it erupted into the air, the result was dramatic. Meli rose, large, sparkling blue white, her hair long and silver, her body graceful and ripe. Callista sat on the beach, rocks pressing onto her ankles, deflated.

"I have waited for you."

"Why?"

Meli sat on the beach, her tail flicking dangerously into the water, hands straightening her locks. "To fulfill your destiny, of course."

And then Callista was crying, shaking, snot running down her mouth. "What destiny?"

"Kill that lady. And you'll find out."

"What fucking lady are you talking about?" Callista screamed out, but then she knew. "You mean Vivian?"

Meli smiled, flicking her tail. The sun glinted on her purple fish scales. "She's always cropping up when you could be here with me."

"She protects me."

"Well, I will protect you instead." She smiled. "I will never let you go."

And then she sang more, a bit like Joan Baez, some sort of rousing folk song that made Callista feel that she wasn't as excited as she should be. She pressed a couple of big, flat stones onto her eyelids to try and soothe them.

"I don't see how I can really move forward without Vivian."

Meli raised her hands towards Callista and stopped singing. A low horn kept blowing in the distance, for a long, clear note, and then the only sound was lapping waves.

"You're not moving forward."

Callista threw the rocks into the water. Even though she hadn't skipped them, they each arced across the bay, skipping endlessly over the water. She was beginning to hate this place.

She stood and ran up the path back to where the summer camp had been, though like in a dream nothing felt permanent. The trees and sky were real, intensely so. But everything else seems to shift and flow.

"Leslie?" Callista called out. "Are you here?"

There was an answering groan.

Instead of camp, Callista was standing on a city street. But it had an unfamiliar, quaint feel.

"Bitch, you have to stop following me." Leslie smiled.

Callista moved toward her. "What happened to you?"

The girl looked older, with hair shorn in an angular buzz cut, and a row of earrings climbing her lobes like the outside edge of a binder. Her face was broken out, her mouth upturned. Callista hadn't seen her smile before. She understood, as Leslie leaned against a half-height barrier in front of a shuttered café, that the girl was stoned.

"Where are you?" Callista said. "In real life?"

"God you're dumb." Leslie hopped on one foot, smiling. "I don't want anyone to know!"

"But what about your mom? Your step-brother, Joe?" Callista's voice trailed off. She felt so tired. Cold was emanating from her feet, and her guts felt leaden. "Adam said someone was hurting you."

"It's all a dream, you, whatever your name is. It's all their dream. You need to wake up."

"Are you awake?"

Leslie closed her eyes as if searching for words. "Don't bother me again. I mean it. I want to forget."

She turned and walked across the street toward an old cast iron building, peeling paint exposing its metal shell, ground floor windows to a record shop on one side, a restaurant on the other. Leslie turned, flipped Callista off, and disappeared into a handsome front door. The edifice read *Longbotham*, 1909.

Callista started to cry. She stepped forward, but then she stopped. Why was she trying so hard to solve other peoples' problems? Why did she care so much about Leslie McCall? No one else did. Girls could disappear. Why was that so hard to accept? A terrible cloud was in her, so dark and thick that she gagged. Her familiar sickness, only more concretely visible than ever before. Was it the tea, or was it always there and only more obvious because of the tea? She grabbed hold of it as she would something solid, and pulled it forcefully, through her throat and out of her body. It stretched forth like gray cotton, thinning as she pulled. She kept going, gagging and retching. Finally she reached the end, and threw the whole mess onto the ground, where it fizzled away to nothing, smoke rising, and she was empty again.

Then she was sitting on the edge of a snow well, in the mountains, and sun was hitting her face. She felt peaceful. In her hand was a Breyer horse, a small chestnut foal with a hoof broken off at the forelock. She felt tears rise, and then an answering sense of deep exhaustion. She threw the foal into the tree well, and stood. When she was standing, the snow was all gone, and she was in the forest above the beach again. A wave broke loudly, the beginning of a wake. A ferry cruised past the inner islands, surreal and majestic. She ran toward it.

As she reached the dock above the rocky shore, the ferry continued past, mirage like. Its wake splashed up onto the Statue of Liberty, who was inexplicably standing waist-high in the bay, her shadow falling onto the clear water. Callista was overcome with yearning to be on the boat, to be moving.

"Meli! Come back." Callista sat on the end of the dock. "Please tell me what destiny you mean."

Meli rose up and pushed the Statue of Liberty forcefully into the water. The structure sank quickly, bubbles rising. Callista felt a disembodied horror. The mermaid smirked, shrinking to her normal jumbo size, facing Callista with her sparkling white face and piercing eyes.

"It's too late, I think. You're too weak for it."

Callista began to scream.

Later, when she woke up in her bed with wet hair, shivering, her mouth tasting of vomit and blood, Callista saw her father's face but wasn't sure if it was real or part of the realm. Her pack and jacket lay on the floor, soaked. Her fingernails were dark with the residue of something foul.

"Honey. I don't understand what is wrong with you exactly," he said, silhouetted by the hall light. "But I think you may need to go to the hospital."

She couldn't answer, but just staggered past him to the bathroom. "I'll be fine by morning. This happens to me all the time, Daddy. All the fucking time."

22

CHAPTER 22

In the morning, Callista sat at the kitchen table while her parents pointedly ignored her. The aroma of their coffee made her want to throw up again. She drank hot water with lemon and honey, thinking about Vivian. Why wasn't she there now? Why had Meli wanted Callista to kill her? As if she could. Without Vivian, what was she? Nothing. A scared kid. The hollow darkness she tried so hard to hide. She began to cry again, drying her tears with a paper napkin. She wanted to slap herself into sobriety again, but she was too tired.

Margaret sat down next to her and scowled. Her eyeliner was gone, her hair back in a blond ponytail, and her cheeks looked sunken. She looked like both the young woman she had been, and the old woman she was to become.

"What the hell is wrong with you?"

Callista was fascinated by her face. She wanted to caress the cheeks, as she had once done, back when her mother had been willing to hug her, to get that close. Was there something vaguely Meli-like about Margaret? Around the shoulders, the tip of her head?

"Jesus, at least have the courtesy to answer me."

"Me?" Callista's voice came out flat, a poor imitation of Vivian's cockiness. "Ma. You know. You have always known."

Margaret flinched back as if struck. "Oh not this again. I might as well just get on a plane back to California right now. Today."

Callista thought of what Vivian might say, like whispers of sarcasm, mean remarks, pointing out things that were hypocritical or cruel. But Vivian herself was like a tracing, not actually there. A ghost of a ghost. The thought made Callista laugh.

"Mother." She said, sipping her hot water. "I don't know what to say to you. You have your life. And I am…I am supposed to have my own. You've made that very clear. But right now…"

"Right now what?" Margaret said, a coiled energy about her.

"Right now…" Callista spoke as loudly as she could, just above a whisper. "I am on the verge of everything. I don't know what to do. And I feel so completely alone."

And to her amazement, Margaret reached for her hand. It felt dry and hard.

"Darling. You're in real trouble. I understand that now. But there's nothing I can do to help you. You are an adult. You have to take responsibility for yourself."

Phillip sipped his coffee, watching.

Callista felt a cool, Meli-flavored breeze wash over her. "I know. I understand that you want to be in California. I don't blame you."

She removed her hand and went back to her room. Phillip had changed the sheets and opened the curtains to the back yard. The breeze felt cool and wet. No doubt he was trying to rid the place of her sour aroma.

She tried to study, but it was hard to concentrate. She cried for a while, took a long shower, thinking of Kevin, her hands moving on her own body to try and get back the feeling of flying, of escape. But she could only half remember his face, the caramel taste of him, his leather jacket's zipper pushing onto her skin. Adam's tears floated in the periphery.

"You idiot." He was saying, "One day you'll look at yourself in the mirror, and realize you can have anyone you want. And on that day, watch the fuck out, world."

But that had been months ago, when they had been driving home after she'd been in a play, and he had been given permission to come see it. Callista smelled that Meli smell again, a fetid salt tang, so she showered again, cleaning her nails until they ached. Afterward, she stood at the mirror naked, pushing her breasts together to make cleavage, trying to affect the blank look of a supermodel,

Patty Hansen or Rose Vela. She was broad shouldered and bulky, though not exactly fat. Callista thought she looked like a naked toddler doll, neither sexy nor asexual. Just a large girl, with long dirty blond hair, and a face that could look very pretty if she did herself up with glimmering eyeshadow and blush. Adam was being kind. He was far prettier that she was. Maybe he'd actually been talking about himself.

She was dressed, hair in a towel, when her father rapped on her door. He sat next to her on the bed and touched her lightly on the arm. He took a deep breath, as if what he was about to say were difficult.

"Darling, I'm afraid things aren't going to be able to stay the same around here."

She looked at the rumpled, dark-haired man sitting on the edge of her bed, his voice so familiar from a million conversations, books read aloud, and interjections about her mother's real intent, efforts to keep the peace. He was a stranger, in that moment, someone she didn't know how to define. A peacemaker, maybe. The link between a girl and her mother, but neutral, someone who seemed to think that both sides were equally as worthy of defending. In other words, Callista saw clearly, like a sinker on a line dropping down, down, into the very heart of her, he wasn't on her side. Not really. Here he sat, his large, soft fingers on her wrist in a gesture that would have been comforting. But it meant only that he wanted her to stop being a problem.

"Father." She said, her voice a rasp. "Why do you think that lying to her is going to protect me? Don't you see that all the lies do the opposite? Something real happened. Something real. Is it worth it to you to see me like this, so the world can go on the way it has?"

Who had said that? Vivian? But no. It was Callista. Simply her, speaking without thinking of the consequences.

He looked at her hard, his blue eyes tired, their usual merry lights so small she could no longer detect them. A middle-aged man in the middle of a complex dance with his wife and a bunch of people in California, with a daughter who would never recover from being twelve.

"You were twelve. Surely you can see how much it hurts her that you are so stubborn?" He smiled gently. "The two of you are a lot alike, you know. Both stubborn. Both brilliant."

She watched his face. Spencer had said something about how her parents would be divorcing if not for their fling with the other couple. And Phillip was still in love with Margaret. Of course he was. Once Callista left for college, he would have nothing, but an abandoned cat and the house in the woods. Callista couldn't find it in her to hate him for it. Even though it meant betraying her, as usual.

"Go on, Daddy. I appreciate you trying to protect me. But apparently, it's too late for that now."

He sighed. "You understand what you're doing?"

"What?"

"You're leaving us without options for how to relate to you, sweetheart. We are a family, of a sort, but you don't seem to want that."

A weariness settled over her. "There's no family to keep together. I understand that you will never see my side. She can tear me to shreds, and you'll sit there watching. I accept that. But don't give me all the credit. It's a choice you two have made."

His face sagged. "Your anger, it's very hard on her. It pushes her to see her father in a whole different way. She doesn't know whom to believe..."

"Exactly. When she should have believed me." She motioned to herself. "I'm not a problem child. Or a 'disturbed youth.' Whatever she calls me behind my back."

"Callista." He said with a small burst of heat. "I have never thought of you as a problem child."

"Thank you, Daddy. I promise, I will always want to be your daughter. If you want me to be."

"Stop." He bent forward at the waist as if in pain. "How can you say something like that?"

She fell silent.

"Darling, I don't want to keep having these conversations. Please can we try to get back to normal?"

"You don't want normal. Please. I love you, but don't lie to me. You and mom have moved on with your lives, and I have no choice but to take a page from your book. I understand. She sent you down here to threaten me. But you can't take away something that I don't have. So don't worry, Daddy. I know you love me, as much as you are able. That's the normal I can offer. Hope it's enough." She smiled. "Good night."

23

—·—

CHAPTER 23

The house was empty when Callista woke. She ate toast and a cup of cold coffee from the Chemex on the counter. Both her parent's cars were gone. She vomited almost immediately into the powder room toilet. Her head throbbed as the menace of her father's words replayed in it, *things can't stay the same around here.*

The phone rang while she was checking off tasks to prepare for her French final.

"Hello?"

"Callista. I got a message that you called."

"Detective Franklin. I'd like to meet with you."

She looked down the drive. "You'll have to come pick me up. I'd love it if you drove a squad car."

The black and white was idling in front of their mailbox within half an hour. Callista had chosen a pair of jeans she hadn't worn in ages, and a fashionable leather jacket she usually reserved for funk shows or school dances. He opened the door for her. Dr. Mere stood staring from their covered catwalk across the street, and Callista waved cheerily. The cruiser's low chassis coasted over the wet pavement like a royal barge. She smiled at the Monroe twins, who watched with evident delight.

"I've looked into Kenneth Kling, as you requested."

"Oh yeah?"

His hands twitched on the wheel. She thought his sideburns might be just a fraction of an inch longer than when they had met in the art classroom. She hadn't been able to see his face at their most recent meeting, in the dark forest.

"It turns out, he has made a number of young people uncomfortable."

She sighed. "Is that a euphemism?"

"What?" He looked at her sidelong, one hand steering. He smelled like Ivory soap.

"Is *making them uncomfortable* a way of saying that he...?"

"I think I know what you're getting at." He spoke quietly. "Something you yourself are familiar with?"

They cruised in silence past Adam's house. Mr. Frazer stood, holding Lobo by the collar, watching from under a billed cap as they cruised slowly past. He stared at Callista, but Franklin leaned over and waved to him, and he flinched, eyes flitting back to her with an expression she couldn't read. It was the first time Callista had ever felt seen by Adam's father, the first time he had perceived her as a person to be reckoned with. Then they were beyond the T, then down Mount Zebulon Drive's treelined corridor.

"What makes you say think I would be?" Oddly, unlike when Grace seemed to be implying that Callista had something shameful to hide, here with this cop, she felt calm and relaxed. Here was someone who had context for her life, who didn't live within the borders of what was considered normal. He saw everything. It was his job, the profession he had chosen. She smiled at him. He flushed with pleasure, sitting a bit taller in his short sleeved polyester shirt, and she understood that he had investigated because she wanted him to. The feeling of power that flowed through her was subtle, but intoxicating. He was here merely because she told him to be. If she asked him to run the siren and turn on the lights, would he?

"So." She said. "What is the name? For what we're talking about?"

He told her names. *Pedophilia, molestation, statutory rape,* and a string of other Latin words that she chose not to memorize, their sound clinically pornographic. As he said them, Callista started to cry. Each word he said felt like a sharp poke, followed by a painful kind of relief, like bursting a blister. There was a compete vocabulary for the thing that had happened. Names of crimes. Categories, degrees, and levels of seriousness. The knowledge pulled at her, like being both in the present and in the past, and in the part of time afterward when she had tried to tell her mother what had happened, and the woman she knew became a stranger.

"Do people really ever get in trouble for those things?"

He shook his head. "It's too hard to prosecute. No one believes the kids. Usually girls. Not to upset you any worse that I already have, but it's boys too."

She sighed. "No one believes them, either, I'm sure."

"You go to Seattle, talk to the runaways there. It's almost always this. Or getting hit. Or both."

"You've seen this? Yourself?"

He smiled grimly. She noticed he had a dimple, which matched the one in his chin. She could easily imagine him as a boy, which felt odd, because in his uniform he seemed almost more than a man. There was something pleasingly exotic about it, the wide belt, the covered holster, the western tooling on leather that was similar to what she had seen that night at the club.

"I've witnessed things on this job that you wouldn't believe. Right here in perfect Fairfield. And let me tell you. Just because people have money or social position, doesn't mean they aren't human. And humans do terrible things to one another."

She snorted sarcastically. "No shit."

He pulled into the parking lot for the Big Ring, a community horse track used for shows and riding lessons. Callista thought what a short walk it was through the forest to Adam's house, how many times she had gone home that way. The place was muddy and deserted. Callista briefly remembered winning a yellow ribbon, in another lifetime. She wasn't that girl anymore, the girl who paraded herself before judges, showing off her skill. She had felt no shame, brazenly attracting the eyes of strangers, then. Because she had been only eleven. She hadn't competed since. She hadn't let herself be seen or judged. The very idea of it made the wave of sickness appear, like mist at the corners of her eyes.

"Are you okay?" Franklin said. He turned the key, and the sudden silence inside the car felt strange. "Leslie McCall's disappearance hit you awful hard."

She wiped her eyes with her hand. "Not because of Adam. You understand? He's not…"

"I know. I put a few things together." He blinked to show how distasteful he found the revelations. But his face was mild, and she could see that wasn't what he wanted to talk about.

"So you're no longer planning to ruin his life?"

"From what I can glean, his dad is doing that all on his own. And there is no law against hitting or terrorizing your own child. So, no. I am not planning to take any action against anyone in the Frazer family." He gazed at her, his hazel eyes soft, lips making an ironic line. "Adam was the best idea I had at first, based on circumstance, and what people were saying. A love triangle would have given him a motive. He would have been acting to protect his relationship with you. To please you."

She laughed.

"Oh, you think it's funny, the idea of a decent man trying to please you?"

She covered her face in her hands. The sickness was replaced with embarrassment, so fast she felt giddy, like screaming with hysterical laughter. Maybe because this news was a relief. Adam was no worse off than he had been before.

"Frazer has other things going on. And the two of you have been letting the world think whatever it wants. Smart of you. But kind of hard, isn't it? If you pretend to date Adam then no one else can ask you out." He looked at her plaintively, his voice rising to show how terrible that was.

"I haven't wanted anyone to. It's been my choice, until very recently. The world does that anyway, you know." She let him see her deeply blushing cheeks. "People believe what they want, and there's not much anyone can do to change their mind."

"Look, I am on thin ice here. I'm kind of a rookie, but I am doing a good job and I don't want to jeopardize that. You saw that." He smiled and shook his head with wide eyes to show how amazing she was. "You knew that threatening my livelihood would count. It was a powerful move, Callista. It really got my attention. You scared the hell out of me, that night in the woods. First that you were out there to begin with. I didn't know that this neighborhood was connected by so many trails. I'm from Spokane, where we use sidewalks, you know? But since then I've learned about this whole trail system, and I guess it's not so weird for a girl to do what you did. Anyway. After you yelled at me like that, I was expecting your father to call me and yell at me, or your mother to serve me papers."

She touched the radio on the console in front of her, making him flinch. "But no one called you. Because they don't know anything about what I do. They don't even know I've been questioned."

He took her hand gently and placed it back on her side of the car. "And then when I found out who your grandfather is..."

Callista sighed.

Franklin raised his eyebrows as if the notion were too incredible to be believed. "A federal judge?"

"Where is Leslie? I mean it. Where is she?"

He shook his head, and his hands strayed to the seat between them, as if picking a piece of invisible hair from the vinyl. "I think you're right about Kenneth Kling. He's a creep. The kids are afraid of him. Especially the girls, though they're nice girls like you, and they don't want to say anything negative about an adult. And, there's nothing to connect him with Leslie's disappearance other than circumstance. I came to tell you, that unless I have something new to go on, I am going to have to move on to other investigations."

"So, she's just going to stay missing?"

"Most kids who disappear are runaways. I think if you went to Broadway or the U District, eventually you'd run into Leslie. She'd be high, probably living with some A-hole in a cheap apartment on the Ave."

"In a cheap apartment. Getting high. Right."

His eyes pleaded. "If there's something more concrete you can tell me, now would be a good time."

"You'd give up?"

It occurred to Callista that his reason for being there was to goose her for more information. She thought of the Realm, and Leslie's pale face, how she'd said she wanted to stay there forever because it was the only safe place. Most missing girls run away. Callista was one step away from being one of them. But Franklin didn't know that. He had her in the other category, *nice*. Because she was rich, and white, and had a voice inside that could sound commanding, like she had resources to make heads roll. She wanted to collapse from the exhaustion of letting people think that about her. The yellow ribbon flapped in her memory, from when she had thrown it onto the fireplace, along with the other girlish items from before the thing that happened, her Breyer colt still covered in sand from when she had buried it in Grandfather's yard, her nightgown printed with strawberries, the *Tuesday* underpants.

"We wouldn't look at it as giving up. Leslie was last seen near a national park. If she can be found, the Feds will find her."

The word *Longbotham* flashed in Callista's mind, Leslie standing on one leg, her shorn head. "What if I gave you a lead?"

He peered at her. "Callista. You don't think that's why I called you. Seriously. Do you really not know?"

Her cheeks burned. She looked into his eyes, and felt a surge of power. And then he was kissing her. And she was pressing herself to him, as if she had wanted this since the moment she'd entered the car. But it felt terrifying and mortifying to understand that she had.

Franklin's hands were large and insistent. His mouth tasted like nutty brine, sesame or cashews. He seemed intent, which made her less nervous. They kissed for a long time, until it dawned on her that she could release her seat belt. And then she straddled him, feeling a dangerous ribbon of recklessness that wrapped around them both. Sometime later, he watched her, unmoving, when she pulled back and caught her breath. She laughed, and he smiled, but his awkwardness was obvious by the way he didn't want to risk adjusting his lap.

"How old are you?" She couldn't stop laughing. "Nothing is funny, I'm just really nervous."

"Nervous? Is that how you act when you're nervous?" He looked delighted. "Do you like older guys? I don't know what excites you."

"Me?" She made a cartoonish, quizzical face. "I have never done this before. That's only the second, third, fourth time I've ever kissed anyone."

He gaped. "You don't know?"

"It depends on how you count. The second time I've kissed someone because I wanted to."

"I'm twenty-four. Too old to be caught with a...wait, you turn eighteen tomorrow, don't you?'

"Oh, I see." She moved away from him, still laughing. "This was premeditated. A planned and executed make out session! Second degree kissing."

He fought off her lightly slapping hands. "You got me. Guilty as charged."

"Wow." She sat back, watching a blackbird trying to find an updraft. "I forgot my birthday."

"You'll be a grownup lady." He said quietly. "Though maybe that doesn't mean a whole lot in your world."

"My world?" She said.

"You know. Prep schools, college, becoming a professional, stuff like that. Where I'm from, you'd be old enough to get married and have a baby."

She didn't answer. She didn't want to get married, but the idea of doing what she'd have to do to get pregnant struck her in that moment in as something she wanted to do. With him.

"Do you have a baby, Randy? Do you have a wife?"

He took a sharp breath. "I thought I was going to get married. But she had different plans. So no."

"I don't know what I want to do. The truth is, I feel like a blank space. Like, there was a person there. But she was erased. Like a chalkboard. And there's no one left, inside me. I'm just a kind of...statue, maybe. And people see what they want to see. And I have no control over it."

"I'm sorry, Callista." Randy motioned for her to buckle up. "That's called *being a victim*. It happens to people. When they're...when something bad happens to them. When they've been hurt or abused. Do you have memory issues?"

She stared at him. "How did you know?"

"It's typical. I'm sorry for what was done to you."

"Does it make you feel different about me?"

His hazel eyes met hers, gleaming with something fierce that almost set her to laughing again. "Jesus. Rich people."

He eased the car out of the muddy parking lot.

"So, you're taking me home, now? Case closed, here's a kiss, have a pleasant day?"

"Unless there's someplace else you'd like to go."

She touched the cold window with her hand. They were pulling by one of the barns, and lights shone out into the rain. "If someone was hurting her, she wouldn't be allowed to say."

"Are you speaking about yourself now? Or just kids like you?"

Her voice grew so small, she almost wished Vivian would show up and start talking. She felt so weak and pitiable. "Kids like us. We don't want to cause problems. We are raised not to disappoint people. And when we do, it's like...all the effort was a waste."

He looked at her sidelong. "Anyone who is disappointed in you is an idiot."

She smiled sadly. "I'm glad you think so. But I'm not talking about horny police officers."

He laughed. "Has Kling ever bothered you?"

"Not in a way to be fired for. I could probably get him to step over the line if I wanted to. But I'll be a legal adult, then. No one's going to make anything out of it. But he creeps me out so bad. I can't even stand to look at him."

"I'm sure Leslie felt the same way. Only, there's not a shred of evidence against him at this point."

Callista thought about the Leslie she met while she was high. Was she a ghost? Or something like a ghost, a spirit? An angel? Would an angel wear red corduroy pants and a turtleneck, or stand on one foot while visibly stoned on a street corner?

"I see her in my dreams."

Randy turned onto Cedar street. "So do I."

Adam's house was dark and motionless in a way that didn't seem normal.

"Can you pull in front of the Frazer's?" She said.

Randy turned smoothly. "How come?"

"I don't know. I just...they are always home. Always. And now..."

She gestured. The house had a foreboding look, but nothing was obviously amiss.

"Do they have a summer cabin? A place in the islands?"

"I don't think so. They have family in Ohio, but they don't visit them. Anyway, it's not break yet. Mr. Frazer wouldn't pull Adam out of school during mid Tri exams."

"They're probably at church or out visiting friends, and just forgot to leave lights on. Maybe they went to see a movie."

It wasn't yet dusk, but the house looked like a dark cavity, blacker than the trees, denser than the surrounding neighborhood.

"Yeah." She said, imagining Adam sitting at a dining table with friends of his family's, smiling woodenly, pretending not to be bored. They might be fixing him up with someone's daughter, a more suitable candidate than Callista. They might be forcing him to listen to an adult friend lecture him on appropriate colleges that didn't border San Francisco.

"Look." She pointed. "His car's gone."

"That's it, then. He went somewhere, in his car. I think you cracked the case."

She didn't return his smile, or explain what Mrs. Frazer had told her about Adam losing driving privileges. Something was wrong.

He stopped at the mouth of the driveway and she jumped out before the subject of a goodbye kiss arose. "Well, officer. Thank you. I'm sure the Feds will solve it all, before long."

"Callista?" He narrowed his eyes. "Answer the damn phone once in a while."

He pulled away.

24

CHAPTER 24

Callista pulled her jacket close against the cold, and considered her next move. There was a sense of light and motion within the windows, as if her parents were cheerfully bustling around the interior. She took the steps down the side of the house.

Her floor was dark, but rang with footsteps from the floor above. Both her mother and father were accounted for, her mother's steps hard and sharp, her father's more shuffling, softer. They were listening to Puccini. Callista smelled frying onions and garlic. It made her stomach ooze with acid, not hunger precisely. More like the beginning of sickness.

She moved silently into her room and changed into a pair of sweats. She washed her face, which was red from kissing. The pleasure of it remained, like a thin layer of quicksilver beneath her skin. Like armor against the parental invasion.

She took the main staircase up to the dining room and watched her parent's reflections as they prepared food in the great room kitchen, talking and drinking red wine. She wondered when they had switched to red, and whether they were really planning to move to California. They would have to give up the practice of law, though. She couldn't see them doing that. What she could see was that they were a complete unit, whole and content, without her. Her mother was speaking, her voice its usual confident alto.

The record ended, and Phillip walked past on his way to the study to change it. He didn't notice her standing there, or perhaps he was ignoring her. Then

Callista had a strange feeling, a kind of deep lurching in her gut. The air smelled a particular way. A familiar, ancient way.

Miles Davis began to pour out from the speakers. An old record. She felt nauseated. Cigar smoke, that was the smell. Her grandfather was in the kitchen, out of her line of vision, lighting up a stogie as he had a thousand times, marking the cocktail hour with a celebratory Cuban. Her mother was cooking him dinner, making ratatouille, and probably lamb chops as well, his favorite meal. As if everything were normal, and Callista…what did it mean, regarding Callista?

That she was turning eighteen the next day. And would be an adult. She felt the vomit in her stomach about to explode onto the dining table. The thought of it didn't bother her, but for the weakness that would follow, the vulnerability of tears and helpless rage that would bubble up. She couldn't let any of them see that.

She rubbed her eyes. When she removed them, her father was standing in the dim dining room, looking at her as if from very far away, though it was less than ten feet. She met his eyes. He made a tiny motion, a kind of semi shrug, to indicate that he wasn't going to let them know that she was there. But nor was he going to invite her to join them. The sound of laughter carried through the door. Her father opened the liquor cabinet and pulled out a bottle of wine, and one of an amber liquid. Scotch for Grandpa.

She watched him. He sighed, looking at her as if she were at the bottom of the ocean, and no line he threw would be long enough to reach her. She blinked back tears. His shoulders sagged, and then he stepped back into the kitchen, and gently slid closed the door.

Callista went to the liquor cabinet and helped herself to a jar of olives, and another of peanuts. She took a can of ginger ale, and a wine glass. In her room, she ate a meal of her pilfered items, and studied. After a while, she heard footsteps again, and a car drove away. Sometime later, there was a soft knock.

"Come in." She said.

To her surprise, the person on the other side of the door was her mother, arms crossed over her nubby sweater and wide legged green pants. Her feet were bare, and her hair in an old fashioned up-do. Callista had once loved it when her mother wore her hair like that.

"Are you going to scream at me?" Margaret said.

Callista wasn't used to seeing her mother intoxicated. She felt the air of danger in it, but also, the still burnished sheen of Randy's kisses. "Would that make it easier?"

"Fine." Her mother came in and sat on the bed. Callista's room was small, the smallest room in the house. She had never taken over Spencer's space, when he'd left. It had never occurred to her that she could. Now, her mother made the room feel miniscule.

"How is your father?" Callista said.

Margaret leveled a gleaming gaze. Callista wondered if she was meant to feel intimidated, or something else. It had been a very long time since she had known what her mother wanted from her, or if she wanted anything at all.

"Callista." She spoke very softly, her voice slightly hoarse. "Is this how you plan to carry on?"

"How I plan to carry on?" Callista said, feeling like a scientist examining a test subject. What is making the rat behave in this way?

"You know what I mean." Her mother exploded, voice rising, her arms swinging around her torso clumsily. "Have you decided to no longer be one of the family?"

Callista felt her face erupting into laughter. But she was tired. She wanted to be back in the Realm, at peace, with the colors and birds and perhaps even crazy Leslie, somewhere she didn't have to explain the obvious.

"Mother."

"Why do you insist on calling me Mother?" Margaret said, her face contorting. "You used to call me Mom! Don't you remember that? When you called me Mom?"

Callista sighed. "I haven't called you that in years. It doesn't matter. You have made your feelings for me clear. Tonight, for the past six weeks, and every day before that. I understand what you're saying to me, Margaret. I'm not a wholly stupid person. And I'm sure you are here to add that as a woman of eighteen,

I no longer have the right to live here anymore. You want to stop paying Mrs. Mackie? I understand. Maybe you want to go to California, and do the fun things you do there?"

Her mother began to protest, but Callista lowered her voice, not stopping.

"Look. You've made your choice. Years ago. And it's taken me a long time to catch on. Because I was a child. And I needed to believe that you loved me. That you would protect me, that you would notice me."

"Don't you dare. You don't think I noticed all your dramatic plays for attention? You don't think I wanted to buckle, and give in, and coddle you for all your little performances? But I didn't. Because it wouldn't have been good for you. And I was right. You have turned out fine. But I have just about had it with your defiance and your whining about how hard it's all been for you. I am just about done with all of that."

Callista watched her mother with Vivian-like calculation. A woman who had convinced herself that being receptive was weak. There was, Callista saw, a grain of truth gleaming in her pile of rationalizations. The parts she knew of her daughter were fine because she accepted the surface. Callista saw what she had to do. Show that she was strong, and Margaret was released. Do what Phillip had implied, and let go of the idea of family. Why not?

"Oh, stop threatening me. I'm not scared of you. You want to have your father over for dinner, go ahead. You want to tell me I'm a fat, ungrateful wench, have at it. I've got midterms. And then, maybe I'll apply to college. Maybe I'll get married and have someone's baby. Who knows?"

Margaret sat back. "What?"

"You heard me." Callista turned in her desk chair.

Callista felt satisfaction at being the focus of her mother's attention, but also fear of the inevitable backlash to come. And she was tired. Her college book sat on the desk, unopened.

"What the hell is wrong with you?"

Callista didn't answer. She was sliding, as she had so many times before, but this time instead of being carried into the Realm, she floated into a hot, red ocean, which hurt all over. She heard herself crying at a distance, and then she was vomiting again, wishing she could pull the sickness out of her as she had the gray fuzz in the Realm. And she was so tired, so exhausted from wishing she could be there, because it was not a good place to go, not a good thing to do.

The thermos lay on its side on the floor next to her closet. Mocking her. Her guts were on fire, especially on the right side.

She whispered. "Please tell Daddy that I think I want to do what he suggested, and go to the hospital."

25

CHAPTER 25

When Callista awoke, the world was pale, and anesthetic was rolling through her like the snap of a clean bed sheet over her prone body. Something had changed. She slept.

In her sleep, there were voices of her mother, her father, and Spencer. Meli saying something about how Callista didn't have to wake up if she didn't want to.

Later, she opened her eyes to a hospital room, everything beige, a soft watercolor print in pastels, curtains all around. It was night. She was hooked to an IV but no machines. Not that sick, she thought. When her grandmother had been dying, she had been hooked up to all kinds of things, with lights and sounds. Her side was still smarting under a large bandage held on with tape over iodine-stained skin. Surgery, then.

She drifted off.

"Callista," a voice said.

She groaned. She had been skiing in her dream.

"Wake up, you big baby." Spencer said. "You slept through your birthday."

She tried to sit up, then remembered her wound.

"Mom. She's awake," he called over his shoulder. "She's about to force the nurses to wake you. I never knew a person could sleep so much."

"What happened to me?" She looked at him pleadingly.

"Appendicitis."

"That's it?"

Margaret appeared. She looked alabaster-pale, with small red spots on her cheeks. Was she hungover?

"Honey." She rushed over and put her hand on Callista's forehead. "How do you feel?"

Callista shrugged "I don't know yet. How long have I been here?"

There was a sound from the other side of the curtain, someone turning on one of the televisions suspended from the ceiling. Bonanza. Little Joe was arguing with a girl in a yellow dress.

Callista spent another night in the room, watching television until Spence brought her books by to study. Her doctor, a slender man with a completely bald head named Dr. Dravus, examined her belly and told her that the scar wouldn't interfere with wearing a bikini. She said a polite thank you, and the hospital let her go.

The Land Rover felt cold and foreign inside, as if she'd ridden to the hospital weeks, not days, before. Adam's house shone with Christmas lights, but the drapes were drawn, and the Goat was under a cover again. Spencer left that night, apologizing for not getting to talk.

"But it was your fault." He sat on her bed. "Man, when Dad called me I thought you were dead."

"I'm surprised they had you come. It must have been so expensive."

He ruffled her hair. "The taps are flowing, money wise. They won that case."

"The California one?"

"And I think Grandpa is talking about trust fundage and all that."

Callista winced. "Is that what the detente is all about?"

He shrugged. "Are you going to be okay?"

"You saw. They took out the bad part of me. I'm all fixed now."

Spencer pressed his lips in a tight smile. "You're bumming my stone, you know. I don't care whatever your thing is with mom. But...you don't seem to be very careful with yourself. The tea is just for fun, right?"

"Of course." She sighed. "I was taken by surprise. When she invited Grandpa over. Just not what I expected. Or wanted."

He nodded. "What do you want?"

There were footsteps on the kitchen stairs. Spencer stood to go.

"For you to come home for Christmas."

He laughed. "You wasted your wish. I was anyway."

"Thank you." She smiled. "I love you."

"Can't believe I flew a thousand miles for this level of abuse."

Phillip brought her tea and sat on her bed. He looked relaxed and pink cheeked. She handed him her American Studies and English papers. "Can you take these to school? Mrs. Webber in the office will make sure they are turned in."

"Where's Adam when you need him?" Phillip said. "I mean, I expected him to visit you, at least. Not to put too fine a point on it, by you could easily have died."

"Adam and I aren't..." She felt tears. Where was Vivian? "I told you this before. We're not..."

He patted her hand. "Well, he's an idiot. Don't worry, I'll get your school-work in."

"Thank you."

"And college applications?" His eyebrows raised. "Do you need some stamps?"

She shook her head. "It's all taken care of."

It wasn't. When her tests were over, Callista felt deflated. No skiing for two weeks. She heard that Brody had thrown an insane party with mushroom tea in china cups, after which kids threw lawn chairs into the pool. Rumors were flying that Callista was having an affair with a cute Fairfield cop. No one had been able to find Adam to ask how he felt about it. His absence seemed to point to heartbreak, but no one knew for sure.

The sky was dark and drippy. Callista was comforted by from the regular noise of her parents' footsteps upstairs, and the Dave Brubeck quartet's preening alto sax. She spent the next few days tucked into bed, surrounded by cards from Harriet and other friends, getting up to walk around the house a few times a day while her incision went from angry red to deep pink.

Harriet herself came by and dropped off pound cake, a stack of supermarket tabloids, and a copy of Helter Skelter. She wafted downstairs smelling like L'air du Temps and scowling at the modernity of Callista's situation.

"Pretentious enough? This place is like mini Falling Water." She sniffed. "No offense. I'm sure Architectural Digest would approve."

Callista smiled. "Have you seen him?"

"Only in passing. He shaved his head. Dropped off the debate team. Eats lunch with Bolt every day. Those monsters he calls parents drop him off and pick him up. Grace tried to talk to Florence on Thursday afternoon, and she refused to even roll down the window. So rude. If you ask me, he's on the verge of a nervous breakdown."

Callista remembered the sound of Adam crying in the car after the club. "Harry. I need a favor."

"You certainly do." Harriet came over and sat on the bed, smoothing its Marimekko cover with her hand.

The following day Mrs. Mack appeared to clean and hover, and she was actually pleasant, telling Callista that her husband Bud sent his best regards for her good health.

"Your mother has been worried sick, Callista." She said while Callista stood watching her change the sheets. "She's a tough lady. But she has a good heart."

"Thank you. Tell Bud I appreciate his wishes."

Then to her amazement, Mrs. Mackie grabbed her roughly in a hug, and planted a kiss near her ear. "You have the things a girl needs for life. Beauty, brains, a good family. You can get whatever you want. I hope you realize that."

Callista sat numbly on the clean bed, her body crawling with embarrassment. That night, she dreamt of Meli, singing and smoothing her silver hair.

The next afternoon she dressed carefully in tights and a skirt, and drove to Harriet's. Her incision twinged slightly when she stepped on the gas. It felt like weeks since she'd crossed the bridge. The Arboretum was ghostly. Harriet's house sat wreathed in woodsmoke, colored bulbs shining out from evergreen swags like an old movie set.

"She's here!" Grace called out when Callista came through the door. Maude barked, her stump waving gayly. A fire spit in the huge hearth under its carved marble festooned with stockings.

"My God." She said. "I've never seen such cheer."

"Why do we invite you?" Harriet said. "Just because you're tall and can reach the high branches."

"Finally! Callista, haven't we missed ya?" Pinch said, poking the ceiling with a huge blue fir tree. "Dammit. That's going to leave a mark."

They removed what seemed like hundreds of intricate glass bulbs from colored tissue paper and hung them carefully on every branch, even ones in the back that only passersby could see. Grace called out encouragement from the kitchen. When they had finished, the Christmas tree was as ornate as any Callista had seen in the Bon Marche, or I Magnin.

Grace put out cioppino and sour dough bread, and they feasted while Pinch held forth about the virtues of a Junior year abroad in Florence rather than Rome. Callista felt the pull of their high spirits, and wondered how they would manage with Harriet away at school, and why they had stopped at only one child. She would never ask. But something about the way Grace smiled at her, as if she saw Callista's every small sorrow, made her think it wasn't intentional.

When dinner was over, they toasted her health. She sipped club soda with lemon and batted away tears. No one mentioned Leslie or Adam. Harriet looked tired but jolly, in a swipe of black winged eyeliner that changed her from retro to fashionable. Callista was able to imagine her friend on the East Coast, holding forth with whatever other weirdos she would meet in her first-year dorm.

"Here." Harriet handed her a shopping bag stuffed with a wrapped loaf of sour dough, a bottle of wine, and a manilla envelope. "Don't forget this."

"You're the best."

Harriet smiled crookedly. "With Adam in hibernation, I suppose I am."

Callista drove over the darkly gleaming lake feeling like she'd had all of the good parts of Christmas without any of the bad. She slowed as she passed

Adam's house. She felt an urge to go beat on the door, demand he come out and explain himself. But she was tired, and her incision itched. Adam must know. Someone would have told him. He must be unable to emerge from his own troubles long enough to notice hers. Or perhaps he had stopped caring about her. She tried to imagine him with a shaved head, or in the throes of a nervous breakdown, and found that it was easy for her to imagine either.

26

CHAPTER 26

T he next day Margaret surprised her with tickets to see the Nutcracker.

"We need to do a mother daughter thing. Will you indulge me?"

Phillip looked on, smiling, as Margaret handed Callista the tickets. Good seats. She must have gotten them from one of the partners, or perhaps the firm had extras.

Callista laughed. "Why not?"

She borrowed a long dress and a fur coat, enjoying the way her breath misted the air as they crossed the footbridge to the Opera House. The ballet had been a tradition when she was small. She had always felt odd, watching the graceful dancers with their limber forms move in ways she couldn't. But now, the whole colorful spectacle felt vaguely Realm-like, dreamy, and impressionistic. She didn't make any effort to feel what the dance conveyed, just let it wash over her, while Margaret closed her eyes and dozed off, a faint glimmer of silver eye shadow on her lids. Callista reached over and let the tips of her fingers graze her mother's wrist.

That weekend Spencer came home, and they got their own tree, a handsome Fir they decorated with wooden curlicues and straw stars. They ate pepper jack cheese on triscuits with hot spiced wine, and played a long and contentious game of Monopoly. The owl flashed by outside, disappearing into the dark trees. It felt to Callista like the day she'd stood in front of Adam's in the snow had been a year before, instead of only a month.

"You can ski now, right?" Spencer said.

It had only been ten days, and she was told to wait for two weeks. "Of course."

"I got you some Goggles that don't fog. Put those in your bag right away so you don't forget."

She grimaced. "I haven't gotten presents for anyone."

"Shut up, invalid. Just the fact that you and mom aren't murdering each other is gift enough. Believe me."

The next day she and Spence rose, opened the small pile of gifts under the tree, and took the Land Rover to Lucent Mountain.

"If you rip open your incision, I will be very displeased." Margaret said.

Callista felt the weight of the thermos in her bag. "Hold on, would you?"

The residue of dark tea smelled foul going down the sink.

"What is that?" Phillip said, wrinkling his nose. He wore an apron.

"Old grog." She said. "I forgot it was in there."

She filled the thermos with cocoa.

The resort was nearly empty, thick with fresh snow.

"It's not Tahoe." She said sarcastically. "But I suppose it'll have to do."

"Deep pow!" Spence made a ridiculous, hog-like squeal.

Burl Ives sang Christmas songs near the lodge complex, but there was no sound but the churning of chairlift wheels and wind on the summit. Sun poked through the nimbus clouds, bringing euphoria even before she hit her first run. Her favorite was Potentate, with its long top and wide bowl so varied she could pick whatever depth of bump she liked.

The powder wasn't as deep as it looked, and at the top the wind was biting. But it didn't matter. Her spirits soared as soon as she and Spencer slid off the chair, not stopping to put on their poles but sliding them on mid-flight. Her cheeks burned under the new ochre-lensed goggles, with made the white slopes golden, the trees bronze. If she didn't push too hard, she could sail all the way to the bottom without stopping. She missed Adam for a split second, knowing he would love carving through the wide, deep bumps. Then she pushed those thoughts away. She found her incision hurt every time she broke rhythm, and she got tired quickly. So she bypassed the moguls for the last few runs, quitting before 3:00.

She found a place near the huge fireplace in the lodge, and opened her pack. She ate a salami sandwich on dark bread, Phillip's work, and drank some of the cocoa. Leslie McCall's stepbrother was sitting with a group of other boys by the snack bar, tossing French fries and laughing. He looked like a slender, leering version of Leslie's stepfather, who had sometimes come to pick her up after ski bus. Callista couldn't remember his name, James or Jacob or Jerome. He met her eye, then said something to the others that made them look. They broke away, laughing at their inside joke. Callista's temper flared, which she assumed was their intent.

"Hey gimp." Spencer sat next to her. "Look at those losers."

"You know them?"

"Just Joseph Auchloss. He goes to St. Augustine's, you know, in Connecticut. Because he washed out of every good school in Seattle."

"Hmm."

"What?"

"It's his stepsister who's missing. Leslie McCall."

Spencer studied the younger boys. "Well, being in another part of the country is a pretty good alibi. That guy is such a smug chode. Old San Francisco. More money than god." Spencer sipped her cocoa. "This is cold. Let's go home and have something better."

The trip down the foothills was dark and clear. Callista dozed off to the sound of Elvis Costello. *She's filing her nails while they're dragging the lake.* She thought about asking her brother if he ever thought she was dragging her nails *in* the lake. But then she was opening her eyes, and Spencer was cursing.

"Those fuckers. Just give them an inch."

A silver Porsche Carrera was parked in front of the front door. Grandfather's car. Callista sat up, wiping her eyes. Her stomach was sore, and she had been drooling. But she felt energetic. It had been a good day.

"I don't care." She said flatly. "He can have dinner with us."

Spencer cursed softly. "The man is a stone asshole. I don't know what he did to you, but it was obviously something terrible."

He turned the Land Rover gingerly around the drive, narrowly avoiding the Porsche.

She smiled at him. "Where were you that day? When Grandma died?"

"I was supposed to go over the Grandpa's with you, but then Jimmy Baxter invited me over. I didn't even know Grandma was sick. I never got to say goodbye."

"Me neither." The last time she had been alone with her Grandfather was the day his ex-wife, Margaret's mother, had died of cancer. Callista thought about Randy, and memory problems, which carried her thoughts to straddling his lap in the police cruiser.

Spencer insisted on carrying her skis downstairs so she could go straight into the shower. She didn't vomit, or start shaking, though she let Spencer talk her into smoking a few puffs from a dube under the eaves on his side of the house. She brushed her teeth, a fresh cotton feeling around her guts. She reached out for Vivian, but realized all she needed was the old strategy, silence. Callista had other options, confrontation, or violence, or refusing to come to the table. But she was hungry. And the Vivian-ish part of her was curious about the old man. Her memories were scrambled, a pain in her throat, his hands on her body, being pinned under his smoke-smelling weight, his muttered orders for her to lie still, and other things that melded together in a confusion of pain and disgust. Then, escaping into the rain. But she had never known exactly what had happened, and in the ensuing five years, she had sometimes wondered if it had been as bad as she had always recalled. Maybe he wasn't. Maybe she could handle him now, the way she handled Franklin.

Upstairs, they were listening to Thelonious Monk. She put on a maroon turtleneck sweater, her grandmother's pearls, and some dark lipstick. In the mirror, she looked flushed from the slopes, but glamorous. Like a woman.

"Vivian, are you really gone?"

There was no answer, not even the smallest of vibrations.

Dinner went by in soft focus. Callista began by drinking the glass Spencer passed her, champagne that hit her tongue like silver-sequined soda pop.

"Callista," Her grandfather began, helping himself to scalloped potatoes. "Meg tells me you're applying to college."

His hands were hairy, a detail that simultaneously amused and disgusted her. She imagined throwing the pan of hot potatoes in his face. What would he do? Instead, feeling her mother's eyes upon her, Callista said. "True."

"Well," His voice was a rich baritone, and she could hear his confidence that it would encounter no opposition, "let me know if I can offer any advice. I don't know where you're considering."

Spencer had stopped chewing, and was watching her face. She blinked, re-calling that her grandfather had put himself through the U by working on the docks, and wasn't altogether pleased that Margaret had gone back East for her college and law school. "Will do."

"Would you do me the great honor of disclosing where you might be attend-ing, Callista?" Now he sounded annoyed.

A long, silent moment passed. Margaret drank her glass of wine.

"Oh," Callista said. "That would be jinxing things."

Phillip pushed a basket of rolls her way. "Here, sweetie. You haven't had any bread."

Callista took one and the conversation moved to other topics. Her grand-father did most of the talking, and Callista tuned it out, like radio static, the background noise between stations.

When dinner was over, she noticed Margaret watching closely, eyes shifting from face to face. She stood.

"I am tuckered out."

"Geeze, Callista." Her grandfather said. "You're too young and strapping to be tired."

"Daddy," Margaret said, rescuing his glass from the edge of the table. "Now, she's getting over surgery. You know that."

"Surgery." He said, unsmiling, his eyes on Callista's midsection. "Let's see the scar, then."

Callista felt frozen. Spencer moved to stand next to her, and she could feel the energy coming off his body. She wanted to take his hand, as they had when they were small and wandering near water.

"It's not pretty."

"Oh, I think I could handle it." He said. "I think you're making it up. Just to upset your mother. I don't believe you had surgery, at all."

"Daddy." Margaret said sharply. "I can assure you. Callista spend three days in the hospital."

"Three days in the hospital." He mimicked in a singsong voice. "I want to see the scar."

Phillip stopped clearing the dishes. "Now Wes, Callista has made her feelings known."

"Feelings. You children and your obsession with feelings. This girl is soft, always has been. Weak and a liar. And you have let her get away with it, all her life."

Spencer made a growling sound in his throat. Callista put her hand on his wrist. "Mother, Father, thank you for a delightful meal. But it's time I took my weak, lying self out of here before Grandfather gives himself a heart attack."

"What did you say?" He moved toward her. He was tall, and strong, but Spencer loomed over him.

"It's okay Spence." Callista said. "It's only Grandfather. He'd never touch me."

And then the old man was cursing and moving around the table, and Margaret was screaming, "Daddy, Daddy, what are you doing?"

But Callista was halfway down wooden stairs to her part of the house, watching her family through the slats.

"Let her go." Spencer said softly.

Their grandfather returned to the table as if nothing had happened. Callista slipped the last few steps.

"Wes, I think you've had enough." Phillip said.

"Daddy, do not speak to her that way." Margaret said. Callista tried to imagine what her mother's face must look like. Her tone was almost pleading.

"She may be a bad seed, but she has turned out remarkably beautiful. She looks like you, Meg, but fleshy. I guess she must be opening her legs for that boy down the lane while you're gone."

There were gasps.

"They're no longer dating." Phillip said. "And I will ask you not to speak of my daughter that way."

"Oh, no. Women can do whatever they like these days, can't they Phil? No one to stop them or tell them they're sluts. But I'm old fashioned. I can see it, always have been able to see it. She must be beating the boys off with a stick. Phillip, that bosom must come from your side of the family. Oh boy."

Time slowed. They were all at the bottom of the ocean, pressurized and silent. Callista wobbled, then crawled into the bathroom where she wretched, her head aching, until nothing more could come out. Her incision ached, but a slight euphoric glimmer rose from deep inside. She washed her hair again, and carefully dressed for bed. She heard footsteps overhead, then doors slamming, and a car engine receding. Something went with it, something heavy and unseen that Callista had been carrying for as long as she could remember.

27

CHAPTER 27

She woke to the sound of her mother crying next to her.

"Oh Honey." Margaret said. "I didn't see it. I just. He never acted that way with me…Your brother is furious. I…"

"It's fine." Callista said. "It's news to you. But not to me."

"What happened between you, that day?" Margaret said in a strained voice.

The curtains made dark stripes of shadow and moonlight. Callista touched the edge of the fabric, wondering who had sewn them. Her breath came easily.

"He let me know how he felt about me." She said, because the details were lost in shadow, and under that, an oozing dream feeling, like the Realm, only much lonelier. "He said things about girls, and how I wasn't being a good girl, because my nightgown was so short, and it let him see my underpants. And.."

Margaret stood. "Stop. I get the picture."

"Mother, please. I've been trying to tell you what happened for years, and you do this every time."

"I know." Margaret sounded shaky. "It just can't take knowing."

"No shit." Callista sat up. "I am aware."

"Stop yelling at me!" Margaret shouted. "I didn't know he would do something like that."

"Why? Because he didn't do it to you?"

"That's right." Margaret cried. "I thought things like that only happened to…not to people like us. Like my…my own father."

"I need to sleep."

"I want to talk about this. I do."

Callista rolled over and pulled over the covers.

"You know what, Mom? If you have questions, ask him."

The next day, Callista and Spencer went to their Grandmother's grave marker on Queen Anne Hill, and left a box of See's candies. Nuts and chews, in dark chocolate. They stood in the rain for twenty minutes, until wind lifted Callista's shell from her hips.

"Do you remember her?" He asked.

"Of course." Callista said, though she didn't really, just a general sense of softness and warmth. "She was so sweet. I can't believe he would leave her."

"For his legal assistant."

"Who didn't even marry him."

"What a shit show."

"Do you think that's why Phillip and Margaret stick together? Because he showed them how not to screw up their lives?"

He laughed. "Mom is having a midlife crisis, and Dad will do anything to keep the focus on her misery, so he doesn't have to look at his own."

"You're going to become a psychiatrist, right?" She said.

"Fuck no. I hate people's problems."

They drove down the hill, and went to the Raison D'Etre for a fancy lunch. Callista took tiny bites from her quiche, her guts still unreliable.

"You're getting so skinny." He said, sipping on his Kir.

"Look who's talking." She said, grabbing an olive off his plate.

Callista spent the afternoon filling out the applications that Harriet had given her, writing out the essays in longhand, then typing them on the typewriter in her father' study while Spencer blasted The Psychedelic Furs. Then she drove him to the airport.

"Fuck you for leaving." Callista said, idling under the Alaska Airlines sign.

"It's your last semester." Spencer said, grabbing his duffel bag from the back seat. "Stop moping around about Adam and get your ass ready for some monumental partying. This is your chance to shine. Don't let me down."

28

— · —

CHAPTER 28

Harriet had clearly learned the route to Fairfield, because she volunteered to drive to Brody's New Year's Eve party even though it meant driving up the east side of the lake. Callista was ready, in clean jeans, new Christmas clogs, and Margaret's fur coat. She thought it gave her a kind of Studio 54 like flair. She half wished Randy could see her, and curse out the rich.

"What the fuck is Frazer's problem?" Harriet said, cruising by Adam's house in Grace's Mercedes. "No word at all?"

"Don't get me started."

"I'm serious. Have you heard from him?"

"No." Callista said, noticing glittering stones beneath Harriet's dark bob. "I like those earrings. Did you get them pierced?"

"Of course not. I'm a lady." Harriet said, gunning it to the T. "These are screw on."

Callista caught a glimpse of Adam's driveway in the rear-view mirror. The lights were taken down, drapes drawn, car in the driveway covered in a dark, leaf-strewn cover. She didn't want to admit to Harriet that she had crept to the woods across the street four times since Christmas. Aside from once almost running into one of the Monroe twins smoking on the trail, she saw no one.

Without Vivian, she found it hard to understand Adam's place in her life. The sharp, aggressive person within always rose up to protect him. Now, all that remained was a sharp shard of failure lodged somewhere below her solar plexus, making it hard to breathe. When a lower part of her body prickled with craving, it was Randy she thought of.

He had called the day before. Phillip had handed Callista the kitchen phone with a questioning look. Randy had asked if she wanted to spend New Year's Eve together, and she had felt a combination of dark annoyance and a flustered confusion.

"Sorry, I made plans with some school friends."

"Yeah," he said quickly. "I guess I thought you would."

The ghost of Vivian asked, *then why are you calling?*

"Any news on Leslie?"

"It's not my case anymore, Callista."

Phillip hovered around the door.

"Thanks for the invitation. Another time?"

"Happy New Year." He said, and hung up.

"Too many beaux?" Phillip asked. "You've gotten so popular."

Callista smiled. "I am on the verge of making a joke about being a slut."

"Please don't." He said. "What a vile thing to say."

"I'll be out late."

"Hon, are you going to keep us in suspense all winter?"

"Suspense? About what?"

He crossed his arms. "About what?"

He meant college. She shook her head. "The fairies are listening, Dad. I don't want my big mouth to arouse their wrath."

New Year's Eve in Seattle, the cars were shabby, streaming smoke and music and laughter. The different stereos warred, small snippets of song passing as they accelerated past. Someone was blasting Born to Run.

"Fuck." Callista said.

"Anyone in particular?"

"What do you think happened to Leslie?"

"Oh that." Harriet merged to the exit lane. "Let's just say that every day they don't find a body I sleep a bit better."

"What if the same thing's happened to Adam?"

"Oh Jesus, Cal. No. There's no connection between the two."

"When was the last time anyone saw him?"

"Okay. I will need you to start drinking immediately. Can you do that for me?"

She could. Brody's house was museum-like in its lines and volume. The place was loud with Blondie and kids yelling gleeful nonsense. Callista located a tub of chilling bottles at one end of the enormous kitchen island.

"Holy shit, York!" Brody said, his light brown eyes dilated under his mop of whitish curls. One of his ears shone with a small silver ball, and his leather jacket bore a scarf-bright silk lining. How had she never noticed how eccentric Brody was? She had not seen much, with Adam standing next to her.

"Holy shit what? Can you open this?" She smiled, and his resulting grin was as gratifying as pushing a finger into a sea anemone.

"Of course, darling." He took the cold champagne from her hands and gave her a paternal nod. "Anything else I can do for you, just ask."

"Tell her just how high you are right now?" Harriet broke in.

"Harry." Brody laughed, struggling with the cork. "I can't do two things at once."

"Give me that."

"I figured out how to make my aunt's tea. You know, bored over the holidays." Brody said, throwing his head back dreamily. "I heard you and Frazer had quite a few tea parties. No fair."

Harriet handed her a red cup full of champagne.

"Ours were dull." Callista said. "We never threw any chairs into the pool."

Brody laughed agreeably. He was joined by a couple of the other Senior guys, and they moved to a pony keg on a table.

"My god." Harriet said. "Ask him for the keys to the Carman Gia. He would deny you nothing."

Callista blushed. "A girl can enjoy a half liter of champagne in innocence, can't she?"

Harriet gazed at her, not answering. Callista raised her glass, then chugged.

As the evening wore on, Callista found herself talking and laughing with kids she barely knew, though she had been in school with them for three and a half years. They asked about her surgery, about her plans for the summer, if she and her family were traveling anywhere. No one mentioned Adam, which she found strange until she realized they were being tactful. The closest she came to learning anything about his life was when a Junior girl mentioned she heard Headmaster was under review from the board, but no one knew why. Then the girl laughed and said she had heard that Lilian was gunning for the Headmaster job, which was a joke, since they would never give it to a woman, and certainly never a woman born in Seattle.

Callista felt thirsty again. In the kitchen, Brody had set up a lemonade station filled with mushroom tea. The mildew smell set Callista on edge.

"So now that Frazer's dumped your ass, who are you moving on to?" Said a voice.

Callista turned. Joseph Aschloss smiled, his eyebrows peaking like crude line drawings.

"Have some tea." She said, and poured him a cup. "It'll relax you."

"What about you?" He said.

She didn't really want to drink, but to spite him, she took a tiny, bitter sip.

29

— · —

CHAPTER 29

T he next morning, waking on the floor next to one of the couches in the TV room, the first thing Callista noticed was that her jeans were unbuttoned. Had she done that? It felt wrong. Nothing too bad could have happened, though, because Harriet was lying asleep on one of the sectionals, black locks peeking out from a pile of coats. Callista jostled her shoulder.

"Harry, come on. Did you tell Grace you weren't coming home?"

"Yes." Harriet said, rubbing her eyes. "Why do people drink?"

Callista was glad Harriet said nothing as they drove home in a drizzle. Memories returned in snatches, of kissing Brody, of someone's rough hands on her and inside her, though she wasn't sure whose. What she remembered was the Realm. Leslie staggered, screaming and crying in front of the Longbotham building, though instead of a city street, it was now in a wetland full of birds and grasses. Joseph was telling his stepsister that she was *worrying her mother sick*, his voice dripping contempt. He wore a shiny deep green suit and rings on every knuckle, his brown hair sculpted high over his forehead like a rock star. He seemed much older than his eighteen years, full of authority and self-importance. Leslie looked even worse than she had before, her skin rough and raw her limbs shuddery as if they didn't quite fit together.

"Fuck off, Joe." She slurred. "My god, leave me alone."

"This has gone on for far too long." Joseph said. "Just get over it, you crazy bitch."

Callista didn't remember what Leslie answered, only that she looked at Callista with a face full of stoned hatred, then collapsed into a raging heap on the sidewalk, a pair of egrets standing sentry over her crumpled form.

"Stop it." Callista said to Joseph. "Can't you see she feels safe here?"

Then she realized how stupid that sounded. Joseph tried to shoo away the white birds. "She's insane. You can see that, can't you?"

Leslie hid her head in her arms. The birds began to peck at Joseph, but he awkwardly Kung Fu kicked at them, and backed away. A smell of cologne came to her.

Callista was crying then, and calling out for Adam. Someone grabbed her arm, hard, and she was between worlds again, Joseph's mouth kissing her deeply, his sharp hands groping under her jeans, Meli calling into her ear.

"Leave me the child." Meli cooed. "And you'll be free to fly to your destiny. You see what being caught here is like. There's still time for you. Not for her. But the child...it's a fair price to pay. To forget."

"What child?"

They were on the shores of the bay, Meli braiding her silver hair, smiling down at a preteen girl on the beach.

"It's raining, Meli." Callista said. "She shouldn't be outside."

And then she was crying harder with recognition. The girl had long, honey-blond hair. She knelt barefoot, deliberate, and blank-faced in a baby doll nightie, hands scrabbling in the sand, burying a toy horse with a broken leg, then covering the grave with stones.

"That's me." Callista said, slowly. "That's me, on the day the thing happened."

She tried to catch the girl's attention, but Meli was between them.

"If you leave her with me, you can go. I'll take her to my queendom. There she will rule alongside me. But if you insist on dragging her along with you everywhere you go, then you will never be free to pursue your destiny." Meli started scat singing.

"Shut up. And fuck my destiny." Callista said. "I can't just leave her here."

"You always leave her here. Remember, she'll be a princess." Meli said.

"Who cares?" Callista said, feeling clear as the water before her. "What's in it for me?"

Meli held out her arms, "Forgetting. Forever."

"Where is Adam?"

Meli's voice merged with Debbie Harry's, and Callista was back at the party. Her mouth tasted like rotting leaves. Brody was stiff arming Joseph, both their faces red with shouting. Harriet was lying in the couch pillows, hiding her face with her hands.

"Get the hell out, you perv. Can't you see York is too good for your raspy ass?"

"She's just right." His voice was teasing. "For one night."

"She doesn't like you, asshole."

"Fuck off, Knapp. Can't you see she wants me?"

Callista made a face. From her vantage point, all she could see was the back of his jeans, where a circle was embossed on the back pocket from a can of snuff. Brody's legs moved forward, and Joseph was knocked back.

"Get out."

"Fine. I didn't know she was yours. But I warn you, she's probably got a disease from that faggot, anyway."

Joseph stomped away.

"What was he doing?" Callista asked. She buttoned her pants. Her crotch was wet, her lips bruised. It didn't feel unpleasant, just confusing.

"Nothing." Brody said, looking away as she straightened her clothes. "Being an asshole."

He handed Callista her fur coat. "This is nice. Can I borrow it some time?"

She put it on. Brody put his arm around her and gave her shoulder a squeeze. "Listen. I can see you're still broken up over the whole Adam thing."

"Oh." She said. Was she crying about it in her sleep?

"That tea..."

"No more of that." She said.

He nodded gravely. "Yeah. It's strong stuff."

"Your aunt was right. It's a bad, dark kind of magic."

"Do you..." His light brown eyes shone with emotion. "Go some-place...weird?"

"Yes." She felt her pockets to make sure her lipstick and wallet were still there. "I liked it at first."

"Yeah, I know. You feel like you get trapped there, right?" He gave her a peck on the cheek. "When you're over Frazer, let's have some good clean fun, would that be okay?"

Harriet was standing behind him, her hair sticking up all over, rolling her eyes in mock disgust.

Callista smiled. Was Brody straight? She started to laugh. "You protected me. Didn't you?"

He blushed and shrugged.

"Thank you."

"What are friends for?" He said, then rubbed his eyes absently and went to see about another guest.

30

— · —

CHAPTER 30

Adam didn't return after Winter Break. Callista invited Randy to Prom, but he just laughed.

"Uh, no. But if you want to go on a real date, I'll pick you up at eight this Saturday."

He drove a Ford F150. They ate hamburgers at the Thunderbird, and she noticed that for the first time in ages, she felt no nausea at all, even though they talked about the missing kids. They went to the drive in at the bottom of Mount Zebulon for a double feature, Swamp Thing and Superfuzz. Swamp Thing was dramatically lit but silly. They talked while the images flashed in front of the nearly empty lot, no one else crazy enough to be out at a drive in during the rainiest part of the year.

"Adam probably ran away." Randy said, looking oddly unimpressive in a T shirt and sweater. His light hair was thin, though when he smiled his dimples were all she could see. "He's kind of the typical runaway, except for being so smart and well connected."

"His family isn't very prominent. His father is an Engineer."

Randy laughed. "God you're a snob. I thought I knew a lot about people when I got hired on at Fairfield. But rich folks are a whole different breed. Here's a man with a good job, a beautiful home, and from what I can tell nothing wrong in his life but a bad temper. And you dismiss him because he's an Engineer?"

"I dismiss him because he's a bully and he hits his son. I respect him for being an Engineer, Randy. God. My snobbery is for what he does, not who he is."

He pushed the lock down on his side of the truck. "Okay. I can see I misjudged. Sorry."

"Look, I am a snob. I was brought up to be one. And because of that, I can tell you that being an aerospace engineer isn't necessarily the kind of position where people do lots of big favors for you. Building airplanes is based on merit, not back scratching. That's all."

"Not like your family."

She sat back, blowing air out of her mouth. "I'm not sure I would be more protected than another girl. I think I'd be judged just as harshly."

"You?" He traced a seam in the upholstery with his finger. "I think you could get away with murder."

"My grandfather called me a slut the other day."

"What?" He laughed. "The judge?"

"Yup." She said. "Great guy."

"He's old fashioned. Older men, where I come from, they think women are to serve them. Any girl who doesn't get married and have children is really a renegade feminist freak. Maybe your grandfather is from that mold."

"He wanted to see this." She pulled up her shirt to show him the scar. He had to turn on the dome light to see it. It had turned into a pink line, five inches long, on the right side below her belly button. He touched it lightly with one finger, and she laughed, pulling away.

"Does it hurt?"

"Not anymore."

He turned the light back off. The Swamp Thing was lumbering into dark shadows below fake looking Spanish moss.

"The irony is, I'm a virgin."

His face shifted slightly. "A perfect woman. Wow."

"Are you kidding?" She sat taller. "The opposite of a slut is a virgin?"

He shook his head and held up his hands, in the same way he had in the woods, as if it would calm her. It didn't. She wanted to slap those hands down.

"Should we talk about something else?"

"Yes." She sat back, facing the screen. Adrienne Barbeau ran through the swamp, crying.

They kissed.

"Where you come from, do girls have sex with men who are six years older? Who aren't necessarily their boyfriend?"

His neck flattened as he drew breath. "I left because that kind of life is too boring for me."

"So you're not old fashioned?"

"I like beautiful girls. If that's what you're asking. I'm with one right now."

"Do you think premarital sex is sinful."

"I don't even know if I believe in God, right now."

They kissed some more. The cab was too narrow for her to straddle him, so he reached over and ran his hands over her thighs.

"Do you live alone?"

His teeth flashed. "My roommate is out of town."

His condominium was sparse, and smelled of dirty dishwater. Callista felt ebullient at the sight of his unmade bed, the ugly red bedspread and geometric sheets, the weight set taking up the rest of the room. He stood uncertainly in the doorframe.

"This is nice."

"You're being sarcastic?"

She pulled her shirt over her head, enjoying the look of hunger that came over his face. "Got a condom?"

"They do offer good sex ed in school over on this side of the mountains. I'll admit that." He moved toward her, and slid his hands around her ribs, grazing her scar. "You know what this entails?"

She kissed him and they moved toward his bed. Randy's eyes widened with amusement as she guided her virginity to its natural death, caught between pleasure and pain.

"Do you need some paper towels?"

"Don't stop." She said. "Cold water will get the blood out."

"Thank god you said that." He grunted. "Because I don't think I could."

31

CHAPTER 31

Phillip and Margaret announced they were returning to California to visit Valerie and Marcus, the Kirsches. The other couple had been waiting patiently to show off their sailboat.

"Fax machines make our work much easier." Phillip said. "And we won't be gone for six weeks, this time."

Margaret looked quizzically at him. "Well. Probably not."

"It's fine." Callista said, "I'll need money for food. And the keys to the Land Rover."

"Only if you promise to answer the phone."

"Done."

"Darling, don't you have anything to share with us? About the new boy you're seeing? I dare not ask about college." Phillip said.

Callista shrugged. "Sharing is overrated."

32

·

CHAPTER 32

Callista took to cruising slowly past Adam's house, but no one emerged, and the Goat sat inert under its dark cover. Bodhi had started sleeping with her, though now they shared her single bed. It was finals crunch time, though Callista felt the same detachment her brother predicted. She could ruin her transcript, but there was little risk of changing her future much. She listened to records and studied, out of habit, to fill the silence of the empty house. She got the best grades of her life.

Spring Tri began, with its exodus of kids doing foreign trips and internships. Callista decided to use her parent's season tickets to the Rep, Intiman, and the Symphony, usually inviting Harriet but sometimes opening her social life up to other kids she hadn't spent much time with. Brody came to see Equus, and they both repressed giggles through the naked scene, laughing about their *chinkle chankle* whenever they saw one another at school.

Callista felt as if she were regressing into a happy teen-hood she had never experienced before. She was coasting through a couple of remaining electives, Art History and Filmmaking. She had never had such an easy course load, but since almost every weekend involved parties at Heron Hall or Brody's, she was rarely idle. As the days passed, the lack of news about Leslie or Adam faded into a nervous coil within her, a gnawing sense that she had better live as much as she could, while she had the chance. People could simply evaporate, and the world would forget them. Still, she didn't have any attacks, or feel the urge to forage in the medicine box. Her body flared from time to time with nausea or hot longing for what she and Randy had done, but it passed. She felt vaguely guilty for being almost happy.

33

CHAPTER 33

Randy called the first Friday in April. They hadn't seen each other since the night she'd lost her virginity, though he'd called twice to ask her out. She declined once out of being busy, and the next out of annoyance that he never planned ahead. She invited him to the theater, and he said a stinging, flat no. But she did think about him often, and wondered if she ought to talk her way back to his ugly condo.

On a Wednesday afternoon, he called, sounded unusually brusque. "Something has happened that you should know about."

"Okay."

"Adam's mother listed him as a missing person."

"Oh." She sat on the bentwood chair by the breakfast bar. "Does that surprise you?"

"Not really." He said. "But she brought charges against Mr. Frazer for assault."

"Wow." Callista said. "Against her?"

"He threatened her with a shotgun. She's fine. He's in jail, but they won't be able to hold him long. It's not that serious a matter."

"Are you kidding?"

"No. Men pull guns on their wives all the time. But she is stalling for time. She refused to put up bail."

"So he's stuck there." Callista said.

"Not necessarily." He lowered his voice. "Even Engineers can usually find something to sell. Be careful."

"You think he'd come after me?" Her stomach tingled. "I haven't seen Adam since before Christmas."

"Has Frazer asked you were Adam is? Because if the mother has filed a report, that means his family doesn't know where he's gone. And if the father is pulling out shotguns, he must not believe his wife's side of things. You understand?"

"And I'm the logical person to ask? So why doesn't Mr. Frazer just call me?"

"How often do you answer your phone?"

"He could stop by. I live a ten-minute walk from the house."

"That's what I'm warning you about." Randy said. "His son is gone. His wife has put him in jail. What's next?"

They set a date to get together to "talk" and then Callista called Harriet.

"That asshole." She said, sounding unsurprised. "Do you think he hurt Adam?"

"You mean, do I think he killed Adam?"

Harriet didn't answer.

"No." She said. "I don't think so. I think Adam found a way out."

Images of Adam in the Realm came, of him running in his little boy clothes, his shorn hair, his pumping boy fists.

"Well. So you won't be coming to prom together. Brody will be happy about that."

Callista dissolved into tears. "Jesus, Harry. He just disappeared. Like in a movie, or a song. Just, poof. It's almost like he was never here." She didn't say, *just like Leslie.*

"Imagine how his mother feels. If she knows what's good for her, she'll start divorce proceedings before that creep gets out of jail."

Callista walked through newly blooming pink dogwoods, down the gully to Adam's. After a tiny moment's hesitation, she knocked on the door. No barking. No sound. She took a step back to leave.

"Oh. Callista dear." Mrs. Frazer sounded not at all surprised. She swung open the door. "Do come in."

The Frazer's house smelled of Lemon Pledge. Callista spent the next hour perched at the edge of a nubby brown couch in the large kitchen, with an art studio in an alcove beyond featuring colorful half-finished landscapes in a dated style. A picture window faced out on a spectacular vista, down the forested mountain to the lake, and city beyond. It provoked her, realizing her parents had chosen a lot with no view of the world beyond their property. She had never even known this view existed. Adam had seen it every day.

She expected Mrs. Frazer to usher her out the door at any moment, but in fact the woman made a show of brewing a pot of Constant Comment and placing cookies on a china plate, asking Callista a series of rote questions about school and her folks. A large family portrait hung on a brick accent wall, young Adam, his blond forelock slicked with water. His father smiled broadly, Florence looking vaguely pert. It was the kind of portrait that was taken at Sears, in the photo studio next to the ophthalmologist. Callista felt undone at the sight of it. Finally, Florence sat across from Callista and settled herself into a forward-pitched position.

"I think it will interest you to know." She broke off, blinking her eyes as if controlling her emotions. "That I have been in contact with my son."

Callista put down her cup. "Oh?"

Florence gazed at her. She was wearing black canvas Keds, and a pair of charcoal gray dungarees with an overstitched front pleat that struck Callista as both home-sewn and rather chic.

"You seem surprised."

"Mrs. Frazer. I was so worried..." Something about the Keds took away her will. She let her tears fall. "I didn't understand what happened with Adam. He told me...almost nothing."

"No. He couldn't, you see. It would have made things harder."

"Where is he?"

"Oh, no. Even I don't know that. It's safer, you see?"

Mrs. Frazer handed her a paper towel. Callista dabbed at her eyes. Adam was gone. Really gone, not hiding upstairs, not hanging out at the elementary school, waiting for her to join him.

"Safer?" She croaked out, imagining Mr. Frazer wandering in from the garage, gun in hand, face askew with anger.

"Mrs. Frazer's eyes fell somewhere in the middle distance. "I have always known that Adam was...who he is. His father...well, he lacks imagination."

Callista sensed something energetic coiling. Mrs. Frazer didn't seem defeated. She picked up her tea and pushed the plate toward Callista matter-of-factly.

"Thank you." Callista said. "I'm not hungry."

"I have something to say to you." Mrs. Frazer leaned closer. "So please don't interrupt or it'll go flying out of my mind. I've been practicing this speech for weeks."

Callista nodded and took a cookie. Mrs. Frazer's pink-frosted lips pressed into a quavering smile.

"I didn't understand what you were doing for my boy. Until November, when he finally told me, you see. And when Dr. Tolland..." She shook her head slightly as if to banish the thought.

"Headmaster spoke to you about me?" Callista asked, then regretted it. "Sorry."

Mrs. Frazer made a silencing gesture. "He said that you've been protecting Adam. It wasn't you being in love with a boy who could never love you back. Sorry to say, but that is what I thought."

Callista felt a gauzy annoyance below her ribs, but she ignored it.

"I have always known who my son is. And I was so focused on getting him the best education, I didn't see...what you were doing to help. And I must say. It worked, Callista. For a long while. It really worked."

"It did?"

Mrs. Frazer looked around the room. "My husband...Adam's father, I should say. You understand how we conspired to let him see what he wanted to see. And you..."

"I was a co-conspirator."

"Yes. You were so young. How could you know? But of course if Adam was your friend, I should have seen you were bright."

Callista sat back, not sure if the water on her cheeks was new tears or old. "I loved him, Mrs. Frazer. Not as a girlfriend. Just...it was just love."

"And he loved you too. I know he did. I'm sure he always will." She closed her eyes, sighing in an exhausted way.

"So he's okay?"

Mrs. Frazer smiled, her blue eyes popping open as if in happy surprise. "He's going to be fine. And he wanted me to give you something. It's from me, too. A kind of thank you."

Callista imagined a letter, perhaps a battered tin box like those neighborhood kids used to bury their drug stashes in. But Mrs. Frazer held out a piece of official looking paper, and a set of car keys.

34

CHAPTER 34

"We won't pay for your insurance." Margaret said on the phone from Sausalito.

Phillip laughed on the other extension. "Yes, we will. Go on, Callista. Go have some fun."

She drove the Goat to school on Monday. Mrs. Weller smiled broadly from her typing. "You're early today."

"I'd like to see Dr. Tolland."

"What light from yonder window?" Came Headmaster's voice.

"Go on in." Mrs. Weller returned to her work. "Stop on the way out, won't you?"

Headmaster's office was booklined and hung with native masks. His desk was the size of a dining table, covered in neat paper piles. Callista had been in the office only a handful of times. She had never lounged in the cozy love seat or Harvard chairs where Adam had eaten so many lunches. It was an exotic world, reeking faintly of dead languages. Dr. Tolland waved for her to sit at the desk, where pale light from the courtyard window shone through his potted plants.

"Well met, Callista."

He gently closed the door. He moved his long, spindly body in a gingerly fashion, settling himself back in his desk chair, his pale gray eyes searching. "How are you healing?"

"Oh. I'm fine." She said.

He smiled faintly. "Mrs. Morgan tells me you refused college counseling. Is that true?"

Callista felt a dark flutter in her gut. She had no memory of Mrs. Morgan asking her about college. Vivian must have shut the inquiry off before it began.

"Sir, I have taken care of that. My parents were out of town, you see, for a long time, and I couldn't make any decisions without talking to them."

"Yes. In any case, Mrs. Webber has kept me informed of where she has sent your transcripts. And you did ask for letters, so apparently you managed."

"I did."

"If you weren't such a reliable student, I would have called you in long before now. It seems to me you've denied yourself the support Peregrine prides itself on."

"I'm sorry, Sir." Callista felt the heat creeping up her back. "It's a bit complicated with my family."

He looked down at his desk. "And is that what you and our friend Adam had in common?"

"In a way." She burned. "I came to ask you where he is."

"Hmmm." Tolland made a quieting gesture with one long hand. "Adam has withdrawn from school. It isn't public knowledge yet, but you probably should be the first to know, given your close friendship."

She hadn't spoken to Adam for five months. He'd been missing for at least three, possibly four. She suppressed an urge to scatter papers all over the Persian rug. "Dr. Tolland, where is he?"

He sat back and seemed to consider. "I would be breaking a confidence if I told you that, my dear. Though I am comfortable sharing that he is safe."

"Are you sure?"

"Yes." He said softly. "I am one hundred percent sure."

"And..." The ghost of Vivian appeared in her mouth. She wasn't going to leave without him giving her something. "And Leslie McCall?"

"Ah. That." His eyes darted to a particular pile of paperwork. "The McCall family have naturally disengaged from speaking to anyone at school, since it seems there is nothing further to discuss at the moment. Sadly, we don't know where Leslie is. But there is no reason to suspect foul play, that I know of. And her case is wholly separate from Adam's. I am sorry if you thought the two were mixed up together."

She touched a leaf, but he didn't raise his eyes from the table.

"Leslie's stepbrother Joseph Aschloss attended Peregrine, didn't he sir?"

"He did." He straightened. "I'm afraid family matters are just that. And there is so little we can do to influence them."

"I see." She rose, mollified by his seeming retreat. "Thank you for attempting to assuage my concerns. I'm sure you are protecting him."

"We try. In Adam's case, I think we were of some use, in the end."

"So, this is the end?" Her heart contracted. "He's definitely not returning?"

"As I said. No." He met her eyes, smiling inscrutably. "I know you understand who Adam is. And your concern for Leslie speaks well of your character. But what do you want for yourself, my dear? What can you and I come up with to forge your bright future?"

"My future? She said. "I...I..."

"You don't think of your own life as mattering as much as the lives of those you love. Sound about right?"

Callista was flooded by hot humiliation. "It's complicated."

"I know." He smiled mildly. "Is there anything I can do? To help get you thinking about what you, you Callista York, want? For yourself?"

"I have to go." Her head was molten tears. She straightened to her full height and turned, releasing the leaf.

He gazed at her. "We will miss you. Next year."

She turned away so he wouldn't see her tears. "Thank you."

On her way out, Mrs. Webber handed her a 6x8 white envelope containing five graduation invitations and ten little cards embossed with her name in block letters. She was tempted to dump them in the garbage can in the foyer. Instead, she went to stuff them in her locker. Adam's hung open, empty but for a note she had left him in tenth grade, and a string of lottery tickets from some fundraising raffle. Callista gave it her middle finger.

"What did that locker ever do to you?" Harriet said, pulling her book bag over her shoulder. She had dark arrows under her eyes. A reminder to Callista to study for midterms, pointless as they were, because at Peregrine learning was an end in itself.

"He's dropped out. Without a fucking word to me, though..."

Harriet straightened. "I guess it's no surprise. But I'm sorry. That's no way to treat his special lady."

"Well." Callista felt a grin coming. "He did leave me the car."

Harriet gaped, then mock punched Callista in the back. "What more proof of his love could you ask for, wench?"

At 3:00 Callista called Randy from Mrs. Webber's phone. It thrilled her darkly to speak to the Fairfield Police department from so near Tolland's office. Randy said he got done with work at 5:00, and he would pick her up, but she said she would meet him at his condo.

"The place is a mess."

"I won't come inside. You'll understand when I get there."

She cruised past the twins, who gawped. She waved gaily, flooring it. Gunmetal rain flattened the lake. She scrabbled for tapes under the seat, popping in Talking Heads and cranking the volume.

"I got three passports." She sang out. "A couple of visas. I don't even know my real name!"

She passed Mrs. Mackie and Bud coming down Mount Zebulon Drive, but they didn't notice her. She parked in the carport and let herself in to the house. There was a foil covered plate sitting on the counter. Cookies. Callista bit into one. Oatmeal. Not her favorite, but she ate it anyway, with a glass of milk.

Bodhi ran to greet her, and she carried him to her mother's closet to find a blouse. "Catch me any mice today? How about some of those annoying robins with their early bird attitudes? Don't they know everyone hates enthusiasm?"

He purred. When she left he stood watching her through the glass.

35

CHAPTER 35

Randy's face clouded when he saw the Goat approaching. He stood looking cold, next to his truck under a wooden carport.

"Rain's going to get in that mouth."

"Did Adam die?" He climbed in.

"Maybe. Maybe not. Wherever he is, he no longer needs to pass as a real boy."

"Do you have insurance?"

She laughed. "I didn't get where I am today by being irresponsible, Randolph."

"Where are we going?"

"That depends."

"On what?"

"Did you bring a condom?"

He blinked. "Always."

"Man of action."

"I didn't get to where I am by being unprepared."

She parked in an empty lot at the entrance to Spirit Falls trail, where her girl scout troop had gone for picnics. The rain had stopped, and the gravel lot mirrored the inky sky from a dozen oval puddles. She splashed through as many as she could, the car jerking up and down. She laughed.

Randy said. "Have you thought about what it means to do it in a car?"

She sighed. "Is this a mistake?"

"I didn't say that." His hand slid into her blouse. "But let's get in back."

She kissed him hard, trying to summon the tingling lust she'd felt in his police car. But the yearning that flowed through her was dark and angry. Callista thought of the twins sitting on the narrow bench seat, all the trips with Adam at the wheel, keeping his secrets, reporting to his violent father, putting concealer on the bruises. *She's filing her nails while they're dragging the lake.* Leslie crying in the Realm. Someone had gotten away with murder, or something like it, a blotting out, a wiping away. *Memory problems*, he had called it.

Randy pulled off her jeans. He tasted salty and warm, and his hair smelled like mousse, but he didn't say anything awestruck or excited, and she felt embarrassed to have rushed him so purposefully. His hands tickled, and she felt large under his bony hips. Then he was inside her, pressing her skin onto the plastic interior, and she had to close her eyes against the sight of Adam's eight track cassettes. A blossoming time lapsed inside her almost in spite of Randy's pushing, a delicate kind of quaver under the strength of his flesh. *Was that an orgasm? Or just pleasure? His slackening was a reli*ef.

She peed under some bushes next to the creek, then strapped back in the driver's seat, brushing out the tangles in her hair.

"Next time, let's get a room."

She started the car, turning on the heat. "Who says there'll be a next time?"

"This was your idea." He sounded exasperated.

"It was fun." She smiled. "I needed to christen this car. So thank you for that."

"My god." He sounded genuinely hurt. "Anything else I can get you, Ma'am?"

"Not so perfect now, am I?"

"I wouldn't go that far."

"Good." She started the car and they headed back. "I need to ask you about Leslie."

"Leslie?" He straightened his cuffs. "Not Adam?"

"Fuck Adam. He's somewhere safe. That's all I get to know."

"His father got out of jail."

"So? He hasn't come around."

"You don't think he'll notice you have this car?"

"My car now. I have the title." She turned onto I-90. Water streamed across the grooves in the highway.

"You're probably right. The Mrs. filed a restraining order. He's not supposed to be within a hundred yards of the house."

"Oh. Well then I'm not worried. He won't come to Mount Zeb."

"What makes you so sure?"

"I want to talk about Leslie."

"Take it easy. You seem kind of riled up tonight. I mean, I'm not exactly complaining but..." He made a gesture she only half saw, throwing his hands up. "Is there something new on Leslie?"

Callista told him about what she had seen in the Realm, making it sound like Joseph had simply told her, instead of the truth, that she had seen it in her mushroom dream on New Year's Eve. "And today, Headmaster made it sound like he knows where Adam went, but they've given up on Leslie. Which really bothers me. "

"Why?" He opened his hands in a gesture she was beginning to understand was to get her to calm down. "What is it about her that gets under your skin?"

"She's a girl, afraid of her awful step-brother, and she disappeared, and the world just...went on. Without her. And that really fucking bothers me." Her voice rose to shouting. "Sorry. I appreciate that you alone cared enough to at least look for her. I really do."

He watched her from the passenger seat.

"Okay. Do you want to go into town and look for her?"

"Detective Franklin!" She smiled. "Could we?"

"I mean, we've eaten dessert first, and you're making it sound like I have to work for my next supper. So why not?"

He was wrapping the used condom inside an old Dick's deluxe paper, folding it carefully into a greasy little packet.

Broadway was sparsely populated. Callista cruised slowly, looking at every kid they passed. She had never really noticed how many wandering, shabby young people there were. A few busked, but most just stood with cardboard signs. After almost running a red light, she let Randy take the wheel. They purred around the University District, with its myriad students, self-talkers, and skateboarders. The night was cold and wet, and few people stayed on the street for long. Heading back to the freeway, they passed through the derelict neighborhood where she'd gone home with Kevin.

And there the doorman was, wearing the same leather jacket and heavy black boots he'd had on in November, waiting to jay walk across Westbay.

"Pull over?" She rolled down the window. "Kevin?"

He turned, eyes unfocused. "Uh, yeah?"

"It's me, Callista."

She smiled. Kevin peered past her to Randy, then met her eyes. "What's up?"

He obviously didn't remember her. Her face burned. "I'm looking for a friend of mine, Leslie McCall? Do you know her? She's sixteen, dark hair, might have been on the street for a while?"

"Oh. Yeah. Everyone's looking for that girl." Kevin straightened. "I don't know her. I work at a gay bar. Not a lot of girls in there."

He ran across Westbay to the overpass, surprisingly light on his feet given how stoned Callista suspected him to be.

"How do you know that guy?" Randy said, scowling.

"I've danced at the place where he works."

"You what?" He said, his mouth an exaggerated snarl. "A gay bar?"

"I wouldn't say I exactly know him." She pressed her knees into the dash, remembering how angry Adam had been that she had gone home with Kevin. She didn't regret it. The murmuration of sparrows he'd sent out of her needed to be set free. "Where to, next?"

"I'm taking you home."

"What?"

"I know your best friend is a fag." They pulled onto the street. "But you dance at gay bars? I...wow. I know your best friend is a fag but, that is not what I would have expected."

She felt suddenly tired. "They have great music. What difference does it make to you?"

"Are you kidding?"

"No." She tried to see his face, but it was flashing in and out of darkness. "Why would you care?"

"I don't care." He sat back. "I just think it's strange that a girl like you would go into one of those places."

"Have you never been in one?"

"No." He said. "Why would I?"

"Why wouldn't you? After all you've seen on the job, how could a few guys in drag get you uncomfortable?"

"Wow." His eyebrows went up, and stayed up for a long time.

He didn't speak to her again all the way back to his condo. He leaned in for a kiss, but she pushed past him.

"Listen." He said. "I know you're mad at me right now. Let me make it up to you. I was thinking about what you said in the parking lot. The step-brother thought she was living in a city with fancy style brick buildings?"

"Yeah?" She grabbed the keys from his hand.

"Do you think the building could be in Portland? Vancouver? Maybe Port Townsend. There are a lot of fancy old buildings there."

"The facade said The Longbotham." She said, sighing with impatience. "Nineteen Oh Nine."

She waited for Randy to say that it made no sense of Joseph to tell her that. It was such a specific detail, that the police weren't familiar with. *Had he shown her a snapshot? How would he know the name of the building?*

Instead he stepped back, laughing nervously. "The Longbotham is in Spokane. Near the university. I've been by it a million times. Why would he…"

"Spokane?"

And then he put it together.

"Wait. Didn't he tell the federal investigators all this?"

"He goes to school back East, so he may never have spoken to them." She forced a smile, moving toward the car. "But you're right. I'm probably confused.

No problem. Sorry this has been such a weird night. And I'm just a crazed teen girl!"

"Okay." He stepped back toward his truck. "The Longbotham…"

"Just an old picture, probably meaningless." She said, changing the subject. "The one loose end is Kenneth Kling. I have a bad feeling about that guy."

"Yeah. I know you do."

"I need to worry about my future. That's what Headmaster said to me. He was right." She felt the need to remind him that she was still in high school, and not his girlfriend.

"So will I see you again?"

"I'll call you!"

She floored it, leaving him in the light next to his truck. "Or I won't. Fuck." She said to the car. "I have to just relax. Leslie is gone. Joseph got away with it. Case closed. Right, Goat?"

The car ticked along happily.

36

— · —

CHAPTER 36

The next weekend Harriet hosted a party to celebrate Ivy League day, though she didn't tell anyone that was the theme.

"Anyone who cares already knows." She said.

It was a beautiful day, with fluffy clouds in a cold blue sky. The ferry was packed. They got supplies at the Port Denham Grocery, and pies at the Rhododendron Bakery. Brody had promised to bring tea, liquor, and a plenty of pot. "No coke, though. I like that stuff way too much."

Loon Landing was so cold Callista kept her down vest on while they opened up, building a fire, and cranking the radiators. The river rock fireplace looked dingy, and the carpets seemed threadbare. They lit sandalwood incense, and turned up an old boom box with the songs of Joan Armatrading.

"Let's go for a walk." Harriet said. "If anyone gets here on the next boat they can let themselves in."

They tramped down to the cove, which reminded Callista so much of the Realm she felt dizzy. They collected sticks for kindling, and broke off some ferns to bring inside for a bouquet.

"Are you going to drink that foul tea again?" Harriet said.

Callista picked a handful of forget me nots near a stump. "I don't know. The last time I did, the mermaid who talks to me said I had to leave a part of myself there or I would never be free."

To her surprise, Harriet didn't laugh. "I drank it. With Brody."

"And?" Callista tied the flowers together with a piece of grass. The bay smelled like rotting kelp.

"I don't like it." She said. "This world is horrible enough, without having to see..."

Callista felt still inside. "What did you see, Harry?"

Harriet sat down on the stump, rubbing her face. "I've never told you this. Because it's so hard to talk about. Please forgive me. But I had a brother, Cal."

"You what?" She shoved herself onto the stump and put her arm around Harriet's shoulders. They were trembling with sobs.

"In that place. I have to revisit when he..."

"What happened to him?"

"He got leukemia." She sighed, dropping her hands to her lap. "I remember sitting in the car outside Children's, you know. There's a little creche in the landscaping there? I would sit and wait, just wait, and wait and once in a while go out and look at little ceramic baby Jesus in the creche. It was in a little garden there. And then."

"I'm so sorry, my love."

Callista rubbed her back through her pea coat as Harriet kept on in a whisper.

"I hate thinking about that time."

"How old were you?"

"Five, six." She hung her head.

Then they were hugging, and Harriet sagged onto Callista's shoulder, and they stood that way until a honk from the drive brought them back.

Callista smoothed Harriet's cheeks. "Thank you for telling me. It's weird, in a way I think I always knew."

Harriet nodded. "Are you going back there?"

"I shouldn't." Callista shrugged. "But I think I need to rescue Leslie. No one else is going to. No one else can."

"Leslie?" Harriet said. "Why? Who is she to you?"

"No one." Callista said. "Me. She's me. In a way. If I didn't have Spencer. If I didn't have you."

Callista marveled as night transformed Loon Landing from a worn old house to a magical place of lights and laughter. She helped Harriet make guests comfortable. Everyone brought snacks, the junkier the better, pringles, bugles, potato chips with onion dip from an envelope of soup mix. They sat around in small groups, some kids mutely stoned, others scribbling in their journals. Twenty friends. Even Mitch and Ben showed up, looking pimply and out of place, but sublimely happy. They made a show of smoking out of a four-foot rainbow bong, as if they had discovered something brand new and exotic. Callista smiled to herself. This was what high school was supposed to be.

"Harriet tells me you have one last quest?" Brody said, tugging on Callista's hand. He had trimmed his hair, so it floated almost vertically off his head in pale waves. He was like someone in a story about taste makers in the East Village, his obvious sense of what everyone was doing, and what it meant. He would make a great cop, she thought. Then she laughed at herself.

"Hi Brody." She said in an exaggerated voice, pretending to be high. "You're so dreamy."

He threw his head back, laughing. "Is that what I sound like?"

She let him take her hand. "Oh, now where are we going? You promised on New Year's Eve that you have something special to show me?"

He pulled her into the study and closed the doors. His face was serious, though still shiny in firelight. "What would be special enough, for you?"

They kissed. His mouth tasted like spearmint and ashes, but beneath that, clean as a swimming pool. Callista felt herself expand, floating in his arms without noticing where they were or what parts of skin were touching, though they were both putting their hands all over. She didn't want the kiss to stop.

"Oh." He said, his eyelids slick with sweat. "You have no idea how good I thought that would be. And it was actually, so much better."

"Brody." She said vehemently. "Brody."

"I know." He said. "Exactly."

They went to the room with the yellow wallpaper, but it was full of kids. The night was too cold to go outside, so they had to satisfy themselves with a butler's pantry off the kitchen, where they made out with such ferocity that just as she was climaxing, Callista pushed a platter off the counter, where it clattered onto the floor with a thud that must have sent the kids in the next room into giggles.

"Do you think they heard?"

Brody opened one eye. "I hope so."

37

CHAPTER 37

When they emerged, most everyone had gone to bed, or were lying in states of deep trance near the fire. Harriet was in the kitchen, staring at a pink bakery box. Brody and Callista wrapped her in their arms, and she sighed.

"Did you think it would feel bigger?" Harriet said in a deep voice that betrayed how much she had smoked.

Callista stepped back to grab an apple fritter. It grated sweetly on the roof of her mouth. "What?"

Brody chucked Harriet's chin. "Everything today is way better than I would have dreamed. And my dreams are fucking wild."

"Is it time?" Callista said. "For the big announcement?"

Harriet looked around the wrecked house. "I think everyone has."

"But you?"

Harriet rolled her eyes. "I got into Penn, duh."

Callista squealed. "Bitch! That is great."

She tried to crush Harriet to her chest. "But..."

"You're not..." Brody said. "Seriously. After all these years of Penn bullshit."

"But I'm going to Barnard!" Harriet said. "And Pinch is fine about it. I thought he'd murder me, but no."

"New York?" Callista said, laughing with delight. "What will you find to keep you busy there?"

Something satisfying clunked into place.

"What about you?" She said to Brody.

He shrugged. "It's between Princeton and…"

She shoved him. "Oh my god."

"Harvard. I know. I know." He shielded his head while Callista and Harriet threw donuts at him.

"All right, prissy princess of Doom." Harriet looked at her.

"I am going to…" Callista thought of the acceptance letter she had left pinned to the wall organizer. "Fucking Stanford."

"Hey."

Her tears were sticky with donut sugar, and a small voice inside told her the only way to get them to stop was to haul off and slap herself, as hard as she possibly could.

"You lousy, lying little bitch." Harriet said softly. "Here and I thought when you asked for so many different applications, you were trying to hide the fact of wanting to take a year off and travel, looking for Adam."

"Oh my God." Callista laughed.

They said as one, "Fuck Adam."

Brody looked back and forth between the two of them collapsing with laughter, a look of delight crossing his face. "Okay."

Callista walked to the cove again before they sealed up the house. Gray waves lapped onto the shore drearily. An otter head rose to look at her with sullen suspicion. She kicked the stones beneath her feet, pulling her collar closed to hide the hickey Brody had left.

Harriet was quiet on the ride back, but Callista didn't try to get her talking. Their silence was better than any conversation.

Turning onto Cedar street, Callista smelled charcoal. As they passed Adam's house, there was a weird shift in physical matter. The shapes were wrong, colors completely off. The house was gone, replaced by a massive pile of blackened logs, surrounded by bright yellow caution tape. For a moment, Callista wondered if she had flashed back to the Realm.

"Holy shit." Harriet said. "My god. That fucking asshole burned their house down."

It was like in a game of Monopoly when a house is changed to a hotel, only this was in reverse. What had been a colonial style split level was now a coal-colored shack, hollow, and near to collapse. Only the white azalea bushes in front seemed normal.

"That bastard," Callista said. She was so tired.

Her beautiful wood-and-glass house sat completely dark under the seawater cylinder of sky.

"I'll just grab a few things. Shouldn't be too long."

"I'll wait here. Too tired to move." Harriet said, shutting off the ignition.

38

CHAPTER 38

The house was silent, and still. Callista moved woodenly down the stairs to pack a bag. In the kitchen, she grabbed the list of important numbers by the phone. Her college acceptance letter was gone. Not on the counter. Not on the nearby floor, where maybe a cat had pulled it down. Simply not where she had pinned it.

She drew in her breath, frozen. The white plastic pushpin that had held the letter was now impaling an old photograph of Callista and Spencer on a dock in the lake, placed directly over Callista's right eye.

Her shoulders trembled, and she felt a film of something cold on her skin. *Get out.* The station wagon gleamed under the trees, Harriet's head partially visible. *It's not far.* Callista's focus narrowed to the door, ten or twelve feet across the room. She glided silently past the breakfast bar, hefting her bag onto her shoulder, fear prickling her diaphragm.

Then three things happened at once. Bodhi jumped up on the counter and meowed loudly, Callista saw her college letter in pieces on the floor in front of the fridge, and a man's voice spoke from the dining room.

"Callista York." The voice said. "You've been a very naughty young lady."

She ran to the door. Bodhi ran with her. *The cat seemed fine*, she said to herself. *If the man had bad intent, he would have hurt the cat by now.*

The doorknob turned in her left hand, and she tried to signal with her right, but Harriet didn't see, and the bag on her shoulder stopped her progress. She was yanked back, thrown painfully onto the kitchen floor, right wrist wrenching. Bodhi yowled as the door banged closed. Callista had never noticed before how small and sleek the cat was, how easy to injure. He streaked out into the forest, his tail crooked where the door had crushed its tip. *How would she explain to Spencer?*

She tried to rise, but hands clutched at her. "Oh no you don't. You have quite some confessing to do."

She tried to turn her head to see him, but he was moving behind her, gripping her book bag to twirl her body, like a kid trying to get another kid dizzy. She threw one of the bentwood chairs behind her, the man stumbling over it, cursing. And then she was scrabbling down the wooden stairs to the lower floor, leaving behind her bag and any hope of getting Harriet's help. It was for the best. Harriet didn't know her way around the house or the neighborhood, the many ways to run.

The exit from Callista's part of the house was only a few steps from the bottom of the stairs. She bumped down them painfully, twisting her right ankle before she caught hold of the bannister. Just as she righted herself on the second to last step, she was again jerked backward, this time by her hair. Her tail bone flared with pain as she collapsed onto the hardwood stairs.

"Let go of me!"

What would Vivian say? But there was no time. He had hold of Callista's hair, and was trying to force her back upstairs. She smelled alcohol and an unfamiliar body odor that made her gag. She wasn't going to break free with her scalp intact, the pain of his jerking starting to sting dangerously. In a moment, she'd be bleeding.

She realized dimly that if she went back upstairs, Harriet might see them and do something, run across the street to use the phone, or drive the car through the kitchen's glass wall. But she couldn't make herself relax. She tried to feint, to dip the shoulder and escape as she had from the bag, but this time the man gripped her right arm, and she found herself stuck between being hauled up the hard stairs, or hanging on with all her left hand's strength to the slats near the ground floor. She still couldn't see his face.

"Fuck off!" She called. It was no use. He was breathing hard, but his hand was powerful.

"Stop fighting me, Cali!" He said. "Just relax."

Callista didn't. She torqued her body back and forth, using the staircase's gravity to dislodge his hand from her shoulder. He lost his balance and fell toward her. She darted out of the way, scurrying down the last two steps and through the laundry area to the outside door, and out, and around to the side yard. A robin watched, its red chest round and healthy, an actual fat worm sliding into its beak. Callista took the steps two at a time, in a cold fury, her lungs exploding with screams.

"Start the car!" She yelled to Harriet. "Now! We have to go now!"

The car was already idling. Callista opened the door to get in, then felt hands on her torso.

Harriet screamed, so loud Callista felt impressed. Then she thought, *this is the last thing I will ever hear, the sound of my best friend, afraid because of danger she never would have faced if she's just stayed in Seattle.*

"Don't you know she's dating a cop?" Harriet said in a shaking voice, coming around the side of the car. "You won't get away with this."

And just like that, his hands released their pressure.

"Oh I know. She's a slut for sure." The man said. "God, I hate you Peregrine A-holes."

"And we feel the same about you, Kling." Harriet said, widening her eyes, which were still bloodshot from the night before. "Get in the car, Callista."

Callista pushed Kenneth Kling's hands away, the fear that had been swirling in her torso erupting into rage. "How dare you come into my house? You criminal." Her voice shook. "What did you do with Leslie?"

Kenneth Kling dropped his hands to his sides in defeat. She got a look at him for the first time. He wore a ribbed ski sweater over sagging corduroys, his red mullet slick with grease.

"Stop. Jesus. I told that cop. I just covered up for Leslie. Little bitch wanted to make some kind of connection at the ticket area, that is all! She did it every week, some friend she met at her brother's rugby match, I don't know. She never said a name." His voice rose in a whine. "But your boyfriend made it sound like I'm a pervert! Because why, I said I liked your braid? Fucking bitch. I never touched any of you kids. I love kids. Normal kids, not jerks like you. Prep schoolers. I wouldn't have fought with you either if you had just fucking listened for two seconds. All I wanted was to talk. I just thought maybe you could call off your dogs, so I can find another job at least." He stopped to sob into his hands.

Harriet whispered, "Get in the car, you stupid cow. Right now."

Callista closed the car door, and Harriet pulled out of the drive, leaving Kenneth standing there. The station wagon squealed onto Cedar Street.

"Turn at the next driveway. We need to call this in." Her voice was calmer than she expected.

"Are you sure?" We could just get the fuck out of here." Harriet said. "Did he touch you?"

"He practically tore the hair from my head." But she felt weirdly remorseful. Kling had helped Leslie. But she believed him when he said he hadn't hurt her. And Randy wouldn't have gone to see him again, if she hadn't made it sound like she'd date him again, if it were part of looking for her. Her scalp stung, and her vest was covered in loose pieces of hair. Her arm ached where he'd wrenched it. No matter what, he deserved to be removed from his job. He had lied. She told herself that she wasn't moved by the man's tears. But she felt sorry for him. And then mad at herself for being so easily pushed around.

They parked in Mrs. Ware's drive. She was already standing in the courtyard between the house and the barn, a look of terror on her gentle face. "I heard screaming. Are you all right?"

Callista forced out, "I need to call the police, Mrs. W. A former staff guy from our school broke into my house. And..." She broke off.

"I called as soon as I heard your voice. You sounded terrified." Mrs. Ware said. "They should be here soon. Where are your folks?"

"Out of town. Mrs. Ware," Callista said, wrapping her hands hard around herself. Her coat had come off with the book bag. "Where is Mrs. Frazer?"

"You'd better come inside. You're shivering. And look at your poor arm."

Her right forearm was turning purple from where she'd landed on it.

39

CHAPTER 39

Randy wasn't in either of the police cars that came to arrest Kenneth Kling. Mrs. Ware had a pot of coffee going, as the fire had raged until four in the morning, and no one on the street had gotten much sleep. Everyone had a theory about who had set it, but so far the Fire Department had refused to theorize. Mrs. Frazer wasn't home. The rumor was she had gone to stay with her sister in Arizona.

"Come on. We have to get you back on the horse." Harriet said, pulling down the drive.

Mrs. Ware's three bay ponies cropping grass beyond a white fence.

"I told you. I hate fucking horses."

"What? You who grew up here. In equine world."

"Yup." Callista said. "But then I learned to ski."

Her breathing returned to normal when she saw the lights left on. The house looked undisturbed, though the police had left a note on the door. Callista had to go downstairs to get in, as they had left the upstairs locked.

Harriet came in through the kitchen. "Have I mentioned that I hate the suburbs?"

"Sit down." Callista said. "If I scream, the knives are in that drawer."

But she could feel that the house was empty, the way she could tell that Harriet was sad. There were so many possible reasons why, but they had the coming evening to talk about it. Mr. Frazer was still at large. Who knew if he was out committing arson, or driving to Tucson? Grace had insisted she come stay for at least a few days, until they got things sorted out.

"Oh, Hon." Harriet saw the shredded college letter. "Look what that maniac did."

She moved to pick up the pieces. "I don't think it matters."

"Of course not." Harriet said.

Callista went to check the rest of the house. Her parent's bed was mussed, but she might have done that. The medicine box appeared to be in order, her mother's jewel case in its hiding spot in the wall as usual. Callista slipped on her mother's engagement ring, for no reason that she could think of except a faint sense of comfort. She didn't seem to be able to get warm.

"Mom's making boeuf bourguignon." Harriet said from the doorway. "I told her we wouldn't be late."

Callista didn't feel the tears until they were halfway down her face. "Would he have killed me?"

Harriet shook her head, blue eyes half closing. "Not you. You fought him like the willful harridan you are. I've never been prouder to be your friend."

And then, as naturally as hugging, Harriet and Callista were kissing. It was soft, and tentative, almost like a hand stroking the side of her face. When they broke off, she felt a surge of hot sorrow.

"I know." Harriet said in a small voice. "But it had to be done."

"Are you..." Callista whispered. "Are we...?"

"No, no." Harriet said. "We're just overwrought teens, caught up in the moment."

"Are you gay?"

Harriet smiled. "I'm like everyone else. Voracious and curious, and ready to get the fuck out into the world and experience it all."

"I love you."

"I love you, too. You pot stirring vixen, you."

They walked back to the car, hand in hand.

Harriet and Callista had benefited from a glass of cabernet and heaping bowls of stew, mopped up with sourdough. They laughed.

"What a creep. Let's never speak of him again." Grace smiled at Callista over her readers. "All that matters is that dear Callista is going to join her brother at Stanford. And our Harriet is going to the hellhole of the Ivy League, where she will no doubt be wildly happy. Can we leave these dark times behind us? Do you think?"

Callista was surprised when Harriet rose from the table, and Grace enveloped her in a hug. Pinch smiled, head to one side, and said, "We'll get you girls to graduation. One way or another."

The phone rang as they were drying the dishes.

"I don't give a damn about anything except you're safe." Margaret said, once Callista had told her the story. "Thank God for the Gambles. As a matter of fact, can you put Pinch on the line?"

Callista felt unreal, handing the receiver over, but Pinch took it with his usual lofty charm, and she soon stopped listening to his noises of agreement and conciliation.

"They're coming home early." He said, hanging up. "And I must say, I'm disappointed. I quite like having an extra daughter."

Callista smiled and hunched her shoulders, suddenly exhausted.

The trundle felt small, and Harriet snuffled in her sleep as if she were coming down with a cold. Pinch had said the sailboat was off Catalina, and the soonest Margaret and Phillip could get home was Saturday. But the next day, Callista drove home from school in the Goat, saying she had to find Bodhi and see about his broken tail. She hugged Harriet long and hard, and they gave one another brave little smiles.

40

— · —

Chapter 40

That night she slept in her parent's bed again, door locked, but Bodhi hadn't come to eat, and she felt more alone than she could ever remember. It sunk in, that Adam was not only gone but his house was a burned shell. The Frazer family no longer existed. Harriet was still there, but nothing would ever be exactly the same.

She slept fitfully, rising to shower in the dark hours of morning, listening to Vivaldi while she brewed coffee, because it reminded her of Sunday mornings when she and Spencer had been small. She picked up the phone to call him, but no one answered. It was 5:30 am.

At 7:00, she locked the house and walked to the carport. Her heart seemed to be beating in her neck, as she came close to unlocking the Goat. A man was sitting inside her father's Land Rover, watching her from under a cap with flapped ears. A rifle poked the window, the hollow hole of its barrel clearly visible. Callista felt the opposite of what she'd been the previous afternoon. Now, she couldn't seem to force herself to move.

It was Mr. Frazer. He had the same pale blue eyes as Adam, though his stared from under shadow, and seemed icy calm. Callista was flattened by a sense of stupidity as he gazed at her. *Why had she come back here?* Seconds passed. When he made no move to come after her, she began breathing again, easing herself into the Goat and locking the door. Still nothing.

The engine roared, and she fishtailed out of the driveway. Mrs. Ware's didn't seem far enough to go. *Mr. Frazer, what was his first name? Henry?* He knew how to get to Mrs. Ware's house via the trail. It would only take him a minute, maybe two. She stopped thinking, just eased the car down the hill, turning away from the lake toward the civic center, where she had spent a thousand afternoons studying in the public library. It stood across the street from the police station, where she had never been, and never expected to go.

The streetlights winked out as she jerked open the front door. Inside, the place was half dark and quiet, but an older, mustached officer behind a desk listened while she stammered out that her neighbor was sitting in her father's car with a rifle, and then shook his head.

"We have been to Cedar Street a lot this week." He picked up a phone. "Domestic drama can be messy, can't it?"

She stared, affronted by his assumption that she would know. "You'll send someone out?"

She thought about saying that she was tired of everything changing so fast, of all the people and institutions of her life suddenly rising up like bears in the spring. Her shoulders shook silently with the memory of Henry Frazer's still, staring eyes.

"Have a seat." The officer said.

"Oh, no sir." Callista said. "I have to get to school."

"Are you reachable by phone at school?"

She shrugged. "If you ask for Mrs. Webber. She knows my schedule."

The officer wrote down the number.

As Callista was turning to leave, she heard her name called.

"Uh..." Randy looked apprehensive. is face looked harder than she remembered it.

"Hi." She said tightly. It was a relief to see him. But he didn't look happy at all. Maybe he didn't want it to look like they knew each other.

"I didn't get a message from you."

She shook her head, following him to a place out of earshot of the desk sergeant. She explained to him about Kenneth Kling attacking her, and then finding Henry Frazer in her driveway.

"Wait." Randy said, face oddly flat. "Can you just wait a quick second?"

She sat on a bench, numbness settling over her with a smell of cheap coffee in an unseen break room. She fiddled with Margaret's engagement ring, a small diamond with two miniscule diamonds on either side in gold. Callista recalled when she had seen her mother wearing the ring last, and it had been years. The sight of it made her feel simultaneously young and old.

"Come with me." Randy said, his face grave. "I'm going to have to take another report."

They sat in a small conference room that Callista dimly registered must be designed for questioning people. She explained again the details of her discovery while the clock ticked past the start of school. He excused himself, and Callista felt relief, then returned in what might have been five minutes, or thirty.

"Okay." He said, swallowing hard. "Officers found Frazer. Just where you said he would be."

She nodded. "Did he say anything? Did he confess to burning the house down?"

"Henry Frazer is dead. Shot in the heart."

"Dead?"

Randy sat back down, crossing his arms. "We don't know yet if it was suicide. Or murder."

"Murder? He might have been murdered? By Kenneth Kling?" She sat numbly, picturing Henry Frazer's dead eyes staring out from the Land Rover. It dawned on her that Randy had his arms crossed over his chest. It was thicker than usual. He was wearing a bullet proof vest. "Do I need a lawyer?"

He stretched his legs out, gazing at her with hard eyes.

"I think you ought to tell me your theories, first. I mean, when I went to ask Kling one last time about Leslie McCall, he admitted to delaying the school bus while she went to meet a friend. Which he never told the Feds. You were right about him holding back information. So I guess you might know what happened with Mr. Frazer. I mean. You're the queen of solving crime. By any means at your disposal."

Her stomach reeled. Was he being aggressive because he was angry, or because he thought she had somehow shot a man in the heart? Or because he felt used?

Which he had been. She had used him. For sex, for help investigating. Why didn't she feel remorse for it? It seemed like he got plenty out of the deal.

"Am I a suspect?"

He looked at her for a long time. She was missing homeroom. Harriet would be wondering where she was. Callista yearned to be in Walker Hall, sitting down to talk about the week ahead. Why had she come here?

"No." He said. "I was just fucking with you."

"What?" She blinked. "Randy."

He shook his head. "Do you think I believe you're capable of murder, Callista?"

"I think you're mad at me."

"I am. I admit it. You make me feel like a fool. So here is one last attempt to impress you, and then I never want to see you again. Okay?"

She nodded, suddenly ashamed, and annoyed with herself for feeling ashamed.

"He broke the restraining order looking for his wife. Who wasn't there. So I think after he burned his own house to the ground, he went looking for you. I think Kling interrupted Frazer in your house. I think Frazer tore up your Stanford letter, found a picture of you and Adam and stabbed it in the face. Then he realized another man was there, and he slipped outside to wait."

But she had been making out with Brody and eating donuts. What if he had found her?

"Why did he shoot himself in my dad's car?" She whispered.

"When he saw Kling go into your house, maybe he just ran out of gas. I don't know. Maybe the adrenaline stopped, and he realized that he'd have to kill two people instead of just you. Or maybe he never meant to kill you, he just wanted to force you to tell him where Adam is. Who can say? He's dead now. If he left a suicide note, it's ashes."

"You're really good at this, Randy." She stood, feeling numb and shaky at the same time. "I'm going to go now."

And then she was across the street, in the Goat, talking herself into keeping her speed below the limit, so she wouldn't get pulled over.

41

— · —

CHAPTER 41

When she got to school, a roaring in her gut told her that she was going to be sick. Where could she go? Mrs. Webber's desk.

"Can I sit in the nurse's office?"

"Of course, Callista." Mrs. Webber said, pushing back her desk chair. Callista made it as far as the tissue-covered bed before she burst into tears. "Mrs. Webber, where is the bathroom?"

She vomited.

"Honey, can I call your mom?" Mrs. Webber said kindly, her dark face as calm as ever under her wire framed glasses. "Do you know what's wrong with you?"

Callista summoned all her self-control to sputter, "I think I need to talk to Headmaster. Will you come too, Mrs. W?"

"Of course I will."

Tolland was staring into the middle distance when they got there. Did he already know?

"Dr. Tolland," Mrs. Webber said. "Are you available?"

He started. "Callista? I had a feeling you'd be back."

She sat down, but words wouldn't come.

"I'll get some tea."

Callista nodded. "Thank you."

"My dear," He said in a weary voice. "I cannot begin to apologize to you for whatever Kenneth Kling did. My understanding is that he...attacked you?"

Callista told him the whole story. She didn't know exactly how to frame her relationship with Randy, but something about Headmaster's revelation that he had been part of Adam's escape made Callista want to go ahead and tell him everything. If Adam had, shouldn't she?

"I don't know how Peregrine is going to weather these storms. We may need to usher in a new administration. The board is aflutter." He said. "I assume you know Pinchon Gamble has been here already this morning. Harriet would transfer out, apparently, were she not so close to graduation."

"Dr. Tolland." Callista said. "Did other kids come to you about Kenneth Kling?"

"Only recently." He considered. "We were unaware of your suspicions, Callista. I wish you had come to us with them."

She sighed. "He just said weird things, called me sexy names. But he didn't touch me. I wish I had told you. Obviously, he knew more about Leslie than he was going to admit unless he absolutely had to."

"It appears he placed protecting himself over her safety. Unconscionable." Headmaster said, rubbing his hand over his face. "When girls began to get word that he had been questioned again, it came out how…"

"Creepy he was?"

He nodded. "It's so strange how no girls said anything at all. Not until Kenneth came here to confront me, very loudly and publicly, accusing me of sicking the Fairfield police on him. I must say, in retrospect I wish I had."

"Did he admit he was keeping Leslie's meeting secret?"

He shook his head softly. "This is the first I've heard. Unfortunately, Kenneth has resigned, so I can't press him on it now. I don't know why this officer took it upon himself to harass Kenneth, since the case is in the hands of the FBI, and the family. Do you?"

She laughed. "I suggested it. I don't approve of his methods, but Kenneth Kling shouldn't be within a mile of any children. Especially girls. And you know, I haven't been able to forget about Leslie. Even though, I know I should."

"I don't agree. I think you are a champion of what appear to be lost causes, but maybe aren't so lost." He reached into his desk. "Do you like shortbread? I have some here. Sometimes if my stomach has been acting up, I like to eat a little something."

He placed a package of Scottish tea biscuits on the desk between them.

"Dr. Tolland." Callista said, as Mrs. Webber returned with a paper cup of tea, depositing it, giving Callista a smile, then going back out. When she was gone, Callista said, "Did you mean what you said? About a new administration?"

He shrugged. "Perhaps. Scandal is the last thing a small, provincial school such as Peregrine needs. We depend on colleges looking upon us positively. They are so likely to forget we exist at all."

"Oh. I almost forgot. I'm going to Stanford, sir." She said, watching her tea bag turn her hot water brown.

"You?" He said, starting. "Congratulations. That is..."

"Where your brother is, presumably, deliriously happy?"

She shrugged. "If I keep my mouth shut about Kling, for a while, at least until after graduation, could we keep word from getting out? So the board doesn't have as much to harangue you with. Maybe I could talk Pinch into stepping down, since Harry won't be here next year."

"I don't know."

Callista sagged, wishing for Margaret's clarity, her ability to cut to the heart of things. She didn't want the man who helped Adam to be punished for it. "A sad thing happened to a former student. Nothing to do with you. Adam can..."

"Yes." He said, sitting up.

Something bright flared inside her. "Adam can come back now. Because he's no longer under threat."

"Callista?" He said softly. "You know that I would never overstep a child's bounds, their personal sovereignty, don't you?"

"I don't know anything about you, sir." She whispered. "But obviously, Adam trusted you. More than he did me, or anyone."

She left him sitting, a small smile playing on his lips, pulling the box of cookies toward him.

"Thank you," She said to Mrs. Webber. "You are a genuine life saver."

Mrs. Webber nodded. "Senior year is sometimes dramatic for kids."

Callista burst out laughing.

Harriet sidled up to her on the way to the cafeteria. "I am going to give you one chance to tell me what the fuck is going on."

Callista did. They stood under the awning in front of the art room, not caring what the passing lunch goers overheard.

"Oh my god." Harriet said, sitting on a bench. "I mean, I am glad that bastard is dead. But..."

"Where are fucking Margaret and Phillip when you need them?" Harriet said. She couldn't help laughing. "God. They'll be here Saturday."

"They you're staying with me, until they get here."

Callista nodded. "Thank you."

"Don't thank me, you conceited cow. One kiss and you turn into a quivering mess. Pull yourself together. We just had to find out. Didn't we?"

"We did." Callista said. "Next time, tongue."

The day was getting better.

42

—◦—

CHAPTER 42

Margaret and Phillip took in the hulk of charcoal that had been Adam's house with serious looks on their tanned faces.

"Oh, Sweetheart." Phillip said, though which of them he addressed Callista couldn't tell. "What a thing."

He went to look at the Land Rover in the carport. Callista had driven Margaret's Volvo. The Goat was parked on the side of the drive, where it collected pine needles but got in no one's way.

"I'm going to see." Margaret said. "Do you want to come?"

Callista hesitated. "Sure."

There was an unbelievable amount of black staining on the striped fabric of the seat cover. Callista hadn't noticed on Monday morning that the back window was webbed with cracks from a bullet hole.

"Are you smiling, Callista?" Margaret said.

"Oh, Mom." She said, "With relief."

"Ah." Margaret said, her hand reaching out toward Callista's. "Let's go see how poor Bodhi is faring."

That night they went to Chinatown for dinner, and Callista let them toast her with cold beer in the bottle. They ate her favorite dishes, and shared their fortunes as if deadly serious about what each foretold.

"Have you spoken to Adam?" Phillip said on the way home. "Does he know about Stanford?"

"No." The words tumbled out without thought. "When people disappear, I assume they stop caring about me."

The comment left them in a pained silence, which surprised her. "I didn't mean that. It's just that I've felt very alone. Between getting attacked and finding a dead body."

To her amazement, Margaret was crying.

"Mom!" She reached over the seat to take Margaret's hand. "It's not your fault."

"No." She said. "But sometimes I think, what fucking thing can happen to you next?"

"I'm sorry." Callista said, too loud. "I'm sorry things happen to me. I wish they didn't. But they do."

Phillip said, "Things happen to all of us. We have had quite an experience sailing around California. And let me say, Cedar Street is looking like quite the pot of gold at the end of our rainbow. Blood stains or no."

"So," Callista said, hand still clutching her mother's, "You're staying?"

"Yes." Margaret sounded stuffy. "This is our home. And we are happy to be here."

Callista leaned back, the lights of Beaux Arts glimmering beyond the bridge, and closed her eyes.

43

—— ◆ ——

Chapter 43

Spring was an abrupt turn, from cool gray to lurid chartreuse. Callista loved the moment the deciduous trees went from bare sticks to fuzzy fronds, and then suddenly leaves broke forth in a fury of dark red and pale green. She was gathering the mail at the end of the driveway when she heard a voice from the trees.

"Hey, stranger."

He looked so much older. She laughed out loud. His hair was stylishly cut, and deeper brown. His face had lost some of its boyish smoothness, and he was taller. She had to look up to meet his eyes.

"You."

They fell into an easy hug.

Callista felt disembodied watching her parents greet Adam, plying him with orange juice, offering condolences for his losses. He thanked them gravely, face a mask.

After Margaret and Phillip headed off to buy food for a nice dinner, he and Callista blasting Heroes because he was in a mood for Bowie, it sunk into her that after the months of complete silence, he was really back. Did he expect her to be the same as before? Before his dead father in her driveway, Kenneth Kling's monstrous attack, having her appendix out, losing her virginity to a cop, making out with Brody, and getting into *his* dream college?

She pinched herself inside her left wrist as a reminder to be less selfish. Adam had lost his home, his father, and the identity he had so carefully built to survive in the world. She ought to be more thoughtful. But in fact, she felt a mix of so many strong emotions, all she could do was wait and see what he expected. She offered him the car back, but he refused, saying he didn't intend to stay in the country long enough to need it, and anyway, it was awfully tacky, wasn't it? And they laughed.

"Are you going somewhere for break?" He said, sipping the glass of scotch she'd poured him the moment her parents had disappeared in the Volvo. They sat in the sunken living room.

"Loon Landing," She said. "My folks are on a big case, and they've taken a lot of time off this year. So it's me and the gang lying around doing nothing. Obviously, you're invited."

"You aren't going to be in Fairfield at all?"

"Do you want to stay here?" She sat forward. "I'm sure my parents would..."

"No." He interrupted, holding up a hand. "This is my last trip to Mount Zebulon. I fucking hate this place."

"So what are you doing, then?"

"Staying with a friend."

It had to be Headmaster. She nodded. "I won't ask who."

He smiled faintly. "Bolt said you're still talking about Leslie."

"Yeah. She's in Spokane. I know why she ran away."

"So, we're going to Spokane?"

Her chest surged with an emotion, hot and confusing. "We?"

There was a long pause. Outside, a group of wrens chased each other through the branches of a Douglas fir.

He swirled the Scotch in the glass, making a show of sniffing it. "I'm sorry I didn't tell you. But I thought you more or less knew. You're always so far ahead."

"No." She realized what she as feeling. It was the need to take control. "Why are you back?"

"To graduate from high school, you silly goose."

"So this whole time you were still enrolled at Peregrine?

He looked at the floor. "I am sorry. Obviously, you're hurt and angry."

"Shut up." She smiled. "I missed you. But mostly I was just fucking afraid for you. And now you're back, looking like milk fed Adam Ant. Obviously, fine."

His face shifted, a blush and devilish grin lighting it. "It's terrifying how you see through me."

"There's just one thing."

"The Realm?"

"I need to retrieve something I left there."

The little girl burying her plastic foal in the rain, her face unmoving, while Melusine sat nearby singing old Led Zep songs to no one.

He crossed his legs. Even his feet looked bigger. "Is it real? Is it...magic? I mean, it can't be, right?"

She rose to put on a new record. "It's real. But not magic."

"Then what? You're talking about a crossover between seeing Leslie in the Realm, and seeing Leslie in the world."

"That's right. We must prove it's really real, though obviously it isn't." She continued in a spooky voice, "With the power of our minds. Who's to say we can't astral project to a different time and place, and meet friends there?"

"The ancients did it." He said.

"Civilizations through the ages have done it."

He smiled easily. "Is it not evidence of ancient astronauts?"

Phillip and Margaret seemed dazzled by the sight of Adam, who explained to them about his internship in England. Upon probing, he admitted, yes it was Oxford, at which point Callista forcibly shoved him out the door. "Jesus Christ. Give it a rest."

"Tolland?"

Adam got in and pulled closed his seatbelt. "There are people in the world who know what it is to need to lose yourself in books."

She rolled her eyes. "Oh, is that what the kids are calling it these days?"

She hadn't seen him laugh that hard for years.

44

— · —

CHAPTER 44

He filled her in on his time in England. Even his voice was different, deeper, and more cultured. He had flown to Vancouver, and then to Frankfurt, and then taken the train to London.

They lay in an ancient hammock outside of Bart Frehl's house on Lake Washington, wrapped in old wool blankets, passing a can of Rainier back and forth.

"I would say it was to avoid being tracked, but it was just cheaper. I will have to pay Tolland back for all of this. The whole time, I was just kind of peeling off my proverbial old skin."

"Like Eustace in the Dawn Treader?"

"Yes, claws and all. You know a boy alone on a train at night, crying, gets attention?"

She shrugged. "You'd get noticed anywhere, handsome."

The trees above them were ruffled by wind, a jet trail so high above it looked like a white eyelash.

"I've seen you get this kind of interest a thousand times, Cal."

She peered at him. Was he crying?

"I have been so afraid." He said. "And then there I was, in fucking London, the most important city in the world, arguably."

"God you're a nerd."

He smiled. "And it was...I don't have words. The most wonderful respite. I had very little money, and my term in Oxford hadn't started yet. Bolt had me staying with an old couple of Wordsworth scholars near Harrow. Just an ordinary row house, but I could spend all day in town, in every museum and gallery. I just…"

"Wound up in a broom closet with a cute boy?" She said.

He laughed. "And more. I met the most glorious people, Cal. The most. Glorious."

She closed her eyes, and he went on talking about his time, his trysts, his tutor, the freedom of walking in daylight without fear. He had danced in clubs on Baker Street, and frozen in the rain waiting for omnibuses.

"I even went to see the Grateful Dead."

"You what?"

He shrugged, "I know. I suppose I was homesick."

"I'm really sorry about Henry."

There was a long silence. Far across the lake, a red ski boat raced along.

"My father was a tortured soul. I don't know if I can express how hard it was for him. If I said he wasn't really angry with me, so much, as I was living the life he couldn't, would that make sense?"

"Your dad was…?"

"Gay?" He said. "Why does a man try to hard to destroy all he has created? Why does he look at his son, and see only something he hates about himself? I don't know. I'll never know."

Wind ruffled his hair, and his face took on a look she had never seen before, a resigned sorrow. His bones had grown, so it seemed even less familiar. She both knew him and didn't know him at all. And the ache it cause was both bitter, and sweet. His cheeks were still flushed, but he knew things now she would never be able to understand. And vice versa. And it was okay. They were both there, listening to a wake hit the Frehl's retaining wall, while someone grilled hotdogs on the patio. Thumps of a base guitar came over an amp, then a kid testing a microphone in preparation for Bart's band to start playing. And she understood in that moment, that Adam had come back to say goodbye. As much to her as to the world around them, to the forest and the mountains and their friends smoking bongs in the house.

"And Florence?"

"Oh, she's a mess but she's putting on a cheery face. I think she is planning to go back to work, which is something she always wanted."

"Are you going to see her?"

"Eventually. She's with friends in New York, having a high old time. They went to the Cloisters." He laughed, eyes widening with mock amazement. "They're going to see Evita."

By the time Bart came down the lawn with a group of friends to greet Adam, Callista was exhausted. She smiled as various people appeared, each one genuinely delighted to see him alive. Adam bore it with stoic good will, rising to go inside and say hello to the debate team, who had brought him a cake.

Brody bypassed the receiving line a came straight over to the hammock, offering her a cold wine cooler. "So."

"Sit down." She smiled. "I'm still over him."

He settled next to her and kissed her cheek. "Thank God."

They lay for a long time, watching the sky, their hands entwined, the summer ahead with all its sun and freedom, the last time they would all be there to swim in the lake, ride bikes in the islands, do whatever they had time for between their jobs and family obligations. Callista had agreed to go work at the law firm, and Brody was taking classes at the university. The time until college was a seamless spring afternoon of green grass, their feet gently rocking the hammock, under a willow tree that smelled only slightly of wet moss.

The band started playing, loud and thrashing with fast guitars and Bart's joyful low growl. They kissed once, long and deeply, then they went inside to dance.

45

CHAPTER 45

Callista pulled up in front of Dr. Tolland's apartment across from Volunteer Park. When Adam climbed into the passenger seat, she felt a sudden sense of vertigo, though she hadn't yet touched a drop of tea. It was his presence in the Goat, where in some strange way, he no longer belonged.

"Are you going to tell Leslie's mother where she is, if we do find her?" He asked, as she pulled onto the freeway.

"Of course." She signaled for the turn East on 90. "But I don't really trust her. Joseph Aschloss is a disgusting pig. Has anyone ever offered Leslie the chance to stand up to him?"

The cruised through the last of the suburban sprawl around Eastgate and into the foothills. The day was starkly sunny, the blue of the sky and river bled of depth.

"Is Leslie worth this? Wherever she is, maybe in some crappy part of Spokane where she's getting high and ruining her own life, isn't that her choice?"

"Does she have a choice?" Callista looked at him sidelong. "When your life is torture, shouldn't someone try to make things right?"

"Ah." He looked at her. "When they hurt us, you stand by and try to fix it. Is that it? A secular martyr?"

He punched his leg. "Fuck you, Frazer. The disrespect. The ingratitude."

He laughed. "It was generous of you to adopt my wayward car."

"Seriously, though." She tapped the wheel, surpassing the speed limit by ten miles per hour. "Would you give up on me? If I disappeared?"

"Of course not. But..."

"What?" She laughed. "What makes us so different from Leslie McCall?"

"You're right. But. I'm thinking of you, right now. Tripping is dangerous. You leave a part of yourself behind every time you go."

"True." She smiled. "Sometimes that's a lifesaver. Right?"

"Yes." He looked out the window. "When we started, all I wanted was to leave my whole self there. Or anywhere."

She thought of little Adam, running from a whoopin'.

"So now...I want to decide for myself. Which parts to ditch, and which to hold onto. Do you understand?"

"I do." He said. "I understand completely. But Cal..."

"It's my last voyage to the Realm. I swear."

46

—— • ——

CHAPTER 46

The pass was sad patches of snow still visible at high elevation, the bare ski slopes reduced to muddy stubble. Callista wondered which tree had been theirs, but the resort passed quickly. They stopped for lunch in Ellensburg at a Mexican place that melted cheese all over everything, and Adam professed he hated the food in England.

"You sure you want to go back?"

He smiled a shredded cheddar smile. "I love it there. I'd eat stale bread and warm beer for the rest of my life if I could stay."

"He must be handsome."

"Well." He drank some coke. "The fellow I'm thinking about is brilliant. But looks aren't his strong suit."

"You've got that covered."

"I must say, you're more stunning than ever, York. The Stanford boys are going to swoon."

"Thank you." She said, unwrapping a peppermint. "Do you think this stuff would taste better over ice?"

In the parking lot, she poured the contents of the thermos into a to go cup. The ice melted immediately, as the tea was still hot from being brewed that morning. A mistake. She held her nose, and drank it down.

"Careful. That's a lot."

The little girl with the broken horse sat, alone on the beach, in the rain. Leslie tottered on the edge of a curb, in front of an old brick building.

"See you on the other side."

She handed him the keys.